All Things New

ALL
THINGS
NEW

LAUREN MILLER

THREE
SAINTS
PRESS

ALSO BY LAUREN MILLER

Parallel

Free to Fall

Library of Congress Cataloging-in-Publication Data
Miller, Lauren (Lauren McBrayer)
All Things New / Lauren Miller. – 1st ed.
p. cm.
1. Love—Fiction. 2. Coming of Age—Fiction. 3. Anxiety—Fiction. 4.Psychological Issues—Fiction.
LCCN: 2017901936

Three Saints Press ISBN: 9780998511108
www.threesaintspress.com

Book Design by Stewart A. Williams

Printed in the United States of America

I knew nothing but shadows,
and I thought them to be real.
OSCAR WILDE, *The Picture of Dorian Gray*

Chapter One

It catches my eye as it goes dark, lights blinking out all at once, upstairs, downstairs, front porch, *snap*, like someone hit a master switch. There are a few others like it, little dark voids in the expanse of bright rectangles below, a constellation of houses and restaurants and nightclubs that all look the same from up here. It's the reason Wren's parents bought this house, for the view. The view, and the fact that everyone knows just by the neighborhood how much they paid for it.

On a clear day, you can see past downtown and almost all the way to the beach from up here. But tonight the sky is muddy with haze. The skyline looks as if someone has wiped parts of it away, the buildings fading into a brown blur, the furthest ones totally out of sight. It's eerie. I bring my eyes back to the house that just went dark and wish that I could do that right now, flick off my lights, done for the night, *Do Not Disturb*. Instead I have to turn back around, look straight into the high beams.

i don't want to have this fight

"Jessa." His voice is impatient. "Are you even listening to me?"

"Of course I'm listening to you," I say, twisting back around. I bring my eyes back to his, resisting the urge to turn away from him again. *i hate when you do that,* Wren said when I did it a few seconds ago, his voice sharp and accusing. I tried to laugh, to make light of it, but the sound got caught in my throat. *why is he being so mean?*

He knows I'm trying. I'm doing the best I can. Neither of us ever says the words *anxiety* or *panic disorder,* but he knows. We weren't dating when things were really bad, but the summer after freshman year, right after my mom had the twins, I stopped being able to feel my feet for a couple weeks and kept tripping over them. I tried to feign clumsiness but Wren didn't buy it and thought something was really wrong with me. So I told him all about middle school and the panic attacks and the therapy that didn't work and the trophy I got, *haha,* for maladaptive coping techniques and how stress sometimes makes the symptoms come back.

Wren exhales and his breath is visible. "It's not even about the physical thing," he's saying now. "I can deal with the fact that we basically don't hook up." He's all magnanimous, as if he deserves a thank you, a gold star, as if it's even *true.* We hook up all the time. Then he adds, "But we barely ever *talk.*" He makes it sound as if talking is the highest aim of a relationship, which it might be for some people, but not for Wren.

Talking is overrated, he whispered right before he kissed me for the first time, two years and two months ago exactly, on Halloween freshman year.

"I want more," he tells me now. "I *need* more. Connection. Depth." He runs his hands through his hair. "I can't do this surface crap anymore, Jessa. It's not enough."

My throat constricts, like someone is squeezing it. *where is this even coming from?* Somewhere deeper, in a room I don't go into, there are answers I don't want. I reach for a strand of my hair and start twirling.

here i go down circle road strong and hopeful-hearted through the dust and wind up just exactly where i started here i go down circle road strong and hopeful-hearted through the dust and wind up just exactly where i started

Two times through and the lump in my throat loosens, slides away.

I look up at Wren. The skin between his eyebrows is bunched up and his lips are pursed in a pout. The face of a cranky toddler, the same face my half brothers make when they don't get their way. *Give me what I want or I will make your life suck*, that's what that face says. But there is no toy to jam in Wren's hands, no fist full of Cheerios to dump on his tray, *there, done, happy now?*

i can't give him what he wants
he wouldn't want it even if i could

I shrug these thoughts off, quickly, before they stick. This isn't about me. This is about Wren, horny and frustrated because I won't sleep with him. He's making it about something else because he knows that's not a good enough reason to pick a fight with me. I could call him on that, but it's New Year's Eve, when everything is supposed to be awesome and hopeful and possible, and I don't really care why we're arguing, I just want to make up.

"C'mon," I say lightly, sliding my hands around his neck. "Kiss me already."

But then his hands are on my shoulders and he's pulling away. "Stop it, Jessa," he says in a rough voice. "Get off."

I jerk back like he hit me, like he's punched me in the face. My spine bangs into the railing. It makes a jarring sound, bone on metal. Bones becoming metal as I steel myself against this moment. I can almost feel them, the little walls that come up inside my skull, tiny compartments of quarantine where the hurt, isolated and cut off, quickly suffocates and dies.

Shaking, I brush past him, *click click click*, my black heels harsh and grating on the deck's polished slate. I wait for the scuff of his shoes on the stone, his voice calling out for me to stay. But the only sounds I hear are coming from the party inside. At the door now, I can either turn around or go inside. I inhale sharply as I open the sliding glass door, one quick motion, like ripping off a band-aid.

The noise on the other side is too much. Not loud, exactly, just discordant, out of tune with the pitch in my brain. I know everyone here, but, really, I know only Wren. The rest are just faces I pass in the hall at school or at parties like this one. Eyes I avoid making contact with, out of habit, out of fear.

Some guys from the lacrosse team stand in the kitchen, drinking champagne from plastic cups. Wren's older sister bought it for us, on the condition that everyone would spend the night. There's a vase filled with car keys by the front door. The girls are scattered around the living room in little groups.

i don't belong here

It's how I always feel, at Wren's parties. At any party. Like the girl no one knows what to do with. I suck at small talk, I hate dancing, I don't drink.

In the hum of voices, I suddenly hear his. I look back at the deck but don't see him, only the outline of my own reflection in the sliding glass door. Hair spilling over thin shoulders, wide eyes and high cheek bones, my almost-button nose.

I step up to the door, peering through it and am confused for a sec, *where did wren go?* I didn't see him come in. But then I hear him, in the kitchen, laughing with his friends. He's holding a champagne bottle, filling a plastic cup to the brim. Heat shoots up my neck, explodes on my cheeks. He came through the door at the other end of the house so he wouldn't have to walk by me.

One of the guys in the kitchen sees me watching, lifts his hand to wave. My eyes drop to the carpet. I fight the urge to run.

out get out

I fumble for my pocket, pretend like I'm getting a call. Press my phone to my ear so hard it hurts. *oh hey how are you oh really that's crazy no way.* I'm moving toward the door now, keeping up my end of this fake conversation, smiling like everything is normal, like I'm not humiliated inside. I glance at the foyer mirror on my way out and feel a tiny flash of relief.

i look fine

no one can tell

Some girl calls from the couch, *hey Jessa!* I tug at my puppet strings, 1, 2, 3. My head turns, hand lifts, and the corners of my mouth draw up into a smile. Then I'm sliding past her, digging out my keys from the bottom of the vase, opening the front door, walking down the driveway to the street. Still clutching my phone to my ear, just in case someone followed me out.

My mom's car is parked around the corner, two houses down.

unlock the doors

get inside

turn the key

Only then do I acknowledge that I have no place to go.

Where I want to be is my bed, buried under the weight of my goose down comforter, but my mom and Carl are hosting a "grown-ups" dinner at our house and have turned my bedroom into a maze of overpriced travel cribs. I imagine walking through the front door as they're serving dessert, the look on my mom's face, *what are you doing here?*, the smile she'd put on quickly but not fast enough.

I pull out my phone and begin to scroll through pictures. *wren, me and wren, mirror selfie, wren, wren, wren.* Three of the same shot, a few seconds apart, taken two nights ago in my mom's car, this car. He's in profile, laughing, slightly out of focus, and my arm is out-stretched from behind the camera, the palm of my other hand flat on his cheek, trying to turn his head. I'm staring right at the camera, my green eyes all lit up and sparkly, blond hair messy around my face. We were parked at one of the overlooks on Mulholland, pretending to look at the lights but mostly making out. We look happy. We *were* happy. He wasn't complaining about us or pushing me away. Two nights ago, everything was okay. We were us, we were Jessa and Wren.

It's not like our relationship is perfect or anything. The eye contact thing really bugs him. And he gets annoyed that I don't make more of an effort when we hang out with his friends. But when we're alone it's awesome. I can almost forget that I don't have any girl friends, and that my grades suck, and that sometimes the panic is so bad I can't get out of bed. Or maybe it's just that none of that stuff matters as much when I'm with him. And, yeah, it's lame that the only good thing in my life is a guy, but isn't love supposed to blur everything else out?

All at once it seems ridiculous that I'm out here, sitting in the car at ten forty-eight on New Year's Eve.

I go back inside.

The girls on the couch glance at each other when I come in, trading looks I cannot read. "I think he went up," Samantha Levin calls. As I'm turning toward the stairs I see the girl next to her jab a pointy elbow into Samantha's ribs. The gesture tries to burrow itself into my brain, *pay attention to me,* but I don't let it. I start up the steps.

I hear his voice first, coming from his bedroom, the first door on the right. I walk lightly in case he's on the phone with his parents. I'm at the edge of the doorframe when I hear *her.* Alexis Duffy, the girl who called to me from the couch before. She was gone when I came back in. I look over my shoulder, expecting to see her coming out of the bathroom behind me. It doesn't cross my mind that she's in the bedroom, too. That he's in the bedroom *with her.*

"I don't want to be the bad guy." Wren's voice. Defensive, like it's an excuse.

"I get that," Alexis says. "Which is why you should do it already. Stop leading her on."

My heart stops.

"Keep your voice down," Wren says.

"It's not like it's a secret," Alexis says. "They all know."

I picture the girls on the couch downstairs, that elbow poking Samantha Levin's ribs, the knowing looks. My face flames. *look at jessa, what an idiot*

"I don't understand why you haven't done it already," Alexis is saying. "It's been two months, Wren. This isn't fair to me."

"I told you," Wren says. "It's complicated."

"I know, I know. Barbie's unstable."

The fire creeps down my neck, explodes inside my stomach, a furnace of humiliation that will swallow me whole.

this isn't happening

he wouldn't do this to me

"Don't be a bitch, Lex."

"I can't help it," Alexis pouts. "I want you all to myself."

I want the sound to cut out, my ears to fall off, anything to keep from hearing more. And through the crack in the door I see her unbuttoning his shirt and I get my wish. I can no longer hear them. All I hear is my heart, banging around my ribcage like a fish in a dry box. My bones cannot contain it. It will burst through my chest.

i am dying

i can't breathe

I jam my thumb into the hollow spot between my collarbones so hard it makes me cough. The vise around my throat releases. Air rushes in. The smell of Wren's cologne.

The breaths come fast now. I am woozy with them. I fumble for a piece of hair.

here i go down circle road

here i go down circle road

The hair slips through my fingers, the rest of the poem slips away. My chest aches. My lungs burn.

I clasp a hand to my mouth, forcing the air through my nose, and start again.

here i go down circle road strong and hopeful hearted through the dust and wind up just exactly where i started

At last, my breathing slows. The hallway comes into focus. The flopping and flapping in my chest goes still. Inside the bedroom, it's quiet. But not completely. Wren's bed creaks.

i can't be here

nobody wants me here

nobody wants me

As soon as the thought forms I am in motion. I can't get out of there fast enough. I can't be far enough away.

Someone calls after me but I don't slow down. Door, sidewalk, driveway, street, and then I'm in the car pulling away. My vision blurs. I blink to refocus, but the clarity doesn't hold. A flash of red to my right, a stop sign I just blew past.

barbie's unstable she's right

I make a left onto Laurel Canyon. Traffic slows and I am stuck. My bones are itching. My skin is too tight on my face. Everything is closing in. There are no side streets, no shoulder to pull off on.

get out of here i have to get out of here

The line of cars in front of me inches forward. There is nowhere to go.

get out of here i have to get out of here.

I ride the bumper of the car in front of me, urging it forward, *please move faster please.* I fixate on its tail lights, the eerie red glow, and for a moment there is silence and peace. But then it stops suddenly and I slam my foot on the brake and my mind cartwheels away.

Red lights blink white and suddenly we are moving again, snaking up Laurel Canyon, accelerating toward the top. The light is green at Mulholland.

I hit the crest of the hill and jam the gas pedal, a surge of elation that I am finally free.

I don't see it. The black Escalade headed east on Mulholland, rounding the curve without slowing down. I only hear the sound of crunching metal as it hits me, and then I hear myself scream.

Chapter Two

Time fragments. Milliseconds split then expand.

Arrested momentum as my trajectory changes. Pressure bearing down on me, swallowing me up.

Pain explodes in my left temple as the side airbag bursts through the ceiling. My neck snaps sideways, torso wrenches. The seatbelt holds.

The window beside me is sucked inward. A vacuum of pins and needles on my face.

The pressure recedes and I am flung to the side again, caught in a spinning, violent whirl. My head slams against the airbag and lights up with pain. The sensation erases all the rest.

Spinning. I am spinning. My brain jostles inside my skull. Through the spider-webbed windshield, another car catches me in its headlights, the car that hit me, *a car hit me*. I spin again and a tree comes into view.

In the eternity before impact, I see Alexis and Wren. Alexis's cheeks streaked with mascara, eyes puffy from crying, a funeral-inappropriate dress. Wren, dark suit, somber face, pretending he gives a crap that I'm dead when really he killed me, ten minutes before I hit this tree. Rage goes off like a bomb inside my gut.

god you cannot let me die

The other car comes into view again, farther away now, and then the tree. Then metal connects with bark and I slam against the headrest and the spinning stops.

☼

Abruptly, sensation returns.

i am not dead

My skull is lead and fire. Sticky feeling on my eyelids, on my lips. There is water rushing somewhere, like a pipe has burst. Every breath burns, acrid and chemical. Asphalt. Rubber. Gas. My wrist is pinned under something heavy. I can't feel my face.

i am not okay

"Can you hear me?" a male voice asks.

I try to nod. My brain aches with the effort.

"You've been in an accident," the voice says gently. "But you're okay."

Sparks of hope, and of doubt. *there is no way i am okay*

"What's your name?"

"Jessa." I barely hear myself.

"Can you open your eyes for me, Jessa?"

"I don't know," I say weakly. "They feel . . . heavy."

Heavy is an understatement. My eyelids feel like they are caked in wet mud.

"What's that sound?" I mumble. "The water."

"You hit a fire hydrant. I need you to try to open your eyes."

Eyelids lifting in slow motion. A face comes into view. A man standing beside the car. The door is hanging open. I blink, try to get the man's face to come into focus. It almost does. He's my dad's age, dark crinkly eyes, curly black hair, a doctor's white coat.

a doctor. My insides flood with relief.

"Good," the man says. He smiles, and I realize we are eye-to-eye. I am not staring past him, or at the bridge of his nose. My eyes aren't darting away like they always do. They are glued to his pupils, shiny black like wet paint. "Now let's see about that hand."

I follow his gaze and see that the heavy thing on my wrist is the steering wheel, bent to the side, trapping my hand like a cage. The doctor grips the wheel and bends it back. Pain ricochets up my arm as my wrist un-flexes. The doctor sees me wince.

"Pain is okay," he says. "Pain isn't permanent. Pain we can fix."

pain. so much pain

My vision blurs. Woozy, I lean back against the headrest. A hand on my forearm. Two fingers on the inside of my left wrist. Another lightning bolt of pain as the man tugs on my hand. A loud *pop* as the bones snap back into place.

"So what happened back there?" he asks, conversationally, a small talk voice.

I am confused. *why does he sound chatty? why am i still in this car?* There is something dripping on my shoulder.

gasoline, it's gasoline, the car is going to blow up

My eyes dart to the wet spot and see that it is blood. I wish it were gasoline. I hear myself scream.

"Jessa." The man's voice is firm now. "The glass from the window cut your face. That's why you're bleeding. I know it's scary, but you are okay. Do you hear me? You're okay." He says it like it's three syllables, *oh-oh-kay*.

he is lying. i am not oh-oh-kay

"The thing is," he goes on. "The circulatory system has a way of overreacting to stuff like this. So we have to convince your body that it doesn't need to freak out. Does that make sense?"

nothing makes sense

"I—I couldn't . . . see it," I say. I am talking about the other car. I am talking about Wren and Alexis. I am talking about this moment, which came out of nowhere and swallowed up everything else.

The man's mouth moves, but this time his words float by me, unheard. My skull feels like the windshield, splintered, a tiny tap and the pieces would scatter.

Blood trickles into my mouth. Salt and rust on my tongue. Bile in my throat.

"Stay with me, Jessa. Just a few more minutes, okay?"

okay okay okay i am oh-oh-kay

In the distance, sirens wail.

"Is that your purse on the passenger seat?"

my purse, why is he asking about my purse?

He leans into the car. "I'm going to reach over you and grab it, okay?"

The man has my wallet now, is pulling my driver's license from its plastic sleeve. He sets it on my lap and checks my pulse again. "You're doing great," he says. He says something else but the sirens drown him out. Red lights flash in my peripheral vision. Someone cuts the siren off. "The ambulance is here," the man says, and rises to his feet. "I'll be back." His shoes crunch glass as he walks away.

Panic flutters limply in my chest. I am too tired for it to take flight.

Voices outside. Doors opening, the slide of metal, rolling wheels. I turn my head toward the sounds and there's a prickling sensation in my cheek. Not pain exactly. But wrong. Something is wrong.

My fatigue evaporates, burned away by fear.

My hand floats to my face. But it's not my face, it can't be my face. *please god don't let it be my face.* It's not skin under my fingers but chunks of ragged broken glass. Pins in a pin cushion, darts on a board.

The bottom drops out inside me and for a moment I feel everything and then I sink beneath the surface and feel nothing at all.

Chapter Three

Through fog, a woman's voice.

intracranial

contusion

edema

lucky

I cling to this last one, *lucky*, and the fog begins to recede. My mom's voice now, simultaneously hushed and high-pitched.

"But she's . . . *okay*?" That word again. Not three syllables this time, a hurried two.

"It's still too early to know," the other voice replies. She has an accent, I hear it now, Australian maybe. "But her scans look really look good. I'm optimistic. Like I said, she's a lucky girl. Let's just see what happens as we try to bring her out."

"Thank god. And . . . her face?"

Cotton edges sharpen. I am awake.

Eyelids spring open. Light floods in. The light recedes a little and two dark blobs emerge. *blob blob blob*, the word pounds in my brain.

"Jessa, honey?" The sound is coming from the blob on the left. *Mom.* I turn my head in her direction and my skull explodes in pain. I can't see her. I can't see anything except darkness and light. No faces, no color, no anything, just two shapeless masses against a bright void. I blink and blink and blink but nothing comes into focus. My head pounds with the effort. "Jessa," she repeats. "Can you hear me?"

I swallow. My mouth is acid and sand.

"Jessa, I'm Dr. Voss," the other blob says, the one on my right. Australian accent. It's the voice I heard before. Now I see a third blob, moving behind her, hear the sound of cabinets opening and closing, the whoosh of an automatic sink. "You were in a car accident last night," Dr. Voss goes on. "You're in the hospital now."

Dread pools in my stomach. I squeeze my eyes shut.

"What's wrong with my eyes?" I ask thickly. My words are garbled, like I have marbles in my mouth.

"Your *eyes?*" Mom. She sounds confused.

"I can't—I can't see."

The dark patches go still.

Then, the doctor's voice. Measured. Calm. "You can't see anything at all?"

"Blobs," I say weakly. "I just see two dark blobs."

"Someone get me a pen light," Dr. Voss says sharply. Behind her, another cabinet opens. Quick footsteps. An almost inaudible click. The blobs shift and then disappear, burned out by light.

"Pupillary response is normal," she says, to someone else, not to me. "Can we bring up her scans on the screen, please?"

"What's happening?" Mom demands. "You didn't say anything about a problem with her eyes. Why can't she see?"

"There's nothing wrong with her eyes," Dr. Voss says calmly. "What Jessa is experiencing is called cortical blindness, which originates in the brain. I suspect that some of the blood vessels in Jessa's visual cortex may be spasming," Dr. Voss goes on, "which is restricting blood flow to the region responsible for sight. If I'm right, then her vision should return to normal as soon as those arteries relax."

and if you're wrong?

Footsteps in the distance. Someone else enters the room.

"Acute bilateral neurological visual impairment with visual acuity of light perception and motion detection only," I hear Dr. Voss say. Each word lands with a thud in my brain. "No evidence of vasogenic edema. Her vitals are normal."

Another blob appears over me. "Let's try five hundred milligrams of methylprednisolone."

I swallow thickly. Out of the void in my skull I have the thought, *I want my dad.* I try to picture his face in my head, but can't. My vision blurs even more. Tears spill over but I can't feel them on my face.

oh my god

I try to sit up. Pressure against my shoulders, someone's hands, pressing me back down. I try to picture those hands, any hands, but can't. *what do hands look like? fingers? ears?* I can't see anything in my head.

"Hold still, baby girl," a new voice says. Female, older, kind. "The doctors are giving you some medicine to help with your vision. Let's give it a chance to work, okay?"

"I can't," I blurt out. "I can't breathe."

"BP spiking," someone barks.

The hands push harder against my shoulders and now the bed is reclining and I am flat on my back. A blob hovers over me. Something cool and rubbery on my chin and both sides my nose. An oxygen mask, pressing against my face.

I suck air through my nose, feel my lungs inflate. The panic sputters out.

As I exhale, the blob above me becomes less of a blob, more of a woman, or at least the form of one. Her face is still out of focus, but I can make out the shape of her head, the curve of her shoulders, the difference between the paleness of her skin and the darkness of her hair.

"It's getting better," I say, muffled under the oxygen mask. I hear the relief in my voice.

The quick step of shoes on my right. Another person appears over me now, out of focus but still a person, another woman, with cropped hair and purple scrubs under her doctor's coat. *pink I can see pink,* and all at once I can see other colors, too. The red of the pen in the doctor's breast pocket, the blondness of her hair, the purple of her scrubs.

There is a sensation in my skull like someone turning up the color volume, every hue saturating, intensifying, driving itself in. Then, everything sharpens into shape, takes on an edge. The texture of the ceiling, the hairs on my forearm, the fibers of my sheet. Every detail screaming, every molecule jutting out.

I close my eyes, dizzy from the onslaught. Behind my eyelids there are no colors, no shapes, no light. Out of nowhere, a tune plays in my head, words I only half remember, a song I can't place.

was blind but now i see

"Jessa?" Dr. Voss asks. The song cuts out.

"It's better," I mumble through the mask. "Normal, I think." *normal, there is nothing normal about this moment.* I force my eyes back open and immediately flinch. The florescent light above me is uncomfortably bright. "I—I need to sit up."

"Sure," Dr. Voss says, and the bed begins to move. Now my mom comes into view. Her sweater is so black it stings my eyes. Someone lifts the mask off my face.

"Hi, honey," Mom says in a voice that is tight with effort, the effort not to cry.

I raise my gaze to her face and blanch. There's a dark purple splotch on her jaw, and another one by her temple. My brain fumbles to name them, then grabs hold of the word *bruise.*

"Mom. What happened?"

She glances at Dr. Voss. "You were in a car accident, honey. Last night. On New Year's Eve."

These words bounce off me, unheard. "But what happened to *you*?" It's not just the bruise. Her hair is too yellow, her eyes are too blue, her freckles too dark. Her chin is uncomfortably sharp.

"Nothing happened to me, honey." Her lips move weirdly. "I've just been here, worried to death about you." She might be trying to smile, but she is failing. Her mouth won't hold the shape.

Dr. Voss steps forward, edging my mom out. "Jessa, it's completely natural for you to feel a bit disoriented right now. Just try to breathe normally and stay relaxed, okay?"

All of a sudden I feel them. The bandages on my face. The gauze wrapped around my head. The words that bounced off me now dig their way in.

you were in an accident last night
you're in the hospital now

"How bad is it?" I whisper.

"This is a lot to take in all at once," Dr. Voss says gently. There are tiny hairs on her upper lip, a narrow gap between her two front teeth. "How about I give you some time with your mom and we can talk about your injuries after you've—"

"I want to know now," I say.

Dr. Voss hesitates, then nods. "Okay. I'll keep it as simple as I can and we can go over it again any time, alright?"

I manage a tiny nod.

"Here's the big picture," she says. "The airbag that saved your life gave you a serious knock to the head. It hit you so hard it caused your brain to hit the back of your skull. It also shattered your left cheekbone, fractured your jaw, and cracked the wall of your left eye socket." She's matter-of-fact, and that makes me feel better, because if she's matter-of-fact it can't be that bad.

Quick breath, then she charges on. "The left side of your face was essentially in pieces when you arrived. Which turned out to be a good thing, relatively speaking, because the shattered bones helped to reduce the pressure on your brain. It gave your brain room to breathe while we repaired your cheekbone and jaw."

"What about my face?" I ask weakly

"She was talking about your face, sweetie," my mom says patronizingly, patting my leg again. I twist out of her reach.

"I mean the outside," I say. I hear hollowness in my voice, empty spaces between the words where emotion should be. But my feelings are trapped in tiny jars inside me, where I need to keep them, because if I let them out they'll swallow me. "The glass. After the crash, I felt chunks of glass in my face."

Dr. Voss nods. "There was quite a bit of glass in your face. Fortunately, because the window was shatterproof glass, it broke into tiny little balls that made fairly clean incisions. We were able to extract them without much tissue damage. As

long as you keep the wounds clean and follow your postopera-
tive care plan, you should end up with thin, mostly flat scars."

scars

In all the *you'll get better*, there it is, the end of the sentence:
but not all the way.

"It was lucky you were wearing that leather jacket," Dr.
Voss adds. "A chunk of glass in your neck and we could've
been dealing with a very different situation."

I look down at the brace on my right arm. One of the
Velcro straps dangles, half open, exposed, hooks pulled away
from loops. I stare at it and something shifts and suddenly the
loops aren't made of fabric anymore, they are knotted wires,
tangled hair, spiders' legs. I feel as if I am outside my body,
pulled away from it, a strap hanging loose.

"I know it's a lot to take in," I hear Dr. Voss say gently.
"But the hospital has resources," Dr. Voss says gently. Outside
the room I hear two sets of footsteps. "People you can talk to
as you—"

"Jessa?" Wren's voice cuts through everything. "Babe, are
you okay? I tried to come yesterday but they wouldn't let me
into the ICU."

A flash of relief. *thank god wren is here.* Then I smell his cologne, and it flips a switch.

Scalding water on frozen fingers. The sharp sting of sensation rushing back.

"No," I whisper, as the piñata inside my gut cracks open.
Fury and envy and sadness and shame, these feelings spew out

like spin art, flinging themselves against the wall, except there are no walls, I cannot build them fast enough.

i am drowning i am gasping for breath

My ears are ringing, roaring, pressure from the inside out. Every part of me is shaking.

The doctor looks at me. My eyes lock on her nose.

"This is Jessa's boyfriend," my mom says, and Wren steps into view. His hair is so dark it burns my eyes.

His lips move *hey babe* but the sound is drowned out by the roar in my head. I squeeze my eyes shut and the room disappears, Wren disappears, everything blinks out.

"You can't be here," Dr. Voss says sharply. "Family only."

"But Wren is *like* family," my mom protests. She touches my arm. I yank it away. "Jessa, honey, tell—"

The doctor cuts her off. "Out. Now. *Both* of you."

"I'm not going anywhere," my mom scoffs. "She's my daughter."

"She is, but she's also my patient." Dr. Voss's voice is iron and ice. "And what my patient needs right now is some space."

My mom makes a huffing sound. Bracelets jangle as she grabs her handbag. Fall collection, blue anchor printed "Dylan" satchel, the only design of hers to ever make it into *Vogue*. Named after one of the twins. None of her bags are named after me.

"Thank you," I whisper hoarsely when the room gets quiet. My lips are sticky plastic, coated in film. Dr. Voss hands me a tissue.

"You bit your lip," she says. I stare at the tissue in my hands, watch it tremble because my hands are trembling. I press my lips together, ball the tissue up in my fist. The trembling stops. I touch the tissue to my mouth, blot away the blood.

"Can I have some water?" I whisper.

"Absolutely," she replies. She fills a blue cup the size of a thimble and holds it to my lips. I tilt my head back to drink it and feel a thunderbolt of pain in my jaw. I focus on the sensation of cool liquid in my throat, the crumpled tissue in my hand. Ignoring the dribble on my chin, the swollen feeling in my lips. I finish the water and hand her the cup.

Dr. Voss is studying me. "Tell me what just happened."

I swallow. "A panic attack, I guess. I get them sometimes."

"How often is sometimes?"

I shrug. "A couple times a year, maybe." *three times last year. seven times the year before that. in eighth grade there were too many to count.* "I don't really keep track."

She points at the empty cup. "More?"

I nod. "Thanks."

"So when was your first one?" she asks, her back to me, from the sink.

the day my dad left. "Seventh grade."

"What do you think caused it? That first one."

I make air quotes with my fingers. "Generalized Anxiety Disorder."

"Ah. Says…?"

"Dr. Rothschild, therapist to the stars and their dysfunctional children."

"So you went to therapy?" She hands me back the cup. "After your parents' divorce?"

I drain it, still thirsty, so thirsty, then nod. "Twice a week for three months. My mom's idea."

"Did it help?"

"No. Can I please have some more water?"

"Sure." She goes back to the sink. "So what's the story on your boyfriend?"

My ribcage contracts. "He's not my boyfriend." These words are agony to say.

"He didn't seem to know that."

She turns off the water. Pulls a paper towel from the dispenser on the wall, wipes off the cup. "Are there friends you *do* want to see?" she asks. "It's important that you don't isolate yourself. Maybe in a couple days, when you're—"

"How long will I be here?" I ask abruptly.

"A week. Maybe ten days." She hands me the cup.

"And then what?"

"Then you get on with your life," she says.

i didn't have a life

i only had wren

Reflexively, my fingers start twirling. Left hand lifts, reaches for a strand of hair. But the piece I touch is stiff and matted, dreadlocked with dried blood. Suddenly I smell it, hair and blood and tea tree oil shampoo. I choke back a gag. The cup jerks. Water sloshes onto my cotton gown.

"I'll send a nurse in to get you cleaned up," I hear Dr. Voss say.

"Uh huh," I say because it's all I can say without throwing up.

I grab at the loose Velcro, tugging it open even more so the whole strap is free, then roll the fabric around my fingers *up and under up and under* over and over again. "Emotional self-regulation," Dr. Rothschild called it, except that back then it was hair twisting instead of twirling, twisting twisting twisting until the blond strands broke. Not (as Rothschild insisted, kept insisting, tried to force me to admit) because I felt "compelled" to rip my hair out, or because I "enjoyed the sensation" when the follicles tore. It wasn't about the hair at all. Not that Rothschild cared what it was really about, he just wanted to give me 100mg of Clomipramine and an "OCD with trichotillomania" diagnosis and call it a day. I hated every second of the fifty-five minutes I spent in his office every week. Hated him. So I switched from twisting to the less "maladaptive" twirling just to piss him off. The Shel Silverstein poem I memorized later, when the twins were born and things got bad again and my mind learned how to un-distract itself, my anxiety like a magnet, always pulling my thoughts back in.

Twirling the strap helps. My pulse stops throbbing in my temples, my breathing slows. My mind starts to empty itself, thoughts draining out, the way I've trained it to do. If I don't think, I can't feel. And I don't want to feel this. I don't want to feel anything at all.

"Hi, Jessa," an older woman's voice says from the door. The nurse Dr. Voss mentioned, here to clean me up.

can you do insides, too?

She takes out the catheter I didn't know I had and hooks my IV bag onto a rolling rack. "Take it real slow," she says as she helps me to my feet. As if there is any other way to take it. Every part of me aches. My brain feels too big for my skull.

I shuffle toward the bathroom. There is a towel hanging over the mirror, tucked in tight at the sides. Its presence there, the fact that someone felt the need to hang it, sucks the air from my chest. I sway on my feet, lightheaded with fear.

"Easy now," the nurse says, catching my arm. She flips down the handicapped seat in the shower, gestures for me to sit. "This'll be more of a half-shower," she says apologetically, as she starts peeling the bandages off my face. "We can't get your head wet. But I can wash the bottom half of your hair with the hand shower. At least get the blood out of your ends."

I stare past her at the grey tiled wall and let my gaze blur. I feel her movements, the brush of gauze on my shoulders as she unwinds the bandage, lets it fall, but cannot feel my face. I have no sense of where my cheekbones are in space, how far my nose sticks out, what is bloodied cotton and what is bloodied skin.

"You're lucky they didn't have to shave any of it," the nurse is saying. "Usually they do, for this kind of thing." *this kind of thing.* The kind of thing where heads crack like eggshells and whole lives come apart?

The last piece of gauze sticks a little, and her brow furrows as she carefully peels it from my forehead. "There," she says when it's off. "Now you can breathe a little." She shoves the mound of gauze into the trash bin by the sink and lets the metal lid fall.

Out of nowhere, my face starts to itch. The sensation doesn't tickle. It's fire beneath the surface, it makes me want to rip off my skin.

My hands fly to my face, but the nurse is quick. She catches them before they touch skin. "Where does it itch?" she asks, holding my wrists with her hands.

"I don't know. I—I can't tell. My left cheek, I think?" The itch is all consuming. I want to claw my skin off, to dig the creepy crawly out with my fingernails. "I just need to—," I pull away from her, trying to get my hands free. Pain erupts in my fractured wrist.

"I can put Vaseline on it, and that'll help, but, sweetheart, I can't let you touch it. Not yet. I know it itches, and an itch you can't scratch can drive a person crazy. But your skin is raw right now and we've got to keep it clean." She lets go of my wrists and reaches into her shower caddy for a jar of Vaseline. She gently rubs it onto my cheeks.

The itch is so intense that my eyes are watering. I dig my nails into my palms, hard. "Why does it itch so much?"

"The nerves are starting to heal," she explains. "It's a good sign, that you're getting sensation back so soon."

i don't want sensation back. numbness doesn't hurt.

She sets the Vaseline aside and unties my hospital gown, sliding it down so it's a heap around my waist. It registers that I am sitting here topless, but this body I am in doesn't feel like mine anymore so the half-nakedness seems irrelevant, like a rumor, something I'm supposed to care about but don't. The nurse is busy with her washcloth, rubbing the blood off my collarbones, gently scrubbing my armpits and my back. I notice the sensation on my skin, the rub of wet cloth, the slippery slickness of soapy lather running off elbows and tailbone and chin, but it feels far off, like I am far off, like I am no where at all.

At some point, the water stops. The nurse pats me dry with a thin, scratchy towel and helps me into a clean hospital gown, this one purple with tiny yellow birds. "Your parents can bring you some pajamas from home," she says as she ties the new gown behind my neck. "You'll feel more like yourself, in your own clothes."

I nod, though I feel like laughing, like screaming, at the absurdity of this.

"Your dinner should be here in a few minutes," she says as she helps me back into bed. "You're on a soft food diet for the next seventy-two hours, so it'll probably be soup, some apple-sauce, jello. Your parents can bring you something else if you want it, a smoothie or ice cream." She smiles conspiratorially. "There's a Pinkberry down the street."

My parents. It's the second time she's said it. I resist the urge to correct her, *no, my parents aren't here, my dad lives in colorado, it's just my mom and carl, the guy she married a year after my dad left, who i can promise won't be doing a pinkberry run because it's the twins' bath time right now and he couldn't possibly miss that.*

"Do you want me to get them?" she asks. "Now that you're all cleaned up?"

"No, that's okay."

"But your mom—"

"Could you just tell her I'm really tired, and I'll see her tomorrow?" I ask. "It's my brothers' bedtime, and I'm sure she wants to see them before they go to bed." I am aware of how ridiculous that sounds. But I also know that my mom will leave as soon as someone gives her permission to go, and that is reason enough to send her away.

There's a knock at the door. "Do you mind if we come in?" a male voice asks. Two police officers, in uniform, are standing in the hall. "We'd just like to ask Jessa some questions about the accident for our report."

"Jessa needs her rest," the nurse says firmly.

"It'll only take a few minutes," one of the cops says, voice friendly, as they step inside the room. He's young, and really cute. The other one is older, the skin on his face twisted with scars.

My stomach churns. Partly for how uncomfortable the older guy's scars are making me, mostly from the realization that I probably look worse.

"It's okay," I say, because the truth is I don't actually want to be alone. "I'll talk to them."

"I should get her mother, then." The nurse moves toward the door.

The one with the scars steps aside to let her pass. "But we're not here to interrogate Jessa. We only need her statement. We know the accident wasn't her fault." His voice is so kind it makes my heart sting because I am staring at my hands to avoid his face. I force my eyes to space between his eyebrows, the only inch of smooth flesh. "What do you want to know?"

"Your recollection of what happened," he replies.

"A car hit me," I say mechanically. I leave out the crunch of metal, the sharp crackle of glass, the sensation of the world being sucked toward me, my hope being sucked out.

"Did you see it enter the intersection? The vehicle that hit you?"

I shake my head. "I— I heard the brakes. Then I was spinning, and then I hit a tree. The guy who fixed my wrist said I hit a fire hydrant, too. But I only remember the tree."

"What guy?" the younger cop is asking. "An EMT?"

"No, before that. There was a man who came to my window. A doctor. In a white coat. He popped my wrist back and told me the ambulance was on its way."

The cop flips back through his notes. "Okay. According to the driver of the other vehicle, *she* called 911. When the ambulance arrived, there was no one else at the scene."

"That's not right," I say. "He was definitely there when the ambulance got there."

The younger cop looks at the older one. "None of the witnesses said anything about a doctor on the scene."

"Let's back up," the older cop says. "Before all that. Your mom said you were coming from a party in the Hollywood Hills."

"I don't want to talk about the party," I say abruptly. The cops exchange a glance.

"Let's start from the moment you turned on Laurel Canyon, then."

the moment i turned on laurel canyon i was having a panic attack

the moment i turned on laurel canyon my heart was exploding in my chest

My hand jerks to my hair. The cops exchange another glance.

I force my mind back to that moment. My foot on the gas pedal, white knuckles on the wheel, the line of brake lights snaking up the hill. I remember the stuck feeling, the sensation of spiders under my skin. But I can't see it.

I can't see *anything* in my head.

"I can't—," I almost say *remember*, but it's not the memory that's missing. The memory is right there, *here*, pressing in from all sides. Headlights. The crunch of metal. Fragments of glass hanging in the air, suspended for a nanosecond, for an eternity, before they're vacuum-sucked into my face.

so why can't i see it?

There's a sharp pain at my scalp. A broken strand in my fist.

The older man's mouth moves with a question I don't hear. I close my eyes and try to picture *him*, the guy in a uniform with scars on his face who's standing on the other side of my eyelids. I was just staring at his eyebrows. *was his hair dark or light?*

I open my eyes. *dark.* His hair is dark.

"It's common to have trouble remembering a traumatic event," the younger cop is saying. His hair is light, his eyes are blue. "It's usually best to go back to an earlier moment and move forward from there." His tone is so patronizing I want to punch him in the face.

There's a commotion in the hall behind them.

I hear my mom's voice first, high and shrill. "She just woke up from a medically induced coma. Can't they wait?"

"She said she wanted to talk to them," the nurse says.

"I should've been consulted."

"I'm consulting you now."

"They're already in there!"

"Lydia," another voice says firmly. "Stop."

daddy

My brain whirls through memories. Dad taking me to Disneyland, Dad making frozen lemonade in the summer, Dad

singing along with the radio as he drives. Dad packing suit-
cases. Dad leaving a stack of old CDs on my bed. These moments are there, but they're not. I remember them, but can't
see a single one in my head.

His face is there but not there also. Wiry eyebrows, eyes
the color of apple cider, a dimple on his chin. I used to press
my finger to it, pretending it was a button that would make
him laugh. He always did.

dad where are you dad?

He's there, right there. He's nowhere in my head.

"We're not married anymore," Mom is saying. "You don't
get to tell me what to do."

Dad sighs. "Can we please not make this about us right
now? I'm here to see my daughter." The cops move out of the
doorway to let him in.

"Hey, Bear," he says, and my eyes leap to his face.

no that's not right

It's not my dad. It can't be my dad. I'm looking at the
wrong man, I'm looking at the police officer with the scars on
his face.

Except I'm not. The police officer is in uniform and he's
holding a clipboard and making notes. The man standing beside my bed is wearing a UC-Boulder t-shirt and jeans and
there is a dimple in his chin because he's trying his best to
smile but his eyes look like maybe his heart might break. The
man standing beside my bed just called me Bear, my dad's
nickname for me, and his voice is my dad's voice. But the man

standing beside my bed is covered in bruises, *so many bruises*, and there's an ugly tangle of scars on his cheek.

The room blurs.

Lightheaded, I fumble for the plastic railing on my bed, trying to catch my breath as black seeps in on the edges.

"Her blood pressure is dropping," someone says.

"Jessa," my mom says. "Jessa, honey, you're hyperventilating. Focus on my voice."

But I don't want to focus on her voice, I don't want to focus on anything. So instead I just give into it. I let myself pass out.

Chapter Four

"I just want to understand why she lost consciousness," my dad is saying.

"She didn't lose consciousness," my mom snaps. "She hyperventilated because she was having a panic attack."

"And that doesn't concern you?"

I pull the oxygen mask off my face. It's been on for ten minutes, ever since I came to with about thirty people in my room. Dr. Voss made them all clear out, including the cops, and then she left, too. I wish she'd taken my parents with her.

"Yes, it *concerns* me, Eric. But if you knew your daughter at all, you'd know that—"

"Stop," I say. My eyes are on the ceiling, the only safe space. "Please, just stop."

They get quiet.

"How're you feeling, Bear?" Dad asks.

"I want to talk to Dr. Voss," I say.

"I'll get her," he says, and walks out.

I feel my mom trying to think of something to say to me. "Where's Carl?" I ask, even though I already know the answer.

"With the boys," she says. "He wanted to bring them up here to see you, but I thought it was probably best to wait."

let's not frighten the children honey

Neither of us says anything after that.

Dad comes back with Dr. Voss.

"Everything okay?" she asks, coming to my bedside.

"I want to know what happened to my brain," I say. "Like, how exactly it got hurt."

"In medical terms or plain English?"

"English," I say.

"Okay. Your brain collided with the back of your skull giving you a big, fat bruise on the outer layer of tissue and making the whole area swell."

"Can that cause brain damage?"

Dr. Voss frowns. "Well, by definition, that *is* brain damage. What specifically are you asking?"

I fiddle with my hospital bracelet. There's a hum of TV noise from somewhere down the hall.

"I think it would help if I spoke to Jessa alone," I hear Dr. Voss say.

"If she's worried about something, we should know," my mom protests.

"Jesus, Lydia. Can you please not argue with everything everybody says?" My dad pats my leg. "We'll be in the hall, Bear."

"You want to tell me what's going on?" Dr. Voss asks when they're gone.

My fingers push the bracelet around my wrist.

"It's two things," I say finally.

"Okay. Let's start with the first."

"Ever since I woke up . . . I can't see anything in my head. When I close my eyes, it's just . . . dark."

"Dark," she repeats. "Meaning there's no visual quality to your thoughts?"

"Right."

She pulls my chart from the tray on the door. "Any issues with your memory as far as you can tell?"

I shake my head. She makes more notes.

"I'd like to run a few tests before I rule anything out, but what you're describing sounds like a condition called *aphantasia*. Mind's eye blindness. People who have it can't form images in their head."

"So it's a thing, then. Other people have it." There's a sliver of relief in this. If other people have it, it can't be that bad.

"Yep. Some are born with it, actually. But we also see it in patients with cerebral cortex injuries, like yours." She hesitates for a sec. "It can also have psychological roots."

My throat goes tight.

psychological roots

code for crazy

like when you see things that aren't there

I spin my bracelet faster. The cheap plastic, jagged where I've picked at it, scrapes against my skin.

"Are you having any psychotic symptoms?" she asks. "Intense feelings of detachment, paranoia, hallucinations, anything like that?"

I stare at the moving plastic, watch my name go round and round.

psychotic psychotic psychotic

I give my head a tiny shake. "Nope."

"Good." The relief in her voice makes my hands shake.

"So is it permanent?" I ask.

"It can be. But there's no reason to assume it will be in your case. Your brain has suffered some pretty gnarly trauma in the last forty-eight hours. I wouldn't be surprised if this resolves on its own within a few days." She makes a note in my chart. "Hey, how's your vision, by the way?" she asks. "Since those few moments of blindness when you first woke up, has your sight felt normal? Because it's common for patients with acquired aphantasia — the ones who aren't born with it — to experience hyper-vivid sensuality while the mind's eye is dark."

A silly flash of hope at the rightness of the phrase, *hyper-vivid*. I bob my head, *yes, exactly that*. "What does it mean?"

"The mind's eye plays a really big role in perception," she says. "We may feel as though we're seeing things fresh all the time, but the neurological reality is that we're predisposed to see things the way we've seen them before. Without mental images, though, the brain has nothing to fall back on. It has to start paying attention again, which can feel pretty intense." She smiles. "So in a way you're super lucky. You're getting to see the world anew."

"Hurray," I say flatly.

Her smile fades. "Look, I know all of this sucks," she says gently. "But I promise you, it could be much, much worse. You're a very lucky girl."

I nod, my eyes filling with tears. Some luck.

"So what's the second thing?" she asks.

It hovers in the air between us for a second. The awful, ugly truth.

Then I shove it into a drawer and slam it shut.

"Oh," I say lightly. "I was just wondering when I can wash my hair."

Dr. Voss grins. "Crucial question. I'd like to wait at least a week before you really scrub, but I'm okay with your scalp getting wet in another day or so as long as we cover your incisions with waterproof tape." She jots another note in my file then slips it back into the plastic sleeve on the door. "Speaking of dirty hair, I need to get out of here and go wash mine before patients start complaining," she says with a laugh. "I'll see you in the morning, okay?"

I stare at the ceiling as she updates my parents. I hear my dad's stillness as he listens, taking it all in. Mom is the opposite of stillness, she is noisy breathing and fidgety hands and constantly shifting weight.

"Bear," Dad says quietly when they come back in. "I am so sorry this happened to you." His voice catches. "It shouldn't have."

"Oh, so now the accident is my fault?" Mom's voice is shrill, like nails on a chalkboard, like nails scraping across my brain. "Because, of course, I'm somehow to blame for the fact that a stranger ran a red light and plowed into *my* Lexus, despite the fact that I wasn't even in it."

"I'm not blaming anyone but myself," my dad fires back.

"And what's *that* supposed to mean?"

"Mom. Stop."

"I don't understand why you were in the car to begin with," she retorts. "You said you were staying at Wren's. And then when he was here you didn't even *acknowledge* him. Did something happen between you two? Are you in some sort of fight?"

I don't answer her. Can't answer her, can't tell her what happened because that would require thinking about it, which it's taking everything I have not to do.

She sighs heavily. "I give up."

and yet you're still here

"Lydia, go home," Dad says wearily, rubbing his eyes, the feature we have in common. Hazel, with blond lashes, same shade as our hair, though his is mostly grey now. "You've been here since it happened. I appreciate that. Jessa appreciates that. But the two of us in this room together isn't helping anything, certainly not our daughter's recovery, so how about you go home and get some rest. I'll stay with Jessa tonight."

Mom bristles but doesn't fight him. "Fine. I'll be back in the morning." She bends over to kiss my forehead then thinks better of it and kisses the air above me instead.

"So how long are you staying?" I ask my dad when my mom is gone. I am careful. There is nothing in my voice to give me away. No hint of how badly I want him to stay. My hand is already in my hair, twirling a crusty strand. Out of the corner of my eye I see him see it. Dare him to comment the way my mom always does. He doesn't. Then again he wouldn't, because my anxiety has never been his problem.

"Well, that depends," he says carefully.

"On what?"

"On you," he replies. He rolls the metal stool by the sink over to my bedside and sits down on it. There is a long moment when he just looks at me, sneakers planted, palms pressed flat on his jeans. "I want you to come live with me in Colorado," he says finally. "Finish high school out there."

Jessa Bear, I'd love for you to come out here, but your mom and I have decided that it's best if you stay here in California with her and all your friends. We'll see each other all the time, though — every Christmas, over the summer, whenever you want.

Try every other Christmas and one summer out of four.

"There are still a lot of details to work out," he's saying now. "I only just mentioned the idea to your mother, so of course we'll have to navigate that, but technically we have joint custody and you're seventeen, so—"

"It's okay," I say, stopping him before it goes too far. Before hope sneaks its way in and I start believing that he means it. "You don't have to do that."

"Yes, Jessa. I do. I should've put my foot down four years ago. But your mother—," he shakes his head. "It doesn't matter. It is what it is."

but it does matter. it matters a lot.

His voice softens. "Look, I'm not going to force this on you. You're seventeen. If you really want to stay in L.A., you can. I know your friends are here, and your boyfriend—"

An urge, overwhelming, to plug my ears, *la la la, i can't hear you.*

Because if I let myself hear him, let myself think about my life here and how little of it is left, my heart will explode in my chest.

"There is nothing here," I say, loudly. Too loud. Dad stops mid-sentence, maybe mid-word. Neither of us says anything. Above us, the fluorescent light hums.

don't ask me what i mean. please don't ask me to explain.

"So," he says finally. "You'll come then."

I hesitate. Live with my dad. In Colorado. A thousand miles away.

My chin jerks, an emphatic nod. "Okay. I'll come."

Chapter Five

There is a new doctor standing in my doorway, his eyes sharp as scalpels on my face. Another shrink. He's the third one who's come by in five days. Each with their clipboards, making notes. "You've had a tough week," this one says.

Contest for most idiotic statement by a therapist, *we've got a winner in room 203.*

I stare at the wall. "Yep."

"How's your mood?" he asks.

"It's fine," I say automatically.

"Fine, huh? No anxiety symptoms?" He is calling my bluff.

"Nope."

"And the aphantasia? Any progress there?"

"Not really." *not at all*

"Can you look at me, Jessa?"

I glance at him now, and immediately wish I hadn't. His forehead is dry and leathery, almost grey. A horrific, disfiguring burn. My mouth goes salty, the feeling you get right before you throw up.

it's not real

It's a daily refrain now, *it's not real, i'm imagining it, i'm making it up.* The janitor with the black eye, the nurse with the scabs, the plastic surgeon with scars like my dad's. All around me, broken faces. Wounds that make my eyes sting they're so gruesome. Wounds that disappear as soon as I look away. Out of my sightline, ghosts in my head.

"Eye contact is difficult for you," I hear him say. I'm staring at the wall behind him now, where it's safe.

I nod. Except it's not his eyes I'm avoiding right now but the burn I hallucinated on his face. This truth I can't talk about, not unless I want to *keep* talking about it, week after week after week, in some claustrophobic office with a fake plant and a black leather couch. *thanks no thanks*

"Do you use other avoidance techniques?" he's asking now. "Avoidance techniques are coping strategies that—"

I cut him off. "I know what they are."

i use them all

"You've been in therapy before."

"Yep."

"You're not a fan."

"I just don't see the point," I say neutrally. "Talking about it doesn't help." *if i'm talking about it, i can't pretend it doesn't exist*

"How do you know?" he asks.

"Because things got better after the therapy stopped."

"Meaning you had fewer panic attacks?"

meaning i don't want to be having this conversation or any conversation with you

But not answering is not an option. Not answering will only prolong this.

"Right," I say.

"Is it possible that you've gotten so good at avoidance that it may *seem* like your anxiety is better since the therapy stopped, when really you're just doing a better job of suppressing your symptoms?"

I shrug. Game face.

"Here's my concern, Jessa," he says. "People who suffer from mood disorders — that's what generalized anxiety is, a mood disorder — are at a greater risk of developing other psychiatric illnesses following a traumatic brain injury. New onset depression, for example, is very common."

what about hallucinating seared flesh?

"In order to treat these conditions," he goes on, "we have to first be able to diagnose them. But if you're not talking about what you're feeling, we can't do that. So if there's something—"

"I'm hallucinating," I blurt out.

He blinks but doesn't react. *His* game face.

"Okay. Hallucinating what?"

"Scars. Bruises. Scrapes. Burns."

"On yourself."

I shake my head. "Other people. I noticed it for the first time when my dad got here. He had these really awful scars on his cheeks I knew weren't there."

"Do you see them on everyone?"

"No. Just some people."

"What about on me?"

"There's a bad burn on your forehead," I say without looking up. "And a scar on your chin." In my peripheral vision I see him reach for my file.

"The scar's real," he says. "I fell off my bike when I was eight." He flips through my file. "Are they always on the face?"

I hesitate. Without mental images, it's hard to be sure. "I think so, yeah."

"What about your own face?"

"What about it?"

He shrugs. "How does it look?"

I don't answer him. He knows I haven't seen it. That little tidbit is most definitely in my file.

He tries again. "Does the thought of seeing your face make you feel anxious?"

"No," I say, just to be contrary. We both know it does.

"How's your mood?"

"You already asked me that."

"Right. And you didn't tell me the truth. Because if you're hallucinating, Jessa, and you're aware of it, then your mood is not 'fine.'" He sets my file down. "If we're going to solve this, you're going to have to be honest about what you're feeling."

"Fine," I say tightly. "I'm freaked out, okay?"

"About what?"

"Um. The fact that I'm *hallucinating* maybe?" All of a sudden I hate this man, I hate this hospital, I hate all shrinks. The incessant questions and prodding and practiced concern.

"What about your own facial injuries? How do you feel about those?"

"Fantastic," I say sarcastically. "I'm totally psyched."

"So you're angry," he says.

"I don't want to talk about this," I snap. "I just want to know how to make the hallucinations stop."

"Therapy," he says bluntly. "You have to work through what happened to you, Jessa. Avoidance isn't an option anymore. Not if you want the hallucinations to stop."

"Isn't there some drug you can give me?"

"Anti-psychotic medication might help in the short term, but there is no quick fix. Particularly if what you're experiencing is an extreme form of dissociation, which is what I suspect. A way for you to separate yourself from your injuries, to keep them literally at arm's length. But, that's a very cursory analysis based on your history and the little you've said. If you want to get better, you have to get down in the dirt. Dealing with psychiatric illness takes work."

psychiatric illness. Pins and needles erupt in my feet.

"It's just— a lot," I say quietly. "All at once."

"I know it is. But it's also an opportunity. To accept that your old ways of doing things aren't working and to try something new. It's not uncommon for people who suffer trauma to experience what we call 'post-traumatic growth.' A radical, positive change in the wake of adversity. A paradigm shift. Instead of setting them back, the trauma becomes a catalyst for growth."

He smiles a little, obviously waiting for me to say something, *sounds great doc I'm in!*

"Let's start here," he says finally, when it's clear that I'm not going to respond. "I'll refer you to a great therapist here in the Valley who specializes in—"

I cut him off. "I can't. I'm moving to Colorado to live with my dad. Next week."

He gives me an encouraging smile. "They have some great therapists in Colorado. I'll talk to your dad about—"

he won't want you. if he knows about the hallucinations, he'll change his mind

"No," I say abruptly. "I don't want my parents to know about the hallucinations. And you can't tell them."

I have no idea if this is true, but I am desperate.

"You're right," he says, and I think *thank god.* "You're seventeen, so by law, I can't disclose your medical information without your consent, unless I think your life is in danger, or you're a risk to yourself."

you're too late, I want to shout. A risk to myself, that was twelve days ago, when I couldn't see what I should've seen, the truth that was so obvious to everyone else. *wren doesn't want her, why would he, she's damaged goods.* That elbow jab on the sofa, *look at jessa, how pathetic, she has no idea.* But of course that's not what he means, he means a physical risk, and I'm not that, have never been that.

"I'm not," I say, but can tell from his face that he knows this already and that I've won.

He takes off his glasses and rubs his eyes. They look tired all of a sudden. He has a wedding ring on and I wonder if he has kids and whether it's made them more or less crazy, having a shrink for a dad.

"What about the medication you mentioned?" I ask.

He sighs. "I can prescribe Quetiapine, but it won't resolve your symptoms on its own. You need—"

"Therapy. Yeah, got it." It sounds brattier than I mean it to. I immediately feel bad.

He doesn't look annoyed or pissed off. Just disappointed. For half a second I think I might explain it to him, why I can't stay in L.A., why I can't risk my dad changing his mind about me living with him, why I'm afraid that if he finds out just how damaged these goods are, he might. But I don't, won't, because explaining it to this doctor, to any doctor, would require talking about it, out loud, with actual words.

"I'll try," I say when he hands me the prescription. As enthusiastically as I possibly can. "To think of this as an opportunity. Radical positive change. Everything you said."

"I hope so," he says wearily. "You owe yourself that." Then his phone buzzes and I know that we are done.

When he's gone I slide the prescription under my pillow and climb out of bed. I've graduated from the gauze into a circus freak appropriate "compression garment" made out of stretchy pink fabric and Velcro in the back. Basically a sports bra for my face. Dr. Voss fitted me for it this morning, suggested that maybe I'd want to look in the mirror before she put it on.

I told her no, my voice about twelve times louder than it needed to be and an octave too high. No one spoke after that. Ten minutes later, in walked shrink #3. Now his words are rattling in my head.

if you want to get better, you have to get down in the dirt

The towel is gone from the bathroom mirror now, so I see my reflection as soon as I swing open the door. The pink fabric hides everything but the eyes and nose, *my* eyes, blue and watery and dilated. Eyelashes so pale they disappear. The left side of my nose is tinged with purple, a creeping bruise. I grip the inside of the door frame, lightheaded with fear.

please god don't let it be as bad as i think

This thought, it sparks a memory, or the edges of one. Kneeling in my bedroom in our new house the summer after eighth grade, begging God to fix me, to take the panic away. I did it for weeks, the entire summer almost, until my mom got creeped out by it and called a new shrink. After one appointment I was done. With therapy, with God, with believing in a fix. I took a shower the next morning, blow-dried my hair, and told my mom I didn't want to talk about my panic anymore.

She took me to Barney's and bought me a new dress. My Bible went in the box for Goodwill.

I'd never thought much about my looks before that shopping trip. But standing in that dressing room in a pretty dress and makeup from the counter downstairs, *just a little honey it'll perk you up*, staring at a girl in a mirror who didn't look panicky or anxious or the tiniest bit afraid, I felt this weird surge of power. *no one can see it*, I remember thinking. *no one has to know.*

I wore that dress three weeks later on my first date with Wren.

I've been hiding ever since.

This is the darkest dirt. Not how repulsive I am now but how repulsive I've always been. The only difference is that it used to be hidden, tucked inside a pretty girl-shaped case. Now that case is cracked, literally broken in pieces, and, yeah, the doctors set the bones but the scars scream the truth.

I have no idea how bad they are. How many I have. Haven't seen them in the mirror, can't picture them in my head. The wounds on the inside, the invisible ones, those are familiar terrain. The rips and tears that mostly closed up over time. Dad leaving, my friends bailing, Mom getting a new family, God completely checking out. If He was ever there to begin with, which I sort of doubt. Over and over again, the same message, *you are not enough.* You hear it enough times and it weaves itself into you, and it's not an idea any more it's who you are, *not enough.*

But then a boy comes along and changes the message. *you are enough*, he says, *enough for me.* And because he is all you have, being enough for him is enough for you, too, even though you know deep down that *good enough* really just means *pretty enough*, and if he really knew you, all of you, he'd bail, too. Because of him, it stops mattering so much that there are gaping holes inside of you because you fill them with panic, hiding both the panic and the truth of you.

At least, you think you're hiding it.

barbie's unstable

Except I'm not Barbie anymore, not unless they make an Accident Victim Barbie, Brain Injury Barbie, *ew mommy that one is scary-looking, take her away* Barbie. As if Barbie can be anything but flawless, anything other than hollow and plastic and perfect. When she stops being that, she stops being Barbie. She's just a broken ugly doll that nobody wants.

The dirt is everywhere, I am sinking in it, *i can't breathe.* Like sewer water bubbling up through a crack in the pavement, the truth of how messed up I am is on the surface now, will always be on the surface now. It's all anyone will see.

I tug at the Velcro, claustrophobic suddenly, *get this thing off.* The tension releases, the mask falls into my hands, and I see myself in the mirror. Tangled blond hair, splotchy bruises, shiny pink lines in oily skin. Instinctively, I start to count them, my scars.

one

two

three

four

Panic explodes in my chest. *there are so many left*

I stumble backward and slam the door shut. Out of sight, out of mind. Literally.

The whirl inside me goes sour. I gag, stomach heaving, but nothing comes out. My body holds onto puke the way it holds on to panic, tight fist, *don't let it breathe.*

"Honey?" Mom. "What's wrong? Are you sick?"

"I'm fine," I say weakly. *so not fine.* I fumble for the pink fabric, pressing it against my face, but can't get the Velcro to stick. *scars there were so many scars* . Tears come so fast I can't blink them back. I swallow a sob.

"Honey," Mom says gently. "Dr. Voss said you only need to wear that thing at night. She said it's a good idea to let your skin breathe during the day, remember?" She comes towards me, brushes my hair off my forehead. "Plus I want to see your pretty face."

I wrench away from her. "Where's Dad?"

"Right here," Dad calls from the hall, then enters the room, an annoying grin on his face. "Sorry, Bear. I was on the phone with your—," his smile fades. He looks from me to Mom. "Everything okay?"

"Everything's fine," I say tightly, before Mom can answer. "Who were you on the phone with?"

"Your new principal," Dad says. "You're all set to start a week from Monday." The grin returns. "Crossroads sounds so cool. I wish I could go."

Crossroads, the *amazing, incredible, we're so lucky they'll take you,* art school in Denver that Dad keeps talking about. The first time he mentioned it I didn't say anything because, well, I assumed he was just having a dad delusion, since I have no artistic talent whatsoever. I pointed this out to Dad the second time he brought it up, and he waved me away, *don't be silly, Bear, your mom's an artist, I'm an artist, you've always had an eye.* Yeah, as if putting your name on overpriced handbags counts as being an "artist," as though landscape design qualifies as "art," as though "having an eye" is a talent, whatever the hell *having an eye* even means.

"Isn't there a regular school I could go to?" I ask, easing myself back into bed.

"Crossroads will be great for you," Dad says. "You'll see."

"Dad, I'm not an artist. I don't even understand how I got in."

"The principal knows your background," Dad says lightly, and, *click,* I understand. My background, code for *my situation,* code for *that poor girl with a head injury and a broken face.*

Inexplicably, I laugh. My dad sort of smiles. My mom nearly drops her phone.

i am losing it. i am losing my mind

And then I think: *i wish.*

Crazy can't hurt this bad. Crazy can't be this much work.

A phone buzzes inside my mom's purse. She's carrying the black leather tote now, last winter's collection, the bag she brings to funerals. She's been pouting ever since I told her I wanted to live with Dad, really laying it on thick, as if she's devastated that I'm leaving. She gave herself away when she offered to pack up my stuff.

"Honey, Wren is calling again," she says. "Again." My face didn't survive the accident but somehow my phone did, not even a scratch. I told my mom to get rid of it last week, but of course she hasn't, she's playing secretary, answering his calls as though my life is just on hold right now, *Jessa can't come to the phone right now, can she call you back?*

The anger rushes back now, whoosh, filling me up.

radical, positive change

"Can I have my phone?"

My mom hands it to me. I palm it, then hurl it at the wall. It clangs against the metal cabinet and falls into the sink.

"Jessa!" my mom shrieks. "What is wrong with you?!"

I look at her. "Really, Mom?"

My dad steps between us. "Bear. Your mom is doing the best she can." *nice try, dad.* No way he actually believes this.

"I asked her to get rid of my phone."

"Your friends are *worried* about you," Mom says from behind him, and I almost laugh. My friends ditched me in seventh grade when the panic attacks started. A year later, Mom married Carl and we moved to the Valley to live with him and I met Wren and the fact that I didn't have any friends didn't matter so much because I had him. He wasn't weirded out by my anxiety. He never even mentioned it. I loved him for that, for not making me talk about it, ever. For letting me be who we both wanted me to be, a girl without issues, a girl who was good enough for him.

My anger wavers a little, tangos with sadness before I sweep them both away.

Chapter Six

Eyes, an airplane full of them, every pair pinned on me. They burn like lasers, searing into my flesh.

they are staring at me, everyone is staring at me

People looking at me has never been pleasant, but this is excruciating, absolute torture, a thousand splinters under the skin.

My own eyes jump around the cabin, not landing anywhere. I fight the urge to run.

As we pass the exit row, a woman turns and whispers something to the man in the seat beside her, *look at that girl, oh my god, what's wrong with her face?*

I drop my chin, stare at the thin strip of carpet, humiliation burning my cheeks. Dad lifts my bag from my shoulder and puts it in the overhead bin. "You okay?" he asks quietly.

"Yeah." My voice is flat. This exchange happens over and over again, every five minutes it feels like. Our meaningless call and response.

He is watching me, but I pretend not to notice. I pretend to be focused on the Sky Mall magazine open on my lap. *The Cocoon! Cocoon yourself in revolutionary comfort!* The man in the ad is zipped up in a full body blanket, and I envy him.

I turn the pages mechanically, willing my dad to fall asleep. His attention is suffocating, like a jacket that's two sizes too tight. It's not just his eyes, it's his focus, the constant scrutiny and concern. I can't breathe when he's watching me, which is most of the time. It's never been like that with my mom. Even before the accident, her gaze seemed to float past me. Now it's been pointedly off its mark, aimed at the wall behind me or a few inches below my chin. Lucky for both of us, she won't have to look at me anymore. Not until summer at least, when I'm supposed to go back to L.A. for a few weeks to see a plastic surgeon about "revising" my scars.

My stomach has twisted just thinking about my face. Out-of-sight-out-of-mind hasn't worked so well, not when my mom won't look at me and my dad won't stop looking at me and my doctors keep commenting on my progress and asking if I want to see it. *if i wanted to see it i would look in a mirror,* I want to scream. But I do not scream, I just shake my head.

It's an avoidance behavior, I know that. I'm fine with that. Avoidance works.

"So," my dad says when we're in the air. He's drinking coffee from a Styrofoam cup. So much for him falling asleep. "Are you even a little bit excited about the move?"

The knot in my stomach gets tighter.

"Sure," I say.

Dad nudges me with his shoulder. "Wow, that's super convincing, Bear." He is angling for a smile. I wish I had one to give. I go back to my magazine. Eventually, he gives up.

❋

Dad's house in Denver is small and kid-free and quiet, the exact opposite of Mom and Carl's house. It looks the same as it did two Christmases ago, though I didn't remember all the mirrors. Two in the living room, one in the dining room, another in the hall. There used to be two more in the guest room, my room now, one above the dresser and another behind the door, but Dad took them out when I asked. I've gotten good at dodging the others. My eyes flick to the carpet when I enter the hallway and stay there until I get to the kitchen. The kitchen, *thank god*, is mirror-free.

So the kitchen is where I hang out, watching the tiny TV on the counter from a swivel bar stool and drinking superfood smoothies. *Eat well*, that's number seven on the list I made before I left the hospital, after *don't avoid, make friends, no boyfriend, work out* and *deep breaths*, all scrawled on a piece of pink notebook paper folded in my bag. Radical positive change. The list feels like a start. At the very least it's a step in the opposite direction, away from my life in L.A., away from my life with Wren.

So far *eat well* is the only item on the list that I can check off, but I'm doing that one really well. I've consumed more kale, quinoa, and cacao nibs in the nine days I've been in Colorado than I have in my whole life. It helps that Dad is big on superfoods, both as a concept and as a word he attempts to insert in pretty much any sentence involving food. Not that eating better would take much effort, considering my diet before the accident basically consisted of Red Vines, cereal, and take-out pad thai, *bon appetit.* The twins ate early with the nanny, and Mom and Carl ate together late, so I ate whatever I wanted, which was usually not much.

"What time do you want to head out?" Dad asks from behind me. He's at the kitchen table, reading the *Home and Garden* section of the newspaper and eating almond butter from the jar. There's a giant bowl of steel-cut oatmeal on the counter in front of me, with almond butter and slices of banana mixed in. It took Dad twenty minutes to make it, but I'm too nervous to eat, so I'm basically just pushing the bananas around with my spoon.

"Never?" I suggest.

"How about seven-fifty?" he asks. "That'll get you to school by eight-fifteen."

School. The word is a grenade in my gut.

School is for smart girls, and talented ones, girls who *thrive* and *excel* and *achieve.* The kind of girl I was before my dad left, *gifted,* before my anxiety took over and I started freezing up on tests. When I switched schools in ninth grade my

GPA was so bad they put me in all remedial classes and even then I couldn't manage better than Cs. But that was okay, because school was where Wren was, and it didn't matter that my grades sucked because I had him. As long as I was his girl-friend, I was enough. I didn't have to be anything else.

"Bear?"

"Sure," I say, and shrug like it doesn't matter, a gesture that's for me as much for him. "Whatever you think."

"You know . . . I don't *have* to take you," Dad says casually. "I usually take the RTD to work anyway, so you're welcome to use the Jeep to drive yourself if you feel—"

I cut him off. "I don't want to drive."

"Okay. You know I'm happy to drive you. To school or anywhere else you want to go. I just don't want you to wait too long to get behind the wheel again."

don't avoid

"I'll drive eventually," I say. "It hasn't even been a month yet."

"It's been five weeks, Bear. Today is February 9th."

"I have to finish getting ready," I say, sliding off my stool. *deep breaths.* I hear Dad sigh.

※

A dark brown ring on the wooden end table. I am fixated on it. The word *knot* is knocking around in my head, is that what this is? I am telling myself that the answer to this question matters so that I won't think about anything else, like the fact that the plexiglass wall behind me is the only thing separating me and the hallway full of kids on the other side.

This end table I'm staring at, I literally see every grain. The handout Dr. Voss gave me when I left the hospital said that all of my senses could exhibit "heightened sensitivity" while my mind's eye is out, but so far it's only been my vision that's amped up. My eyes feel like they've been coated in magnifying glass, like they're constantly zooming in. The space between my eyebrows pretty much always throbs.

I follow the grain as it curves around the dark spot near the edge of the table, the *knot.* Hair knot, wood knot, it seems weird now that they are the same word. I absorb the details, every gradient of color, every curve of every line, then quickly press my lids closed before the image fades.

But it's already gone. It was never there at all.

circle. table. brown.

I am a magician trying to pull a rabbit out of a dark, empty hat.

what does a rabbit look like?

a hat?

My jaw aches from clenching, my mind aches from straining.

table! circle! rabbit! hat!, these words are a soundless shout.

The turn of a knob behind me and my eyes pop open. Someone enters the front office from the hall. Footsteps, then a pair of brown leather work boots appear in the corner of my view. The boy wearing them stops beside me. I keep my eyes on the table as he fumbles through his bag. My mind randomly leaps to Wren's shoes, the linen loafers he always wore, never with socks. The tops of his feet were always peeling a little from the sun. I remember this all so clearly but can't picture any of it in my head. Not his sunburned feet or his perfect ankles or the way his face looked when he told me he loved me on Christmas Eve sophomore year. The void in my head dilutes the realness of him, as if my memories are coated in cotton, dulled to the point of irrelevance, like I'm thinking about a movie plot, or something that happened in a dream. But instead of making it better, the far-off feeling makes it worse, because my brain won't stop reaching for them, these images I've lost.

"Jessa Gray?"

Surprised by the voice — a girl's voice, lilting and almost lyrical and the exact opposite of the boots — I look up.

The girl's face totally feminine, pretty even, in an I-don't-give-a-crap-if-people-think-I'm pretty sort of way. Her auburn hair is cropped in a sort of asymmetrical bob, chin length on one side and buzzed almost to her scalp on the other, and she's not wearing any make-up. Her outfit is like her haircut; stylish, but not especially flattering. Wool pants cuffed above boys' work boots, a silky white t-shirt under a bulky brown cardigan. She reminds me of the models I saw hanging out backstage at my mom's one and only runway show two years ago. Exotic cranes in boys' clothing, twiggy and unassuming in hoodies and beanie caps and Ugg boots. But unlike those girls, this one has her guard up. She wears her caution like armor, stiff and opaque.

"Are you Jessa?" the girl asks again. Without meaning to, I look her in the eyes. They're hard and bruised and wary.

is that how my eyes look?

"Yeah, that's me," I say, dropping my gaze as I reach for my bag. One of my mom's designs. I never would've carried one of her bags back in L.A., but I had to get rid of the one I had with me the night of the accident. The smell of asphalt and burnt rubber was seared into the leather. The hardware on this new bag seems garish and clunky to me now, and sharp somehow, as if the edges of the gold-plated buckle might slice my skin.

why am i carrying this heinous bag?

"I'm Hannah," the girl says.

"Hi," I say, and stand. I force myself to look at her, pretend not to notice that she's staring at my scars. "Sorry you have to do this. Show me around, I mean."

"It's no big deal," Hannah says, and shrugs. Her whole body appears jostled by the movement, like the Tin Man in *Wizard of Oz*. She awkwardly shifts her weight. "Um. So. Do you have your schedule?"

I nod and dig it out of my bag. When I hand it to her, our eyes meet briefly again. The caution has faded a little, the hurt has mellowed out. She's mostly curious now.

She glances down, scans my list of classes. "Performing or visual?"

"Huh?"

She points at the letters *CM* at the top of my schedule. "The comparative media program. Which concentration are you in?"

I shrug. "No clue."

Hannah has questions but doesn't ask them. She hands the schedule back. "You wanna go now or wait?"

"Wait for what?"

"The bell. If you come in after everyone is sitting, you'll get the whole new-girl routine when you walk in." She shrugs. "If you want that."

"No," I say quickly, stomach clenching at the thought.

do i look like someone who would want that?

"Then we should hurry," she says, pulling open the door. "We've only got two minutes 'til the bell."

The noise in the hallway nearly knocks me over. So many voices, so many decibels, so much sound. My hands fly to my ears.

don't be a freak

I quickly drop my hands.

too late

Hannah is staring at me.

"I was in a car wreck," I say, because I have to say something, and *my hearing is on overdrive because I'm experiencing aphantaisa as a result of a traumatic brain injury* is too many words.

She blinks, and now empathy is everywhere; in her eyes, on her forehead, around her pale, chapped lips. "I'm sorry," she says softly.

My throat clamps up.

A group of boys passes us. They get quiet when they see me. One of them nudges another, nods at my scars.

"We can walk around the building," Hannah says quietly, nodding at the metal door just a few feet away. "It'll be quieter. And faster." I nod, grateful, and zip up my puffy coat. I realize then that Hannah doesn't have a jacket with her. It was sleeting when Dad dropped me off.

"But you'll freeze," I say.

"I'll be fine," she says, and heads toward the side door. I follow her. I don't even know this girl, but I suddenly don't want to be without her.

The metal latch grates against the door frame when she pushes the door open with her hip. The icy air rushes in, a storm of tiny needles on my cheeks.

Outside the sky is a pale, dimensionless void. It's still sleeting. I keep my head down, watching the soggy wetness, heavy in the dead grass, darken my boots.

Hannah leads the way around the building, hands jammed in her pockets, cardigan pulled up around her neck. I tilt my head back as I follow her, eyes open, staring down the sleet. It's as if I can see the snow melting into rain, as if I'm watching it transform in mid-air. Something beautiful and delicate shifting shape, becoming hard and heavy and mundane. And yet, from this vantage point, even the ordinary rain has its elegance. Tiny teardrops in flight.

"This is the G hall," I hear Hannah say, metal door opening, a surge of voices and movement and sound, as a raindrop smacks me in the eye. I blink quickly, vision blurring, a chill settling in behind my left eyelid, seeping out to the rest of my face. "English and history are on G, and the student lounge. Technically it's for the alternative school, but anyone can use it."

"Alternative school?" I ask. "Like, for pregnant girls?"

"Pregnant, anorexic, bipolar. Kids like my brother who suck at regular school. We've got a wide array of dysfunction here."

And now, *click*, it makes perfect sense, why Dad was so keen on my going here, how he was able to get me in.

"Oh," I say, because I can't think of anything else.

Hannah glances over at me, then looks embarrassed suddenly, like she's put her foot in her mouth.

"That wasn't pejorative," she says quickly. "Dysfunctional in the most interesting sense."

dysfunctional is only interesting if it doesn't apply to you

Just then, the bell rings. Loud and shrill, the sound knocks me off balance inside.

i don't want to be here

Around us, bodies and backpacks in motion, a swirl of color and movement and noise. Lockers the shade of basketballs. Bright, screaming graffiti on the walls above.

Somebody's idea of art, no doubt, but the onslaught of pigment feels like an optical assault. It's all too harsh, too saturated, too much. I keep my eyes on the back of Hannah's muddy brown sweater, distracted now by my inability to picture actual mud in my head. For an eerie second, I wonder if mud even exists.

i am losing it. i am losing my mind

"This is you," Hannah says when we reach my classroom's door.

"Thanks."

"I'll meet you here after class," she says, and smiles a little. "Good luck." Then she's off, the back of her brown sweater the dullest shade in the over-colored hallway, yet somehow the brightest, too.

I keep my legs moving, don't let myself consider not going in. *be normal just be normal.* Heads turn as I make my way toward an empty desk in the back, curiosity so potent I feel it on my skin, but I ignore it, ignore them, focus on the speckled surface of the floor beneath my feet. There is a strand of dark hair wrapped around the silver leg of a desk, a smashed chunk of banana I recognize by its smell, hunks of mud somebody in sneakers tracked in. My stomach churns as my brain clocks these things but doesn't store them. *hair, desk leg, banana, mud.* Words that do not stick, words that are just words.

There's a worn copy of *The Picture of Dorian Gray* on my desk, a class syllabus tucked inside the cover. The desk looks new, but the chair attached to it is cracked down the center and someone has etched the word TRUTH onto the surface of the blue plastic seat. At the front of the room, a woman is writing on the white board. The teacher, I guess, though she's not like any I had in L.A. Black leather pants and combat boots, spiky platinum hair and a tattoo of a rose on her neck. Its petals stand out in crisp detail, even at this distance. Its thorns seem to prick at my eyes.

"We're on chapter three," this teacher says, and I flip to the appropriate page and spend the rest of the class period pretending to listen as they talk about the book. Creepy looking man on the cover, tissue soft pages inside. I flip when they flip, force myself to blink, to nod like I am listening. But I'm not listening, I can't listen. I'm too aware of the girl in the desk beside me who keeps looking at my scars. She's trying to be subtle about it, but every few minutes she completely turns her head in my direction. I imagine myself whipping around to face her, calling her on it, *I CAN SEE YOU*. But I never would.

The bell rings eventually. I wait for the girl beside me to leave. I put the book in my bag.

"Hey," Hannah calls from the door. "You ready?"

"Yep," I say, and slide out of my desk. One foot in front of the other, *deep breaths*.

"So where were you before?" Hannah asks when we're back in the hall. "Public school?"

"California. I moved here to live with my dad."

"Were you in an arts program out there?"

I shake my head. "This school was my dad's idea. I suck at art."

Hannah gets quiet. "I feel like a jerk for what I said before," she says finally. "About the dysfunction thing. I didn't mean—"

"It's fine," I say quickly. "Really."

"Seriously, though. I don't want you to think I feel superior or some crap because I'm in the certificate program. It's not like there's some big divide. It's the opposite actually — that's the whole theory behind the school, that there shouldn't be a distinction. Everyone takes the same classes, does the same things. We just have a performance element, and an extra set of grades. The asshole aspect is optional," she adds. "Apparently, I opted in."

I smile a little. "What kind of art do you do?"

"Music. I play the piano."

"Is this a really good school for that?"

"It's okay," Hannah replies. "Mostly I'm here because my parents can't afford to send me anywhere else and I haven't been able to get a scholarship to somewhere better yet. And because Marshall's here."

"Is Marshall your boyfriend?" I feel a twinge in my chest where my heart would be if Wren hadn't torn it out.

"Ew. Gross, no. Marshall's my twin brother. I don't have a boyfriend."

I feel it coming, *do you?*

"My mom has twins," I hear myself say. Not, *I have twin brothers*, what a normal person would say, *but my mom has twins*, as though they have nothing to do with me. Which is how it's always felt, but still. I don't know why I'm even bringing them up. "With my stepfather," I say, to clarify. "They're my half brothers."

I can almost see them. Dylan's dark eyes, Wyatt's freckles, their matching devilish grins. Almost, but not quite. Almost, but not at all.

"Identical or fraternal?" Hannah is asking.

"Fraternal. My mom had in vitro. There were actually three of them but one of them died."

Hannah's face registers discomfort, sadness, shock.

"It wasn't a big deal or anything," I say quickly. "It happened really early on. Before they were born."

why am i telling her this?

"That must've been hard on your family," Hannah says, her voice like a greeting card now, stilted, too formal, *I'm sorry for your loss*.

My family. Is that what they are, Mom and Carl and the twins? It always felt like *a family* and then, separately, *me*.

My mind disengages from our conversation, like the latch on the heavy door we just walked through. We are back outside again, in the quiet, in the cold.

✻

Hannah comes to get me after chemistry, taught by a man with shaggy white hair and a matching beard, like Santa. Or maybe not like Santa at all. I kept trying to picture him, *rosy cheeks, white beard, red hat,* beads of sweat on my forehead when his face wouldn't come. When the bell rang I barely heard it. I sat, gripping the edge of the lab table, *cheeks! beard! hat!,* as the room cleared out, convinced that Hannah wouldn't come for me, that I wouldn't recognize her if she did.

But then I heard my name and there she was, standing in the doorway, like a lantern in the dark. I could let go of the table and stand up.

"The cafeteria's across from the office," Hannah is saying now. "But I need to practice during lunch."

"Got it," I say, taking the hint. "I'll catch up with you later, then." My voice is casual, nonchalant even, but inside I am desperate, *please don't go.* My eyes jump to the GIRLS sign behind her. I can feel the toilet seat against my calves, the crinkle of the paper cover under my butt. My eighth grade daily ritual, pre-Wren, perching cross-legged on a toilet during lunch time, eating a sandwich out of a sack. Holding my breath each time the bathroom door opened. Dropping broken pieces of hair into the water, watching them float on the surface, flushing them when I left. My chest aches with the memory of it.

i don't want to be alone

"You can come if you want," Hannah says casually. She shifts her weight, fiddles with the hem of her sleeve, suddenly insecure, as if she's worried I might turn her down. It's so absurd I almost laugh. "I mean. No pressure, obviously. Just if—"

make friends

"Yeah," I say quickly. "That'd be great."

Hannah smiles. "Rad."

The practice rooms are on the music hall, a length of windowless doors, a space that reverberates with contained sound. Hannah goes to the room at the end, holds open the door.

From inside, voices. Girls talking. I wasn't expecting others. My eyes dart to where the door's hinges should be, to the place where a space should have appeared but hasn't. I can't picture it, but I know this should happen, the creation of a space to peek through, a *crack* between door and frame. *Crack,* another word, like *knot,* that doesn't fit. Windshields crack, and cheekbones and cuticles and confidence. Sometimes all the way through.

"Jessa?" Hannah pops her head back out. "Are you coming in?"

"Yeah, sorry." I force a smile and follow her inside.

The room is nicer than the hallway. Berber carpet, wooden walls, a grand piano, music stands in a cluster at one side. When the door shuts behind me, the noise from the hallway abruptly goes out. The door is soundproof, I realize, designed without hinges because hinges make cracks, and cracks leak.

The other voices belong to two girls with violins. They are packing up their instruments now, gathering their things. They stop when I walk in.

"Hi," the taller one says, staring me down. I swallow thickly. Her forehead is puckered with scars. "I'm Janet. This is Chloe."

"Jessa," I say, sweat cooling the backs of my knees. *they're not real, i'm imagining it, i'm making them up.* The refrain kicks in automatically even though I haven't needed it in over a week, not since the barista at Starbucks with the bruises and the burns. Then again, I haven't left the house.

"What instrument are you?" Chloe asks coolly. She looks normal, almost. There's a brownish bruise on her right cheek, edged in yellow, the shade a bruise turns as it fades. I stare at it, weirdly thrilled by its color. The color of progress, of healing, a wound on its way out. If my brain is making up old bruises now instead of new ones then maybe it means my mind is finally working its crap out.

"She's not in the music program," Hannah says when I don't answer. She's on the piano bench with her back to us, playing scales. Her fingers move up and down the keys the way mine twirl hair; fast and fluid, no effort at all.

The girls' faces relax. "Oh," Janet says, and now she's not hostile, just confused. "What are you doing in here, then?"

"Do you guys mind?" Hannah calls over her shoulder. She doesn't stop playing. "I only have forty minutes."

As soon as the girls leave, she pulls her hands off the keys.

"Sorry about that," she says. "They also opted-in."

I smile a little. "I thought the shorter one was going to stab me in the eye with her bow."

"Only because she can't reach Janet. Chloe's second chair and it drives her insane." Hannah rifles through her bag and pulls out a piece of sheet music, sets it on the stand.

"Is everyone here that intense?"

"Not everyone," she says, laying her hands on the keys. "Only the ones who are good."

At first I think she's joking but then she doesn't laugh.

"So how many hours a day do you practice?" I ask.

"Normally, two or three. Right now, six."

"A *day*?"

"I'm applying to Interlochen," she says. "It's a boarding school for the arts in Michigan. Literally the best music program in the country. It's basically Juilliard for high school kids. Going there would change my life. But their admissions rate for rising seniors is less than five percent, and I can only go if I get an Emerson scholarship, which only forty kids in the world get. I tried for one last year and didn't get it. This is my last shot."

"When's your audition?"

"Twenty-six days."

Her dark eyes are the only thing moving as she studies her music. The rest of her is still, steady, muscles taut like she might pounce on the keys. Abruptly she turns her head to look at me. "Can you sit or something? You're sort of throwing me off."

"Sorry," I say, and drop to the floor. "Is here okay? Where do people usually sit?"

"They don't," Hannah replies, eyes back on the music, fingers drawn up on the keys, every ounce of her focus hovering in that space between her hands and her face, shoulders rising and falling with long, steady breaths. "I've never had anyone in here with me before."

"This is Liszt's *La Campanella*," she says then, and starts to play. Slowly at first, left hand then right, back and forth, taking turns on the keys. Then her right hand plays faster, a delicate pitter-patter on the high notes. The left hand stays lower, more measured, precise. Faster, and then faster, the tempo picks up. Her hands leap from one end of the piano to the other, her fingers like hailstones on the keys.

"Wow," I breathe when she's finished. "That was—"

"Sloppy," she mutters sharply under her breath. She looks over at me. "Sorry," she says. "I'm off my game."

"Are you joking? That was incredible. I've never heard someone play like that."

"I'm having trouble with the two-handed trills," she says, ignoring my compliment, flexing her wrist. "The parts where it alternates between adjacent notes." She demonstrates with her pinky and ring finger on her right hand, fingers fluttering like a hummingbird's wings. "Ugh!" she says suddenly, clenching her hand into a fist and banging it down on the keys. Self-loathing darkens her features, pulls on her brows.

i know what that's like

Then, as fast as it appeared, the darkness is gone, painted over with confidence, and I think to myself *i wish i had that.* "From the top," she says, straightening up.

She starts again, but this time only gets a few bars in before she stops, abruptly, and curses under her breath.

i should offer to leave. i'm throwing her off

"Hey listen," I say, reaching for my bag.

"Don't go," she says suddenly. "I mean. . . Unless you want to. If you're bored or whatever. But don't feel like you have to." She smiles a little. "I'm glad that you're here."

She starts playing again before I can say anything, which is good, because my throat is too tight to speak.

me too

Chapter Seven

what if I don't recognize her?

It's less of a question, really, more of a statement, *i will run into hannah and not know it's her and she'll drop me or hate me or think i'm a freak.*

I try to tell myself there's nothing to worry about. According to the handout from the hospital, most people with aphantasia have no trouble recognizing familiar faces. Which has been true so far for me. I knew who my parents were right away, and eventually my doctors. But Hannah's face is hardly familiar yet. I've known her all of one day.

And there it is again, that all-consuming thought, running on a loop in my brain: *i will run into hannah and not know its her and she'll drop me or hate me or think i'm a freak.*

It's all I can think about as my dad pulls into the school parking lot the next morning. The sidewalk in front of the building is crowded with bodies, kids hanging out before the bell. As the line of cars in the drop-off line inches forward, fear erupts in my chest.

"Can you drop me off across the street?" I ask abruptly.

"Across the street?" Dad looks confused. "Why?"

"I just— I want to walk. I need some air."

He points at the clock on the dash. "It's already eight twenty-five, Bear."

"I'll walk fast," I say, fighting panic, *i don't want to get out here.* "Please."

He nods and pulls out of the line of traffic, looping around to head back toward the street.

I point at the red brick building across the street. A bank. "You can drop me off there."

Silence. Not, *sure, honey* or *whatever you want* or any of the other things I expect him to say. Still, he pulls out of the school parking lot and across the main road. "I'll wait here until you get inside school," he says when he parks.

"You don't need to—"

"I wasn't asking, Bear."

I get out of the car without looking at him.

"I want to talk about this," he says, leaning across the passenger seat. "This afternoon, when I pick you up."

"There's nothing to talk about."

"Jessa," he says calmly. "I know I haven't been there. I know you've been handling all of this on your own. But that doesn't mean you should be."

"Pick me up here," I say brusquely, and shut the door in his face.

There's a handful of kids waiting at the crosswalk with skateboards and bikes. I feel my dad's eyes on my back as I join them, willing the light to change so we can cross. When it does I follow them across the street, hanging back a little to make distance between us, walking faster when the little orange hand starts to blink. On the other side, they stick to the sidewalk, hop back on their skateboards and bikes. I walk across the grass instead, my hands jammed in my coat pockets to keep them out of my hair. My left wrist, the one I fractured, aches from the angle and the sharp, grey cold. My eyes, those are pinned on the patchy brown grass. The yard gives way to sidewalk cement then a slick concrete floor. The cold, still quiet becomes heat and movement and noise. I'm inside.

I follow the route I drew on the inside of my hand, paranoid I'd get lost, even though Dr. Voss told me that most people with aphantasia can find their way around without a mind's eye. Down the main hallway, take a right on C. I get there without using my map. My locker is in the bank at the far end, number 413, on top. I wrote my combination on my hand, too. The hall is too crowded now, people on both sides, so much noise. There's a kid two lockers down with giant burns on his face. My hand is shaking as I turn the dial.

The little pink rectangle is the first thing I see when I open my locker. It wasn't there yesterday because I definitely would've noticed if there were a slip of paper the color of baby Tylenol laying on top of my chemistry textbook. It's impossible to miss. I can't remember the last time I took baby Tylenol, the last time I saw those chalky chewable pills. The color, though, is somehow lodged in my brain. I couldn't picture it if I tried, but the second I see that pink piece of paper, that's the thought I have, *baby Tylenol*, then, just as quickly, *office slip.*

I could ignore it. Grab my book, let the paper slide down between my other books, pretend I never saw it, get on with my day. But then tomorrow there'd be another slip in my locker, and maybe that one would be yellow, or blue, which ever color means *second warning, last chance before we call for you over the intercom, you should've just come on your own.*

I have experience with office slips. In eighth grade I got them all the time. Every Friday, practically, after being tardy to fifth period four times in a row. My math teacher didn't care why I was late to class every day; she never even asked. She just reported me to the office every fourth time, protocol, and carried on with remedial math. Not that I wanted her to ask. If she had, I would've shrugged and said I lost track of time, the same thing I told the principal every Friday. He never did anything about my lateness, which means he must've known about my anxiety, or at least about my parents' divorce. He'd just sigh and ask me to please try to do better and then give me a pass to return to class. I couldn't tell them the real reason that it took me until ten minutes after the bell to feel calm enough to leave my perch in the girls' bathroom, when I knew the sinks would be empty and the halls would be too.

Just thinking about eighth grade makes my stomach hurt. It was so much worse than seventh grade, the year the panic attacks started, when I still didn't know how bad they'd get, or how completely my friends would bail when they did. Eighth grade was when I found all that out. I didn't know Mom would start dating Carl on Valentine's Day and marry him in Vegas three months later. I didn't know we'd move to the Valley that summer and I'd go to a new school that fall and a cute lacrosse player would ask me out, changing everything, changing me, pulling me out of the dark. My insides squeeze. I also didn't know that lacrosse player would break my heart two years later. In eighth grade all I knew was how sad and scared I was, and how impossible it seemed that I'd ever be anything other than that.

Pretty much exactly how I feel right now.

Someone opens the door at the end of the hall and there's a whoosh of cold air. The pink slip flutters. I grab it before it slips behind my books.

"Hey," someone calls. "You're Jessa, right?"

he's talking to me

Now that I'm aware of his presence, I see him in my peripheral vision. A guy, a few lockers down. Baggy blue cords and a hooded sweatshirt, wavy brown hair that's sticking up in places, maybe like he styled it that way, maybe like he just woke up. For a second I am frozen, puppet strings jammed. Then I give them a yank and my head is turning and I'm trying to smile but can't. In the same motion I crumple the office slip in my fist.

"I'm Marshall, Hannah's brother," he says, slamming his locker shut. I jump a little at the sound, metal on metal, that particular crunch. Marshall notices, and winces. "Sorry," he says quickly.

I feel myself recoil, retreat back into myself, embarrassed by whatever Hannah said to make him react like that.

i met this girl yesterday she has issues she's a total freak

"So Hannah said you're from L.A.," he says easily, slinging his backpack over his shoulder.

make friends

deep breaths

I try again to smile. "Yep."

"I love L.A.," he says.

There's no way this is true.

"I see the doubt in your eyes," he says, grinning. "You don't think I'm *L.A.* enough to love L.A. The pasty whiteness of my skin screams I hate sunshine and attractive people."

The smile finally comes. He's right, it sort of does.

"And you aren't wrong," Marshall goes on. "I do sort of hate sunshine and attractive people — present company excluded, obvi — but I will always love L.A. because Kelly Taylor lives there."

I try to keep up. Sunshine, Kelly Taylor, *he called me attractive.*

"From *90210*?" I ask, and gently push my locker shut. Metal sliding into metal, I see the latch catch.

He nods solemnly. "Kelly was there for me during a really crucial time in my life."

My mind darts to That Summer, shades drawn, air conditioning turned all the way up, when I didn't take a shower for three weeks, when I couldn't get off the couch in Carl's basement. The slickness of my pillowcase, the smell of dirty hair. The gnawing feeling in my stomach because I could never remember to eat. The theme song I heard once an hour for days on end. Hundreds of episodes in random order, the original series mixed in with the new. It doesn't matter that I can't see it in my head, the memory lives in my gut. The sensation of it. The emptiness, the longing, the fear.

"Diet pill Kelly or guidance counselor Kelly?" I ask, making an effort, trying not to be rude. But my voice sounds wrong. Too tight, too heavy for this moment. Because I am not in this moment, not any more, I am back on that microsuede couch, drowning in the darkness, buried in it.

If Marshall hears it, *he has to hear it*, he doesn't let on.

"Both," he answers. "But only because Netflix tricked me. I was nine episodes into the new series before I realized it was a totally different show. And by then we knew about Harry's illegitimate son and I mean, c'mon. Who could stop there?"

A few seconds pass, then a few more. This is the part where I'm supposed to say something, the birdie comes to me, *this is how conversations work*. Marshall blinks. His eyelashes are ridiculous, thick and long and unruly, like blades of wild black grass.

deep breaths

I fumble for my hair. It's braided today, pulled forward on the left to hide my scars, but I can feel them peeking out, pulsing with a tingly sensation, *look at us.* Marshall fiddles with the zipper on his hoodie, the teeth on the track coming apart and then clamping together again, *open shut open shut,* a mechanical, maniacal mouth. I swallow thickly, clutching the base of my braid like it's a rope. Marshall is smiling casually, naturally, as if this isn't completely awkward. But it is awkward, so awkward. I can't remember what he said, what I'm supposed to say next. The pause is too long, I am out of sync.

"So you and Hannah are twins," I say finally, randomly, so painfully. "That's cool." I die inside, killed by the excruciating awkwardness of this conversation, *please just let it end.* It's not just the conversation that's awkward, it's me, my stiffness, the weird way I'm holding my head, chin angled away from him to block my scars, *nothing to see here folks.*

"Allegedly," Marshall says easily, zero weirdness, as if I didn't jump topics mid-thread. "But she hates cake so I have my doubts." The randomness of his non-sequitur somehow diminishes the weirdness of mine.

"*All* cake?" I ask, on time this time, totally in sync.

He nods. "She says it smells like skin."

"*Skin?*"

"Only the chocolate smells like skin," comes Hannah's voice from behind me. "The vanilla smells fine, it just tastes gross." She appears beside us, in a dress and tights with the longer side of her hair in a dozen tiny braids and as soon as I see her my fears that I wouldn't recognize her disappear.

Marshall looks at me. "We had to have a cookie cake at our birthday every year, which, in case anyone is wondering, is just a big cookie with frosting on it. Not a cake."

"I see you've met my brother," Hannah says wryly. It's obvious, now, that they're related, even though her hair is red and her skin is darker and his eyes are deeper set. They have the same wide mouth, identical freckled noses that scrunch up when they laugh.

"I was just about to ask Jessa how you did yesterday," Marshall says. "Whether you covered all the really important stuff, like where the attendance nazi keeps the late passes and the exact spot on the vending machine to pound with your fist to get free SunChips." He turns to me. "It's actually more of a triple punch — one, two, *three*." He karate chops the air with his hand. "The technique is crucial."

"Ignore him," Hannah says. "His awkwardness is a disease."

"You are not a regular human," Marshall says to her. "Regular humans need SunChips to survive this place. And copious amounts of cake." He looks over at me. "Unless you're like my sister and completely obsessed with your *craft*, this place sucks the first week."

Hannah rolls her eyes. "Marshall hates the Arts."

"Not so," Marshall says. "I love the Arts. The Arts are not pretentious and self-important. The Arts do not uses phrases like *verisimilitude* and *transversal.*"

"He literally submitted a petition to the principal saying he needed a language interpreter for Art Criticism," Hannah tells me.

"I maintain that the class was not in English."

Hannah rolls her eyes. "Shut up. Art Crit is a great class."

"No joke, there were moments when I legitimately thought the teacher was punking us," Marshall says to me. "There is no such thing as a *'carnival of ephemeral futility'*! It doesn't even work as a metaphor!"

I laugh unexpectedly. This laughter is lightness, helium in my chest.

"I knew it," Marshall says, and grins. "I have an ally. In this carnival of ephemeral futility, I am not the only circus freak."

step right up ladies and gents come see the girl with the broken face

"Don't ruin it for Jessa," Hannah says, punching her brother in the arm. "She might like it here. There are things here to like."

"There are," Marshall says. "Like the fact that the classes are pass/fail and we don't have a football team and the cinnamon rolls are made of Crisco and crack."

"Maybe if the classes weren't pass/fail you'd know what verisimilitude and transversal mean," Hannah says dryly.

The bell rings. The pace of the hallways picks up. Lockers slam, bags jostle. Everyone is in motion, on their way to somewhere else. I am going nowhere. I am standing still.

"You coming, Jessa?" I hear Hannah say.

I yank the puppet strings, *head up, smile, nod*, and follow her down the hall.

"Meet you on G at lunch?" she asks when we get to my English class. So casually, like it's not even a question. Like we're already friends. Immediately I have the thought, *if only it were that easy*. And then I have the thought, *maybe it is*.

※

I wait until the morning announcements have started to uncrumple the pink wad of paper in my fist, smoothing it out on my desk.

Jessa Gray is handwritten on the line at the top. Then, in pre-printed type, *please report to:* and a column of options, five checkboxes. The square in front of the words *the guidance counselor's office* is marked with an oversize X, as if the person who filled out this out did it with flourish. Or glee. Chest tight, my eyes drop to the bottom of the slip where that same person has written in loopy script, *Please stop by Dr. I's office to schedule a new student consultation. Welcome to Crossroads!* There's a smiley face drawn at the end.

A "new student consultation" sounds generic. NBD. An invitation more than a request. The band around my ribcage loosens a little. I wad the paper back up and shove it into my bag, telling myself I'll deal with it later, knowing I probably, *definitely*, won't.

For the next fifty minutes I try to focus, but there's a girl two rows over with a jagged scar down her cheek. I can see it in my peripheral vision, daring me to look. I hear almost nothing my teacher says.

Hannah is waiting for me by the water fountain after chemistry. Her fingers peck at her thighs, the notes of a song only she can hear. It's as if the activity of the hallway is happening somewhere else, or maybe it's just that *she* is somewhere else, on a piano bench somewhere, in a music room, on a stage. Watching her, I feel a sharp pang of envy. *she has an escape.* I've never had anywhere to go, nothing separate from me to hold my thoughts, to keep them from spinning out of control and going everywhere and nowhere all at once. No matter where I go, there I am, stuck in a loop on the Circle Road, round and round again, *strong and hopeful hearted through the dust and wind up just exactly where I started.* It's the reason I picked that particular Shel Silverstein poem when I read online somewhere that reciting verses from memory can calm the mind down. The words just fit.

Hannah sees me and her hands go still.

"Practicing?" I ask.

"Trying," she says, making a face. We start down the hall toward the practice room. "It's the second piece I'm working on for my audition. *Mad Rush* by Phillip Glass. I have to play eight eighth notes per measure in my left hand against four eighth note triplets in my right. I should have it by now, but I keep tripping up on the triplets."

"You'll get it," I say.

Annoyance flashes on Hannah's face.

"Or maybe you won't," I blurt out. "Honestly, I don't even know what an 'eighth note triplet' is. I was just trying to be supportive."

The annoyance evaporates, palpably, *whoosh*. "Ugh. Thank you. Can you and my brother please hang out?"

"Um. What?"

"He's always telling me how great I am, that I'm too hard on myself. But he knows nothing about music. Literally, nothing. Unless you count rap, and sorry, I just don't."

For some reason, this makes me laugh. "Marshall's into rap?"

"I know, right? I'm pretty sure he started listening to it just to annoy me, but now he's obsessed. It's mostly just awkward because he's *so* white and so, I dunno, I-grew-up-in-Colorado-with-a-heart-condition, but he walks around listening to Chance The Rapper and wearing ridiculous oversized headphones."

My brain stalls on the words *heart condition*. I remember what she said yesterday, about her brother not being able to do regular school.

"Is he— okay?" I ask, my own heart weirdly pounding at the thought of something wrong with his.

"Oh — yeah. He has a hole in his heart. Which, when you get to know him, is, like, the greatest irony ever."

"Wow," I say. "An actual hole?"

"Pretty much. His is in the wall between the two upper chambers. They saw it on the ultrasound before we were even born. The doctors were hoping it would close on its own, but it never did."

"And that's okay? A person can have a hole in their heart and be fine?"

"If the hole is small enough, yeah. His is right on the borderline, I guess. The longer he goes without any symptoms, the better the chances he never will. And he hasn't had any symptoms yet."

We reach the practice room. Hannah pulls open the door.

"I think he's secretly happy they never fixed it," Hannah says as she follows me in. "He likes being the weird guy with the heart defect. It means he doesn't have to try to be anything else."

There's an odd note in her voice when she says it. Jealous and judgy at the same time.

"That must've been hard for you," I say neutrally, knowing somehow that if I probe she'll shut me down. *i know because it's what i would do*

"Yeah, I guess," she replies, just as neutrally.

She drops her bag on the floor by the piano bench and digs out her music. There are chairs arranged in a semi-circle in the center of the room today. *were there chairs here yesterday?* As

I try to remember, I find myself wondering what exactly I'm doing with my brain. What is memory without a mind's eye? Pages of a diary I'm trying to read in the dark. Panic flutters in my gut as I strain to picture it. Something, anything. This room, the ocean, my mom's face.

"My parents couldn't afford to pay for lessons when I was little," I hear Hannah say. "We were born eight weeks early and had to be in intensive care for two months, which I guess is crazy expensive and my parents barely had insurance. Then there was all the stuff with Marshall's heart and a billion specialists that didn't take insurance. There wasn't a lot of money left over for music lessons." She sets her music on the stand and gets situated on the bench.

"So how'd you learn to play?" I ask.

"YouTube," she replies. "I just watched instructional videos over and over again until I could play whatever song they were teaching, and then I'd move on to the next one. From the very first song I was hooked. I mean, I sucked obviously. I couldn't read music, I didn't know the notes. I was pecking out *Happy Birthday* on a paper keyboard. But somehow even before I could play, I knew. Piano was my thing."

My thing, emphasis on the *my*, as if everyone has a thing. *does panic count?*

"So what's Marshall's thing?" I ask.

"People," she says without hesitating, and starts to play.

Chapter Eight

"So how's school going, Bear?" Dad asks on the ride to school Friday morning. I'm impressed he managed to hold off this long.

"Fine," I say automatically.

"You seem to be adjusting well," he says casually.

"I guess."

I don't know why I'm being like this. He's trying. But something about the attentive father routine bugs.

Beside me, he is trying to decide what to say next. I can feel him toying with different approaches, looking for the magic words, exactly the right question to get me to open up. "Why didn't you tell me Crossroads was an alternative school?" I ask abruptly, cutting him off at the pass.

He hesitates, but only for a second. "I wasn't sure how you'd react," he admits. "I know there's a stigma associated with them, and I didn't want you to read anything into my decision to send you to one."

my decision. I never thought of it that way, as his decision, a choice he made on my behalf. But of course it was. Before I even left the hospital in L.A. the details were all worked out.

I grit my teeth, angry suddenly, *why am I so pissed off?* It's a raw, unbridled feeling, a rope cut loose inside, fury flapping like a tarp inside my chest. Pain shoots up my jaw.

"Does it bother you?" he asks.

"The fact that it's an alternative school? Or that you lied to me about it?"

"I didn't *lie* about it," he says, and now his voice is tight. "I may not have mentioned it, Jessa, but I didn't purposely hide it from you. Please don't accuse me of that."

"Whatever." A few minutes later he pulls into the bank. I get out without a word.

"Have a good day," he says quietly. I slam the door. As soon as I do, I regret the drama of it. But he's already pulling away.

Hannah is waiting for me under the stairs that go down to the gym. Our meeting place since Wednesday, when Dad had a client meeting and had to drop me off early and I went looking for a place to hide out and found hers. She was sitting cross-legged with a notebook in her lap and a wool cap on her head, all her auburn hair tucked in, and for a second I didn't recognize her, but then she smiled and her brown eyes crinkled and I did.

Today it's a calculus textbook and a black fedora and a scowl.

"Kill me now," she says as I sit. "The bell's gonna ring in three minutes and I have twenty-two problems left."

"Out of how many?"

"Twenty-five."

"Yikes."

"I was up late practicing and slept through my alarm," she says without looking up, her pencil moving methodically down the page.

Her phone is on the floor next to her, counting down the seconds until the warning bell. Two minutes and forty-three seconds. Now forty-two. Now forty-one. She had the timer going yesterday, too, when it was a music theory worksheet instead of math. "It keeps me from getting distracted," she said when I asked her about it, shrugging like she hadn't given it much thought. The time, meanwhile, was suddenly all I could think about. The changing numbers, the pressure of moments passing, the awareness of something scarce being lost. My pulse keeps pace with the racing seconds. Anxiety escalating, taking off.

Hannah's timer buzzes just as the bell goes off. She closes her book and shoves it into her bag. "I have to stop by Dr. I's office before class," she says, getting to her feet.

please stop by dr. i's office

The crumpled pink office slip. I haven't thought about it since I dropped it in my bag on Tuesday morning.

"He's the guidance counselor, right?" I ask casually, fiddling with my bag.

"Yeah, but don't tell him that," Hannah says. "'I'm a psychi*iiiiii*atrist, long I, like my name.'" She rolls her eyes. "He went to med school, so apparently the counselor label is a real ego slam."

"What are you seeing him for?" I ask. It's weird that I haven't stood up yet, but there's no way I'm going with her to his office, no way I'm getting near the a school shrink.

"I'm gonna see if he'll get me out of the English paper I have due next week," she's says. "Prioritizing my music career over a stupid essay won't fly with him, so I'm gonna try the overwhelmed by stress angle and see if that works." She starts up the stairs.

"I should get to class," I say, so focused on the fact that I don't want to go with her that it doesn't register until she's halfway up the stairs that she hasn't even asked me to.

She waves over her shoulder. "See you at lunch."

※

The practice room at lunch, that's become the second half of our routine. There are six rooms total, but only one of them has a piano, so that's the only one we ever use. Chloe and Janet are usually there when we get there and there's a guy with a guitar waiting in the hall when we come out. Hannah says most of the kids in the music program have a free period they use to practice, but since she's taking a double load of classes for Interlochen, for her it has to be during lunch.

Today, Hannah's not at the water fountain when I get there, so I go down to the room. Janet and Chloe are on their way out.

"Is Hannah inside?" I ask.

They exchange a glance. Chloe smirks. "Nope."

Janet has her hair pulled back in a ponytail. The scars on her forehead are all I see. The expression on her face is more apologetic than smirky.

"What?" I ask.

"Nothing," Chloe says before Janet can answer. "We just finished practicing in the room we reserved. Now we're going to lunch." She pulls Janet down the hall.

As they round the corner at the end of the hall, Hannah comes through the side door from outside, her cheeks pink from the cold. She seems happier than she did this morning. Less stressed.

"Hey! Sorry I'm late," she says brightly. "I had to run down to Rite Aid." I start to tell her about the weird exchange I just had with Janet and Chloe, but she's already pulling open the practice room door. As she steps in front of me I notice that her backpack is coming unzipped. A paper Rite Aid bag is caught in the zipper, the kind they put prescriptions in.

Hannah steps inside the room then stops abruptly. There's a girl at the piano. Blond ringlets, tan that looks natural but has to have come from a can because it's January in Colorado and the sun hasn't been out all week. The girl has her eyes closed, playing a song I recognize but can't place. The heavy door behind us shuts and the girl's eyes spring open, a whoosh of mascaraed lashes like a butterfly's wings. Her hands go still on the keys.

"What are you doing here?" Hannah demands.

"This is called a piano," the girl says calmly, tapping her finger pointedly on the highest key, a shrill, repetitive scream. "I'm playing it."

"Not in here you're not," Hannah says coldly. "There are five other practice rooms. You can go to one of those."

"But this is the only room with a piano," the girl replies. "Which is why I signed up to use it." Hannah's eyes dart to the wall by the door. There's a print-out taped there, with the days of the week and time slots in a grid. The name *Logan Dwyer* is written in the 12:10-1:00 pm block for the next three weeks.

"You've got to be kidding," Hannah retorts. "Nobody uses those sign-up sheets."

"I guess Mr. Tanaka does," Logan says innocently. "I asked if I could reserve a practice room for the next couple weeks — you know, to help me get ready for my big audition — and he said to just sign the sheet."

I can see Hannah in the corner of my eye, all angles and edges, balled hands at her hips. "What audition?"

Logan arranges her fingers on the piano with a smug smile. "I'm trying out for Interlochen."

Hannah stares at her for several seconds. Then she turns and walks out.

She doesn't stop in the hallway. She pushes through the side door. I follow her out, the sharp cold stinging my face.

"Where are you going?" I call.

"Marshall has my physics book," she calls over her shoulder, not slowing down. "If I can't practice now then I'll have to put in an extra fifty minutes tonight, which means I'll have less time for homework. Are you coming?"

I hurry to catch up to her.

"If I get my physics problem set done now," she's saying, "and I read for history on the drive home, then I'll only have calc and music theory to finish. And those I can probably do in the morning. If I don't sleep though my alarm. I should get a back-up clock." She's blinking fast, thinking, working it all out in her head.

"Wait, can we talk about what just happened? Who was that girl?"

"Logan Dwyer. She plays the piano too, obviously. Of course she's sitting in there playing the freaking *Moonlight Sonata*. God. Could she be a bigger cliché?"

"Is she good?" I ask as I follow her back inside the building.

"Good enough," Hannah says. "I mean, her technical skills aren't great, but she makes up for it with expression. Which is all you need when you're playing the freaking *Moonlight Sonata*. Or some crap by Mozart. Ugh. I *hate* Mr. Tanaka. He obviously told her about the Emerson. Not that she needs it, her parents are loaded. The only reason she wants it is because there's a bunch of press when you get it. Do you see my brother anywhere?"

We've reached the windowed wall of the cafeteria, a fish-bowl of tempered glass in the center of the main hall. The room is overcrowded, bodies jammed around tables, girls doubled up in blue plastic seats. "He usually sits on the far right," Hannah says, craning her neck. "At the Aspie table." She glances at me. "He doesn't have Asperger's, obviously. He just sits with the kids who do." Her eyes go back to scanning.

"Why?" I ask.

"He says they're the only people at Crossroads who don't talk about themselves all the time," she says, and I have the thought *he would've hated wren*. She taps the glass. "There he is. C'mon."

She tugs the door open, and when she does the volume cranks way up. Without meaning to, I take a step back.

Instantly she's back at my side. "I wasn't even thinking about the crowd. I'm sorry. I can totally text him, tell him to come out."

The concern in her voice makes me cringe.

barbie's unstable

"It's fine," I say, and step past Hannah into the cafeteria.

Marshall is waving us over, so I keep my eyes on his out-stretched arm and try to ignore everything else.

"Hey," Marshall calls. "What happened to the practice session?"

"Change of plans," Hannah says flatly. She kicks out a chair and sits down. "Can I have my physics book, please?"

I take the only other empty seat, next to Marshall, across from a girl with carrot-colored hair.

"You're new," the girl says bluntly. She's looking at a spot in the air to the left of my face, blinking super fast.

make friends

"Uh, yeah," I say. "I'm Jessa."

"Are you on the spectrum?" the girl asks.

Hannah rolls her eyes. "You don't have to be autistic to sit at this table, Sophie. She's here because I'm here, and she's my friend."

"You don't have any friends," Sophie says.

"Shut up, Sophie," Hannah says.

Beside me, Marshall leans forward, elbows on the table. I can't tell who he's looking at.

please don't be looking at me

"Do you play an instrument?" the boy beside Sophie asks. "Hannah plays the piano. I play the trumpet. The trumpet has been around since 1500 BC."

I shake my head, wishing I could leap from this table and run. Away from all the talking and the questions and the eye-balls on my face.

The boy across the table keeps talking at me, his voice sort of like a trumpet, *ba ba ba ba da ba*. "The precursor to the trumpet, the cornetto, didn't have valves or keys," the boy is saying now. "Modern trumpets have three valves and can play forty-five distinct notes." He pauses now, abruptly, like it's my turn to speak.

"Wow," I say.

The boy doesn't blink. "Are you saying that because you don't believe me, or because you find it surprising, or because it's something people say when other people tell them things they don't care about?"

"I—," I don't know why I said it. I said it because it was something to say.

Marshall laughs. "Brendon, buddy, you're supposed to ask yourself those questions, not the person you're talking to."

"But that's stupid," Brendon says flatly. "If I ask myself, how will I know if I'm right?"

"Leave Jessa alone," Hannah says. As she works through physics problems, she picks at a red, scaly patch of skin on the inside of her wrist. "She doesn't need to be interrogated over lunch."

"But she's not eating lunch," Sophie points out.

"Sophie. Shut up."

"I'm getting more pizza," Brendon says, and abruptly stands up.

"Are you guys gonna eat?" Marshall asks us.

Hannah picks up the piece of pizza on her brother's tray and takes a bite.

"Brendon," Marshall calls. "Get me another slice." He looks over at me. "You want one?"

"Sure," I say, then remember the lunch Dad packed for me this morning, the almond butter he ground himself, the local blueberries in a half pint jar. *eat well.* "Actually — never mind. I have stuff." The sack is at the very bottom of my bag, buried under my chem textbook, flattened and smushed. A piece of my hair slips from my braid as I'm digging for it. I push it back, tuck it behind my ear without thinking.

"What's wrong with your face?" Sophie asks, and Hannah and Marshall go still.

The sack slips from my fingers, lands with a thud in my tote.

here I go down circle road strong and hopeful hearted through the dust and wind up just exactly where I started

The leather strap is wrapped around my wrist, cutting off the circulation to my hand. I hadn't realized I'd been twirling it. I fumble for the piece of hair I tucked behind my ear and accidentally pull another chunk free.

"Jessa?" Hannah says my name in a way that makes me think she's said it a few times already.

"I was in a car wreck," I hear myself say.

"Did anyone die?" Sophie asks as I straighten up, her eyes darting from my face to the air beside it. The way a person would look at something gross, quick glances, too uncomfortable to stare. Steel walls partition off this thought, a *Do Not Enter* zone. I force another explanation, literally force my mind to form the thought.

she's autistic. she looks at everyone that way.

"...suppressing internal thoughts," I hear Marshall say in a low voice.

"I understand that," Hannah snaps. "But she needs to know that she's being super rude."

don't avoid

"It's not a big deal," I say, as breezily as I can, which isn't breezy so much as stilted and heavy, the opposite of breezy, a boulder in the snow. I look directly at Sophie's eyes, hiding in her one blind spot. "No, no one died. No one else was even hurt."

"Move over, Sophie." Brendon is back with the pizza. "Your chair is touching my chair. You know I don't like it when other chairs touch my chair."

It's a diversion, and I should be thankful for it, because all the eyes have turned to him. But I just . . . can't.

be here, do this, make small talk with these people i don't know

"I'm gonna go," I say abruptly, jerking to my feet. My chair scrapes noisily against the floor. I fumble for my bag.

"Jessa," Hannah says.

"I'm fine," I say, and force myself to look her in the eye, ignore the pity I find there. "Really," I add, as convincingly as I can. "I just need a second." She nods, and I see on her face *I believe you.* And I am grateful for this, for my ability to pretend.

this is what i'm good at

this one thing

Except I actually suck at it now because my face gives me away.

The bodies around me blur as I push my way toward the door.

The hallway is empty, *thank god*. No one to see my chest heaving, my fist balled at my mouth. Knuckles digging into my lips, pressing into my teeth. I move toward the girls' bathroom, but then I think of the mirrors, *there will be mirrors*, and I freeze.

don't avoid

But I can't do a mirror right now. Not yet.

A surge of crowded voices behind me, cafeteria noise. Someone has opened the lunch room door. Hannah, maybe, coming after me, checking that I'm okay.

"Jessa," Marshall calls.

His voice disorients me. I was expecting Hannah. I'm not prepared for him.

"I said I was fine," I say loudly, too loud, without turning around. "I just need some space."

The cafeteria door shuts, and the hall is quiet again.

"I need some space, too," he says. "I *really* do not like it when Brendon's chair touches my chair."

Despite myself, I smile.

"It's a problem," I say, and turn around. Marshall is standing in the center of the hallway with his hands in the pockets of his cords. Dark hair falling in his face.

"We have to do something," he's saying. "In this carnival of ephemeral futility, the chair touching really has to stop."

My eyes are on his chin, his forehead, then, finally, his eyes, which leap at me like they did yesterday, swallowing up the air between us.

let go of me

But he's not holding on to me. He's not even touching me. He's just *looking* at me.

I want to look away, but that feels like cheating, or giving up. My pulse thumps in my neck.

"Mostly because people are so messy," Marshall goes on. "Their stuff gets all over your stuff. And the next thing you know, you're completely invaded."

like how i feel right now

The cafeteria door opens again, and it's Hannah this time.

"I'm gonna go outside," she announces, then looks at me. Her eyes are so much gentler than his. "Come with me. You need some cold air." It isn't a question and she isn't wrong.

"Yeah," I say. "Okay."

I look back at Marshall but he is already pulling open the cafeteria door. "Be brilliant," he tells Hannah, then disappears inside.

Her features crunch, an irritated scowl.

"He's an extrovert," Hannah says. "It's annoying as hell."

agreed

I follow her out the side door, around the building to the practice field in the back. The chain link fence is rusty, and the grass is patchy in places, weeded, dotted with brown. My old school had a sparkly stadium, with Astroturf and a rubber

track. The cheerleaders used to hang out on the bleachers before school, passing lip gloss around and taking pictures of
themselves with their phones. There were seven of them, maybe eight, but without their faces in my head I can't distinguish
them, they are just *those cheerleaders*, they are just *blond*. I doubt
they all had the same hair color, but I never paid enough attention to know.

We climb the metal bleachers and sit on the top row. It's
freezing out here, the kind of cold that makes your bones ache,
but the starkness of the air is a comfort, a relief. It numbs everything else out.

"You wanna talk about it?" Hannah asks quietly.

The answer is automatic. "No."

"You sure?"

don't avoid

"Not right now," I say, the best I can do.

"Okay," Hannah says simply, and pulls her physics book
from her bag. Her wrist looks even worse in this light, thick
and scaly and red. She sees me see it.

"Eczema," she says, tugging her sleeve down to hide it.
"It's disgusting, I know. I shouldn't have worn this sweater.
The wool makes it worse."

"Trade you," I say. "My face for your wrist."

Her irises go glossy. The pity is back.

"I should read," I say, looking away. I dig *The Picture of
Dorian Gray* from my bag. We're supposed to read through
chapter nine by Monday, and I still haven't opened the book.

This happens when my panic gets bad. Homework stresses me out so I don't do it, which only stresses me out more. I was in the gifted program before Dad left, honors track, but after That Summer school became another chance for me to second guess myself, *it's too much i can't do this*, and after a couple months I'd proved myself right.

My mind pings to that pink office slip. If my grades drop they'll send me another one, whatever color means *you're majorly messing up*. Someone will call Dad and action plans will be made and I'll end up in Dr. I's office staring at an Ansel Adams print on the wall.

I flip past the preface and start on chapter one. The words are like bricks, the yellowed page an impenetrable wall. I grit my teeth and start again.

"*The ugly and the stupid have the best of it in this world*," someone named Basil says on page two. My left cheek aches from clenching, from the cold, from the dense prose I can barely muddle through.

if he's right then I'm in luck

Chapter Nine

"I'm going home at lunch," Hannah says when I come down the stairs on Monday morning. "We live close, so it'll give me at least a half hour to play. It's not the same as fifty-two minutes in the practice room, but it's my only option at this point." She's cross-legged on the floor working through another calculus problem set and doesn't look up. "You'll be okay without me, right?"

Something dark inside me flares.

i can take care of myself

"Don't be silly," I say lightly. "I'll be fine."

"I don't want you to think I'm bailing on you," she says. "I just need the practice time, you know?"

She glances up at me then, and my anger shapeshifts into fear. There's a bruise under her left eye; a purple crescent moon. A bruise that wasn't there before. A bruise that screams *YOU'RE NOT GETTING BETTER* and whispers *you might be getting worse.*

Sweat behind my knee caps, I stare the bruise down, *you're not real, I'm making you up*. It doesn't budge.

"Jessa?"

"I get it," I say thickly. "No big deal."

At lunch I skip the cafeteria and hide out on the bleachers. The lamp in Dad's guest room, *stop calling it the guest room bear it's your room now*, burned out last night, so I went hunting in the living room cabinets for a new bulb and found my dad's Discman and a stack of old CDs instead. Most of them were eighties hair bands, *so dad*, but there were a handful of random classical albums mixed in. I took the only one with piano in the title, meant to ask Hannah if it was any good. But I got so distracted by her bruise this morning that I never did.

I don't want to think about the bruise but I can't not think about it. I've been thinking about it ever since I saw it, trying to convince myself that I didn't actually see it. That it could've been a shadow. Dirt. Blue marker on her face. Anything but an imaginary bruise I invented because my brain is still completely jacked up.

I shove my earbuds in, turn the volume all the way up. The first track starts with banging chords, so loud my earbuds crackle, still not loud enough. I used to do this with *Heart of Steel* by Manowar on my phone, the only song I owned. Full volume on repeat until the panic in my gut sputtered out. One man on a piano doesn't really have the same effect, but the repetition of the melody helps. It reminds me of spinning hair, a Circle Road, the same thing over and over again until it's all there is. I'm halfway through the song when Marshall shows up.

I feel him before I see him, the bleachers rattling beneath his Vans as he climbs to the top.

"So here's the thing about space," he says when I pull my earbuds out. "It's overrated."

"Says who?"

"Says me," he says, and sits down right beside me, so close we're almost touching. He's warmer than I am, his body heat seeping out through his sweatshirt. "I mean, sure, it keeps chairs from touching and other people from leaking all their weirdness onto you, but what happens to all your own weirdness? Where's it supposed to go?"

"Nowhere," I say. "That's sort of the point."

"But then you're stuck with it."

My gut clenches. I stare at my book.

Marshall shrugs out of his backpack. Our legs are touching now, his baggy jeans rub against mine when he moves. "What're you listening to?" he asks.

I fish the CD case out of my bag and show it to him.

"Phillip Glass," he says, sounding surprised. "How elevated."

"It's my dad's, actually. I raided his CD collection last night."

"Hannah would approve of your dad's taste," Marshall says. "She's less enthusiastic about mine."

"Which is what?" I ask, remembering what Hannah said about him liking rap and remembering what she told me right after that about his heart. It feels weird to know these two things already.

"Rap, mostly," Marshall says. "More Kendrick than Kanye."

"How elevated."

He grins. "What about you? When you're not listening to manic piano solos. What's your jam?"

i used to listen to guns 'n roses and ac/dc, until my dad left and i broke all of his cds

"You'll make fun of me," I say, because Wren always did. "But I mostly just listen to the radio." *except when i'm pounding heavy metal to silence my brain*

"The radio. You're so vintage."

"Right?"

We smile, both of us, at the exact same time.

"So is that why I've never seen you with a phone?" Marshall asks. "You refuse to use anything but a rotary dial?"

I feel my smile fade. *you've never seen me with a phone because avoidance only works if you go all in.* Having a phone, even a new one with a new number, would make it too easy to check in on Wren, to maybe accidentally call him one night. To stalk Alexis Duffy on Instagram, to die all over again when I see pics of her and Wren.

"Something like that," I say finally. The ease of the prior moment slips away and the space between us is awkward again, crowded with all the things I don't want to say. I fiddle with the book in my lap.

"How far in are you?" he asks.

"Um. Page four. If you count the first two pages twice."

"Yeah, the first fifty pages are rough. It gets better when Dorian meets Sibyl. But don't get too attached because she kills herself a few chapters later. It gets really good after that."

"I mean, obvi," I say wryly. "Suicide makes everything better."

"Not *everything*," he says. "But for sure nineteenth century novels and 90210. Tell me it wasn't supes intense when Jasper jumped off the Hollywood Sign because he was depressed about Annie. That hooked me for another five episodes at least."

I nod seriously. "Supes."

"You're mocking me."

"A little bit."

"People say supes!"

"What people?"

"I can't believe you're shaming me right now. I'm very sensitive about my use of cool vernacular."

"Then we're good. Because you haven't used any." I flash a grin.

"Oooh, cool girl L.A., schooling the Denver dork." He leans all his weight into me. "For that, I'm putting all of my weirdness on you. And p.s., it's a lot."

I hear myself laugh and for a few seconds I'm not TBI Barbie or Wren's jilted girlfriend because Marshall doesn't know me as either of those things. But then I have the thought *he doesn't know me at all* and the sound dies in my throat.

"I should probably at least try to read," I say awkwardly, scooting away from him. Marshall straightens up, reaches for his backpack. "You don't have to go," I say quickly.

Marshall pulls his phone and headphones out of the side pouch of his backpack. "Good," he says, slipping the headphones over his ears. "I didn't want to."

He stays until the bell rings, then walks me to my locker. As we pass other people, they say hi to him, call out his name. It's different than being with Hannah. No one says anything to her.

"So who else does Hannah hang out with?" I ask as I turn my lock, thinking about what Sophie said on Friday, about her not having any friends.

"My sister hangs out with her piano," Marshall says. "And sometimes, with other girls in the orchestra. But mostly just her piano. And now you."

"Does she date?"

"Nope. She decided freshman year that high school relationships were too distracting."

isn't that the point?

"So the loner thing, that's what she wants?"

"I doubt she thinks about it," Marshall replies. "She's super independent — always has been. Being alone has never been a big deal for her the way it would be for me."

"You need a buddy," I say.

He grins. "Obvi."

The warning bell rings. We both just stand there. It's awkward, suddenly, but at the same time I don't want the moment to end, because when it does I'll be alone in this hallway, and I need a buddy, too.

"So I have a *supes* important question for you," Marshall says. "Which I will ask and then sprint awkwardly to the D hall because if I'm late to drawing one more time our instructor is gonna make me pose for her advanced composition class which means staying after school and being completely still for an hour which I'm pretty sure is the definition of hell."

"Got it. Go."

"Cool if I hang out at lunch again tomorrow?" He's already moving away from me, walking backward down the hall. "There's a new addition at the Aspie table and there's a lot of chair touching. I need some space."

"As long as you don't bring your weirdness."

"No promises," he calls. Then he turns the corner and is gone.

Chapter Ten

Hannah and I keep meeting under the stairs before school, but as the days pass we talk less and less. She always beats me there, even when I ask Dad to drop me off super early, and she always has a textbook in her lap and the timer on her phone ticking down. She waves to me when I come down the steps but she rarely looks up. "Chem," she'll say, or "History" or "Calc," whatever assignment she's hurrying to finish before the bell, and I'll sit down and pull the tattered paperback from my bag and read another chapter, sometimes two. Today it's four, as I race to finish the whole book. Marshall was right about Sybil; the story gets good when she dies. That's when the portrait of Dorian starts changing. It's never really clear how the canvas becomes a reflection of Dorian's soul, it just sort of does – the painted version of him getting uglier and uglier while real life Dorian stays the exact same, until finally Dorian tries to destroy the painting and ends up killing himself instead.

I'm still thinking about that final scene as I stop by my locker before lunch. I've started bringing my history book with me to the bleachers so I can stay out there with Marshall until the warning bell rings, turning fifty-two minutes into fifty-four. Meeting outside is our unspoken arrangement now. Even when it snowed last Thursday, we both showed up. We spent the period under the bleachers instead of on them, with Marshall's backpack laid sideways on the bench above us, a makeshift roof.

"Have you seen my brother?"

Hannah's voice comes out of nowhere, makes me jump.

"You're still here," I say, swinging my locker shut. The bruise under her eye is the first thing I see. It looks more like a half moon now than a crescent. *did it get bigger or was it always this shape?*

Frustration pecks against my forehead, *buh buh buh buh*, incessant and ineffectual, a finger pounding a broken key.

"Only because Marshall freaking has the keys. Ugh. Have you seen him?"

"He's probably outside already," I say, forcing my eyes up to hers. "He usually beats me out there."

"Out where?"

he hasn't told her
why hasn't he told her?
why haven't i?

"Um. Down at the field. We've been eating out there the last few days." More than a few, exactly nine, every day for almost two weeks.

Surprise, confusion, hurt, *zing zing zing*, like lightning flashes across her face.

"Oh," she says finally, with a smile that's definitely forced. "Cool."

"It's not, like, a thing or anything," I say quickly. "We're just out there at the same time. Sometimes we don't even talk." This is true, sometimes we don't, like when I'm listening to a song on his playlist, absorbing lyrics he'll then proceed to explain, or when he's reading some passage from my book that I've underlined for him, bobbing his head the tiniest bit, a thing he does when ideas are sinking in. He does the head bobbing thing when I'm talking sometimes, as if what I'm saying is making him think. Sometimes we don't talk. But most of the time we do. We talk more than I've ever talked to anyone, so much talking that by the time the bell rings, I'm completely spent. "Anyway. That's probably where he is."

Hannah's already moving toward the door. "You coming?" she calls. She doesn't wait.

Marshall has his headphones on, doesn't hear us approach. Hannah climbs the back of the bleachers, whacks him with her hand. "You have the keys," she says, impatient, when he pulls the headphones off. He turns, sees Hannah, then sees me.

"Hey," he says to me.

"Hey."

"The keys," Hannah repeats, and holds out her hand. "I'm already late." Her palm is hidden in the sleeve of her jacket, fingers wedged to the inside seam. She sees Marshall clock this, answers the question he hasn't asked. "I haven't been picking it," she snaps. She shoves up her sleeve, turns over her wrist. The flesh is bumpy and pink, islands of eczema from wrist to elbow, but not a single scab. "Happy, Dad? Now can I please have the keys?"

Marshall digs them out of his pocket. "Don't speed."

Hannah grabs the keys and hops down. "Enjoy your lunch," she says neutrally, and turns to go. Fear sparks in my chest. It feels like I am choosing him suddenly, her brother, *the boy*, over her.

"I'll come with you," I say suddenly.

She shakes her head. "You can't."

"I promise I won't bother you," I insist. "I won't even talk. I want to hear how it's coming, that's all."

"It's not that," she says. Her eyes flick to Marshall.

"What?" I ask.

"We're not supposed to leave campus during the day," Marshall answers when Hannah doesn't.

"But she's been going home every day at lunch for two weeks," I point out.

"I'm allowed to," Hannah says.

"It's only the alternative school kids who can't," Marshall explains.

I don't let this register. Don't let myself think about the reasons behind this rule, how horrifying it is that this rule applies to me.

"Whatever," I say lightly. "We'll be back before fifth period, right? No one will even know."

Hannah hesitates, debating. Then she shrugs.

"Yeah, okay," she says finally. "But we have to go now."

I look up at Marshall. "Thanks again for keeping me company," I say in a weird, department store lady voice, *why do i feel the need to do this, i can't help it but i do.*

"No problem," he says, and slips his headphones back on.

✺

Their house is a couple miles from school, which in L.A. would be a different zip code but in Boulder is a five minute drive. Hannah pulls their Camry into the driveway, flings the gear in park.

Their house is bigger than Dad's but much older, more run down. Hannah's already inside by the time I get to the front porch. Without a word she shrugs out of her jacket, drapes it across the kitchen counter, and gets situated at their piano, a baby grand just off the kitchen where a breakfast table would normally be.

I wander into the living room. Mismatched frames line the mantel over the fireplace, a catalog of family photos that go back to the twins' birth. Marshall was the smaller baby, but in the pictures he doesn't look sick. In one, his dad has Hannah on his shoulders, and his mom has Marshall on her back and they're all making goofy faces from the top of a mountain peak. My throat tightens as I move down the mantel.

this is what a family looks like. these are the things that real families do

We had some of these moments, I remember them. My family at the beach, my family in the snow, my family at Benihana eating chicken-fried rice the night before my family fell apart. But without a mental image, these memories feel like fiction, a bedtime story I made up. *once upon a time there was a mommy and a daddy and a little girl. and then the daddy left and the mommy got a new family and the little girl discovered there was no one she could trust, and they all lived unhappily ever after, the end.*

In the other room, Hannah fumbles a transition. "Ugh!" she explodes, pounding the keys with her fists.

My heart keeps tempo with her banging, off kilter, too fast.

does she do this when she's alone?

I peek my head in. "Hey," I say softly, and she immediately stops banging, embarrassment flooding her face, and I have my answer. She'd forgotten I was here.

"Sorry," she mumbles.

"Maybe you should eat something," I suggest. "What do you normally do for lunch when you're here?"

"I don't," she says.

"You've been skipping lunch every day?"

She doesn't answer me.

"Hannah. You have to eat."

"No," she says, refusing to look at me. "I actually don't. I don't have to eat, and I don't have to talk about why I don't have time to do anything right now but practice this song." Her voice rises. "My audition is in *nine days*, Jessa."

"I get it," I say, stung. But she doesn't hear me. She's already begun to play.

I let myself out the front door and walk to the driveway. The music is muted out here, muffled by wood and window glass. I sit down on the cold cement, that familiar whirl in my ribcage, Hannah's words pounding against my forehead like her piano notes, *buh buh buh buh buh*, like a machine gun in my brain.

you don't understand

leave me alone

Not the words she spoke, but what I heard. What she wanted me to hear.

And she's right. I *don't* understand. I don't know what it's like to be that good at something. "Such beautiful bone structure," I overheard my dance teacher tell my mom when I was seven. "A little music box ballerina!" Except that music box ballerinas can pirouette without face-planting and don't forget to point their toes. After ballet was soccer, then ceramics, then horseback riding, then singing lessons that lasted two weeks. *Not her thing*, the instructor would eventually say, and we'd stop going, and Mom would sign me up for something else. Then dad left, and the lessons stopped.

My breath is visible when I exhale, rising like steam. Inside, Hannah is banging again.

what am i doing here?

At this house, with this girl, in this city. It seems so strange, suddenly, that this is my life.

My eyes dance around the yard for a distraction, land on a patch of trees beside the driveway. They're tall and thin and pencil straight, their pale trunks knotted in black. *Knotted.* There it is again, that phrase. *Knot in wood.* But knotted things are tied together; shoelaces, strands of twisted hair. These trees aren't knotted, they're broken off; dark spots where branches once were. *Spots*, not the right word, either. Curved lines and circles, lids and sockets, a trunk full of Aspen eyes.

Eye to eye, I stare at one. Pupil bulging under a heavy black lid. My dad told me about aspen trees the first time I came to visit him after he moved, when I was so mad at him for leaving that I could hardly breathe. *"Aspen trees, they have deep roots, they are impervious to fire, like us, Jessa Bear, like you and me."* Except the earth between us was scorched already, no roots left, just desolate dirt. He kept repeating, over and over again, that what happened between him and Mom had nothing to do with me, *it's just between the grownups, sweetheart, you understand that, right?* The answer was yes, I did understand that I was irrelevant. How kind of Wren to remind me four years later when I almost forgot.

My vision blurs and the eye loses its shape. Not just this eye, but all eyes, in trees, through needles, on faces. I blink and there it is again, vacant and staring, unmoved by my tears.

The banging inside has stopped. Through the bay window, Hannah is gathering her things. I rub my tears away with frozen fingers, pretend I can't feel the raised skin on my cheek.

"I do get it," I say when she appears at the door. "I mean, I've never been that good at anything, or wanted something as much as you want this scholarship. But I know what's like to have other people act like they know what's best for you when they have no freaking clue. And it sucks."

Her brown eyes go glassy. She opens her mouth, but whatever she wants to say gets caught in her throat. She nods, a nod that says *thank you*, and *me too*, and *we are the same*.

※

Hannah drops me off in the teacher parking lot, behind the building, since it's closer to my fifth period class and I can't afford to be late.

"Thanks for coming with me," she says as I climb out. "Sorry I was such a jerk."

"No sorries," I tell her, something Wren used to say, his way of skating over arguments, before things changed and he started picking fights. "Thanks for letting me come with."

"This audition is really throwing me," Hannah says quietly. Her hands tighten on the steering wheel. "I don't know why. It wasn't nearly this bad last year."

"You got in, right?"

"Yeah, but getting in is only half of it. I need an Emerson."

"That's the scholarship?"

She nods. "My parents can't swing the tuition without one. Loans aren't an option because there's already a second mortgage on our house because of Marshall's medical bills. My dad lost his job when were in third grade so things were really tight for awhile."

"Are there other music schools you could try out for?" I ask. "Just for back-up?"

"They're all just as expensive," she says dully. "And none of them are as good." Her eyes flick to the clock on the dash. "You should go. The bell's about to ring."

I want to say something else, something that'll take all the stress away, but I know there aren't words that'll do that. I know because I've heard them all.

"Hang in there," I say instead.

As I weave through a maze of SUVs, I'm thinking about Hannah and her audition and not at all about the fact that I'm in the teacher's parking lot without a pass. So when I see him, a man in jeans and a white lab smock it doesn't dawn on me that I'm caught.

"The front door would've been a better option," the man says when I step up onto the sidewalk, and it's at that moment that it hits me, the delayed *oh crap*. "This door doesn't go any-where other than the teacher's lot, so it's harder to make up a good excuse for where you've been." The man has a brown bag lunch beside him and a dog-eared library book in his lap.

"Oh," I say, because there is nothing to say, nothing that will get me out of whatever punishment is coming, *how big of a deal is this?* Then I say it again, because it's all I have. "Oh."

"You're Jessa, right? Started three weeks ago, moved here from L.A. Steadily ignoring every invitation to the school psy-chiatrist's office that you've received?" His voice is friendly, no trace of accusation. I wonder for a half a second how he could possibly know all of this, and then, *duh*, it clicks. It's not a lab smock he has on but a doctor's coat, the kind a pretentious school psychiatrist would wear to make sure everyone remem-bers he has a medical degree.

dr. i.

"So how's it been so far?" Dr. I asks when I don't say any-thing. "Settling in alright?"

I shift my bag to my opposite arm, not sure what to make of this man, this school authority figure, this white-coat-wear-ing shrink. I can't tell if this is a conversation or a trap.

bell ring why won't the bell just ring

"It's been good," I say finally. "I like it. More than I thought I would, actually."

"And your classes are going okay?"

I nod. "Yeah. Still getting caught up."

"Good. I know it can be an adjustment, coming to a new place, starting over in the middle of a school year. If you ever feel underwater, don't be afraid to speak up. I'm here to help."

"Thanks," I say, my throat going weirdly tight. I feel like I should say something else, apologize for ignoring the pink slips, explain where I've just been. But just then the bell rings and I have my escape. "Well. I guess I'll see you later," I say.

"I hope so," he replies, and goes back to his book.

※

"You have to give me a ride," I hear Marshall say. "Penance for bailing on lunch." The final bell rang ten minutes ago and I am at my locker putting books in and taking them out again, stalling until the hallway clears. The sidewalk in front of the main office is crowded after school, freshmen standing in clusters waiting for their parents to pick them up. Dad comes twenty minutes after the bell, when the sidewalk is nearly empty and the gym coach in the orange vest has gone back inside, idling in the bank's parking lot like a getaway car ready to flee. I come across the courtyard, bypassing the sidewalk all together, eyes pinned on the grass until I hit the street.

"I don't have a car," I tell Marshall.

"Neither do I," he says.

"Where's Hannah?"

"Left before sixth period." He holds out his phone. There's a text on the screen, *going home. find a ride.* "So can you?"

I hesitate. Not because I don't want Marshall to meet my dad. But because I know my dad will make a big deal out of meeting him, when it isn't a big deal, it's just a ride home. Which is why I have to say yes, because if I say no, then I'm the one making more of it than it is.

"Sure," I say finally. "My dad picks me up across the street."

The Jeep is exactly where it always is, in the far corner spot, closest to school. Marshall doesn't comment on how quickly I stride across the courtyard, though he has to half jog to keep up.

"Hey," Dad says when I pull open the passenger door.

"This is Marshall," I say as neutrally as I can, not wanting Dad to read anything into this, knowing he will anyway. "He needs a ride home."

"Hi, Marshall," my dad says. "I'm Eric, Jessa's dad."

"Nice to meet you," Marshall says, sliding into the back seat.

"How was school?" Dad asks as he pulls out of the parking lot.

"Fine," I say automatically.

"My day was sort of depressing," Marshall pipes up. "The girl I was supposed to have lunch with bailed at the last minute."

"That's too bad," my dad says.

"Maybe she got a better offer," I say.

Dad flicks his eyes toward me, trying to figure out if I'm being funny or being mean, and sadness kicks me in the ribs. He doesn't know me well enough to know.

"Either way, she's definitely making it up to me," Marshall says from the back seat. "I charge one nighttime outing for every missed lunch."

My heart hiccups in my chest. Nighttime outing sounds a lot like a date.

no boyfriend

Another flick of Dad's eyes, and this time I know he's caught on. A smile tugs at the corners of his lips. More than tugs, actually. Blatantly yanks.

"A nighttime outing, huh?" I say lightly. "That doesn't sound like a fair trade."

Dad's grin is out of control now. It's embarrassing, for him and for me.

"Only because you don't know how soul crushing it is to be stood up for lunch," Marshall is saying.

"I didn't stand you up! I thought Hannah needed the moral support."

"Who's Hannah?" my dad asks, his voice practically bubbling with the idea that I might have friends, plural, that there might be others beyond this boy in the backseat.

"His sister," I say.

"So how's tomorrow night?" Marshall asks. "Assuming it's okay with you, Mr. Gray."

The formality makes me squirm. "It's fine," I say shortly. My dad granting his permission will be even weirder than Marshall asking for it. "Turn left at the next intersection."

I say it without thinking. *Turn left*, like I know the route. And when Dad flicks on his blinker and slows for the turn and Marshall doesn't say anything, I know that I am right. "Take the next right," I say, testing myself. Navigating the school hallways without a mind's eye is one thing; finding my way to a house I've only been to once feels significant, like progress at least.

Dad glances over at me, understandably surprised, but for different reasons. I don't drive, don't leave the house on the weekends, and he drops me off and picks me up at school every day during the week.

"I was at their house earlier today," I say, distracted by the next turn, *is there another turn or is this their street?* "With Hannah. She comes home to practice piano at lunch." I try to envision the house, or their piano, or Hannah's face, something, anything, but I am sucking air from a drained glass, scraping a spoon against the bottom of an empty bowl.

"It's that one," I hear Marshall say. Dad pulls into the driveway and puts the car in park. Now that we're here, the house is familiar, stone and painted wood, aspen trees out front. I try again, looking down at my lap for sec, trying to hold the image of their house in my head.

nope

"Thanks for the ride, Mr. Gray," Marshall says from behind me.

"I'm happy to offer my chauffeur services again tomorrow night," Dad says jovially, winking at me. "I can dress in all black and speak only when spoken to."

"That's okay," I say quickly. "Marshall has a car."

"So that's a yes, then," Marshall says. I twist in my seat and he is grinning at me, the sun behind him like a backlight, casting his face in shadows, and I notice for the first time that his brows are the perfect shape. It seems impossible that I could've missed them, two effortless arches in the middle of his face, so maybe I saw them before but never made a point of remembering them, or maybe his eyes always distracted me, the way they're doing now. All intensity and focus, burning everything else out.

I shrug, as casually as I can, but my heart is *BAM BAM BAM*ing in my chest, my dad's grin like a school yard taunt, *you like him you like him*. Wren used to give me butterflies, but this is more like a frog on speed, thumping in a jar. "Sure," I say, almost add *whatever* but don't, too much nonchalance and the edges start to show.

"You better be at the bleachers tomorrow," Marshall says as he hops out of the car. "Or else you're mine on Saturday, too."

Chapter Eleven

My suede pants feel rough and uncomfortable, too tight, like sausage casings on my thighs. The cashmere turtleneck I borrowed from my mom on Christmas Eve and forgot to give back is making my neck itch.

i dont want to do this

i don't even know what this is

Today at lunch Marshall barely mentioned the fact that we were hanging out tonight. Only that I should wear something "kinda nice," and that he'd pick me up at seven. Both of which made it sound suspiciously like a date.

i can't date

Not now, not yet. The idea of it makes my armpits prickle with sweat.

There's a knock at my door. "Come in," I call out, and the knob turns. Dad is wearing that obnoxious grin again, the one that says he's thrilled about tonight's excursion and is totally on board with Marshall despite the fact that he spent all of seven minutes with him.

"You look great, Bear," he says enthusiastically. Not *beautiful* or even *pretty*, just *great*, a generic nothing that makes me even more self-conscious than before. My outsides are supposed to *hide* the broken parts of me. Not put them on display.

Fingers at my hairline now, I am tracing the tracks of tough flesh. This has become my thing now, doing this instead of twisting my hair. *such improvement!*

"They feel a lot worse than they look," Dad says gently. He rubs the raised scar on the inside of his thumb, from the time several years ago when a broken saw blade almost took the whole thing off.

I look away. "I wouldn't know."

"You can't avoid mirrors forever, Bear. You can't let fear hold you hostage like that."

"I'm not afraid of mirrors," I say stiffly.

"No," he says gently. "You're afraid of what you'll see inside of one. A girl with scars. A girl you don't know how to be yet. But that girl, she's *you*, Jessa."

"You think I don't know that?" I snap, angry suddenly, rage seeping out from every pore. I can't remember ever yelling at my dad, not even that first Christmas when I hated him so much I couldn't breathe. "You think I need a mirror to help me accept how screwed up I am? FYI, I'm pretty clear on it, thanks." These words cut through the room, shrinking the space between us the way the truth always does.

Dad doesn't say anything right away. This is how he's different from Mom. She can't let a silence sit, she has to tear through it with her voice, always. Dad decides what he wants to say before he says it. I can literally see him doing it now, weighing his words in his head before speaking them; he wants to get it right.

"I blame myself," he says finally, his voice so heavy it makes my stomach clench. "For what you went through— have been going through. Since the divorce." He rubs his forehead. "But, sweetheart, you are not 'screwed up.' On the inside or the outside. That's not—"

"Marshall will be here any minute," I say, turning away from him. "I have to finish getting ready."

"Okay, Bear." The disappointment in his voice makes my heart clench. *i didn't mean to be mean i just can't do this right now.* "I'll be in the kitchen."

When the door closes, the tears spring to my eyes so fast I can't blink them away. Instead, blinking sends them over my lower lid, a pair of hot, fat drops on each cheek.

i miss mom

Even as I think this thought I am aware that it is a half-truth. I do miss her, but mostly I miss the way she let me be invisible. Being with Dad is a constant interrogation. Every conversation is a question in disguise, him asking and probing and trying to assess. Mom answered more questions than she ever asked, and she let us both pretend that I was okay.

oh-oh-kay

The funny pronunciation pops into my head, a single spoken word, three syllables inside my skull. The voice, a guy's voice, is familiar, but without an image attached I can't place it.

oh-oh-kay

I close my eyes, the memory just out of grasp.

you are oh-oh-kay

Bits of context bounce to the surface. The voice was kind, his hands were warm.

The man from the accident. The doctor in the white coat that nobody else at the accident saw. I'd almost forgotten about him. Remembering him now, it all comes back. The awareness of headlights coming toward me, the crunch of metal, the sharp crackle of glass, the sensation of the world being sucked toward me as I sat pinned, powerless, in my seat. The man appearing at my window, telling me I was *oh-oh-kay*, that the pain would go away. I can't see any of it, but I remember it, in my brain and also in my gut. The fear, the tiny sparks of hope.

I hear the sound of a car pull into the driveway. Engine cuts out, door opens then closes, steps on the sidewalk up to the front porch. It's 6:58, he's two minutes early.

wren was always late

The thought is a sharp pang in my chest.

no boyfriend

deep breaths

"Jessa!" Dad calls.

"Coming," I yell back, and grab my coat.

Marshall is standing inside the front door in a dark blue button up and khaki pants. For half a second he is unfamiliar, a stranger in preppy clothing I have never met.

marshall isn't collars and khakis, marshall is skating sweatshirts and baggy jeans

But then he smiles, and though his smile is nowhere in my head, it must've been hiding somewhere else inside me because seeing it lights me up.

"Hey, Fancy," Marshall says. "Look at you."

Instinctively, my chin drops.

no please don't look at me, look at anything but

"Well, you two have fun," Dad says cheerily. "Just be home by eleven, okay?"

I glare at him. "*Eleven?*" I expected a curfew — it's Dad after all — but eleven is inhuman.

"Yeah, eleven is pretty ambitious," Marshall says. "I'm pretty convinced she'll be sick of me by nine forty-five."

Dad laughs. "What can I say? I'm optimistic."

Marshall follows me outside and down the sidewalk toward his car. "So where are we going?" I ask him as he steps around me to open the passenger door.

"A carnival."

"A carnival," I repeat, looking down at my clothes.

"Yup. Of ephemeral futility. Otherwise known as an art exhibition at a super pretentious gallery in LoDo."

"Really?"

"Well, in all fairness, I don't know if the gallery is pretentious because I've never been there," Marshall says. "But I assume it has to be because it's in a hipster neighborhood next to the most painfully hipster coffee shop in all of Colorado, quite possibly the world." He shuts my door and jogs around to his side, his breath making tiny clouds in the cold night air. Seeing his breath makes me think about his heart.

"Whose art is it?" I ask when he gets in the driver's seat.

"A guy I skate with. And other people, but he's the only one I know." Marshall turns the key and immediately the heat blasts, a burst of dry air lifting the hair around my face. I angle the vents away from me, smooth the hair back down.

"Does he go to Crossroads?" I ask.

"Oh – no – he's old. I mean, not old, but not in high school. Early thirties, probably."

Autistic kids and thirty year olds. And his twin sister. And me.

He glances over at me. "Why don't I have normal friends?"

"Well… yeah."

"Laziness. Normal people are too much work."

"Makes sense why you're hanging out with me, then." I mean it as a joke, but my voice is too tight to pull it off.

"Oh, we're not hanging out," Marshall says, backing down the driveway. "'Hanging out' implies a pre-date situation. This is absolutely a date."

"I can't date," I blurt out, so awkward.

Marshall slams on the brakes. "That's it. Get out."

"Hilarious," I say wryly, but my heart is ping-ponging in my chest, *he's not serious he can't be serious.*

"Just kidding, you can stay," he says, easing his foot of the brake. "But I'm super mad at you for withholding this information until now, *after* I went to the Gap to buy slim fit khakis."

"They look very nice."

"No, they don't. I'm basically Woody from *Toy Story* right now. Also, why are we going to a lifeless art show if this isn't a date? We should be going to the skate park."

"I wasn't involved in the planning of this outing," I point out. "My attendance was somewhat compulsory, if you recall."

"It was, and I apologize. I generally only force girls to go on dates with me. Hanging out is usually optional." He slams on the brakes again. I bounce forward in my seat. "That one was a little dramatic, sorry. But I just remembered that there's a skating invitational happening downtown. You game?"

I look down at my cashmere and suede. "Can I change first?"

"Do you see how I'm dressed? No way." He guns it backward out of the driveway.

The skatepark is crowded when we get there, people everywhere, in makeshift risers and on folding chairs, packed in every inch of flat space.

"Are you cool with this?" Marshall asks me as we pass through the fence. "I didn't think about the people. More specifically, about the fact that you hate them."

"Hey. Not *all* people." I point at a little boy, nine maybe ten, doing tricks off to the side. "He's seems cool."

"Ugh. I hate that kid. There's this trick I've been trying to learn that he nailed in like three tries last week."

"You should steal his lunch money."

"Already did."

We're making our way toward the biggest bowl, which Marshal keeps calling a "pool." I'm trying not to feel the weight and heat of the people around us, the sheer number of humans in this claustrophobic rectangle. From every direction, the sound of skateboard wheels on pavement, incessant rolls and clicks.

deep breaths

The risers are packed but we find two empty folding chairs at the front. A skateboarder comes up the side of the pool and sails into the air, then grabs his board and spins it mid-flight.

"Can you do that?" I ask Marshall.

"Yeah, but it never looks that good. Maybe because I can't figure out how not to make a panicked face when I'm doing tricks."

"Demo, please."

He pulls a face.

I burst out laughing. "You look like a cartoon character."

Marshall nods vigorously. "I know. Like Roadrunner when he speeds off a cliff. It's horrible. The worst part is it's not even a fear thing anymore. It's literally the only way I can do the trick."

"Have you ever actually fallen?"

"Oh, I fall all the time. That was never it. It was more the thought that my heart would crap out mid-trick. To be clear, there was very little chance of that happening with a hole the size of mine, but no one told me that back then."

"Hannah mentioned the hole," I say. "Can you feel it?"

"Nah. Though I guess I really don't know because I've always had it. But it's not like there's a huge gaping sensation in my chest. I mean, there is, but only because you said this wasn't a date."

I flush, unexpectedly. It's not the joke so much as the proximity of his face to mine as he says it. We're both leaned forward, knees on elbows. The bleachers are crowded so our bodies are touching, which means that when we look at each other, like right now, our noses are six inches apart. He smells like spearmint gum.

"Does it freak you out?" I ask, face back to the front, scars out of sight, *thank god he's on my right.* "Knowing that it's there?"

"It used to. Though I always tried to act like it didn't. Mostly because I didn't want my parents to worry more than they already were. I could almost forget about it during the day, while I was preoccupied with trying to convince the popular kids I was cool. But at night it was all I could think about. I'd lie in my bed with my heart racing, which only made things worse because I was convinced the racing itself would kill me."

I try to imagine Marshall as a little boy, laying in his bed with a hand over his dysfunctional heart, terrified but not wanting to burden anyone else with it. I can't see it, but the thought alone makes my own heart sting.

"So what happened?" I ask. "You seem pretty chill about it now."

"Well, my parents saw through the act, for starters. Or Hannah ratted me out. Either way, one Saturday morning my dad announced that he was taking me to a support group for kids with disabilities. I wouldn't get in the car at first — I didn't want to think of my heart condition as a disability, and I definitely didn't want to sit in a room with kids with actual disabilities. But then my dad said he'd take me to Little Man after, so, obvi, I went."

"Little Man?"

"Best ice cream on the planet. We are one hundred percent going there tonight. Anyway, we got to the group, and there were maybe eight or ten other kids there, all different ages, all different kinds of health issues, most of them a lot worse than mine. And right out of gate the doctor in charge of the group had us go around and say three things: what was wrong with our bodies, what was hurting our souls, and which of the two made us sadder."

"Oh man," I say softly.

"Yeah. Brutal. Since I was the new kid, he let me go last. So I sat there for an hour, listening the other kids talk about how scared they were, how they didn't want their parents to worry, how they thought they'd never make friends at school. Exactly the way I felt. It didn't matter if they had tumors on their face or cancer in their blood. We all had the same stuff going on inside." He shrugs. "That flipped a switch for me. Realizing that I wasn't alone in it somehow made it easier to admit the things that I was feeling. To let it be okay that I wasn't okay."

My throat gets tight. *but what if it isn't actually okay?*

"So you got your ice cream," I say.

"Ha. No. Because when my dad came to pick me up, I informed him that I'd decided to live at the hospital with the other kids. Him explaining to me that you couldn't just move into the hospital didn't deter me. I feigned chest pains until they were forced to admit me."

"You did not."

"Heck yeah I did. No parents, as much TV and jello as I wanted, absolutely no piano music anywhere? C'mon. So much better than ice cream."

My stomach goes sour at the mention of jello. The bright artificial taste on my tongue, the slippery slide down my throat. With the thought of jello comes the rest of it, harsh lights, frigid air, the incessant hum, rough papery sheets on my bare legs, the socks that didn't fit. No images, just sensations and feelings and thoughts that send a shudder down my spine.

"I hate jello," I say quietly. *and hospitals*

"Do you want to talk about it?"

"My hatred of jello?"

"Your accident."

My instinct is to say no, right away, without thinking. But in this moment I do want to talk about it, if only to get out from under the weight of it, even for a second, for one breath.

"It was bad," I say finally. "The other car ran a red light." I take a breath and try to steady the waver in my voice. "The airbag shattered my cheekbone and...I guess the physics of it or whatever made my brain slam against the side of my skull." I swallow. "There was a lot of glass in my face, too, from the window . . . that's what the scars are from."

"Were you by yourself?" Marshall asks.

I nod. "I was coming home from a party. At my boyfriend's house. He's not my boyfriend anymore."

Marshall touches the back of my hand with the back of his. "Do you want to talk about that?" he asks.

I shake my head, move my hand away. "No."

We're both quiet then, staring forward, thinking our separate thoughts.

A few minutes pass. Then the music changes and a new pair of skaters enter the pool. My eyes leap from one face to the other as they crisscross the pavement, heart thundering in my chest. One is covered in bruises, the other is striped with scars.

they're not real, i'm imagining it, i'm making them up

"I can't see things in my head anymore," I hear myself say. The thing I really want to say, *i'm hallucinating*, is lodged in my throat.

Marshall turns his head. "What?"

"It's called 'aphantasia,'" I say, not looking at him. "The inability to form mental images. I woke up with it after the accident. The doctors thought it might get better after awhile, but..." I shrug.

"You can't see anything at all?"

"Nope." I fiddle with the sleeve of my sweater.

"Whoa," Marshall says quietly. "That's intense."

"Yeah," I say flatly. The rest of it — the all-consuming anxiety, the hallucinations, the fact that the anti-psychotics haven't helped — hangs in the air between us. A shroud, a storm cloud, a fog. "It sucks."

All of a sudden Marshall comes around the front of my chair and puts his arms around me.

"What are you doing?" I ask, instantly uncomfortable, too stiff, too aware of my scars pressing against the slick fabric of his coat.

"I'm hugging you," he says. "I'm not letting you do the thing you do. Emotionally disengage."

"How do you know what I do? You met me three weeks ago. Not even."

"I pay attention," he says simply. Then, quieter, almost too quiet to hear, he whispers into my hair. "I'm sorry. For what happened to you. For the awkwardness of this hug."

The stiffness gives away and I smile.

"And now I'm not sure how to extract myself from it," Marshall says, leaning further into me. "What happened to my chair?"

"It's right here," I say, laughing, and reach for it. His head drops a little as he fumbles for the seat, and for a second his breath is on my neck.

no boyfriend

My body goes rigid again. Marshall straightens back up. For a second all I can feel is the absence of him, cold air replacing his warmth.

I force myself to focus on the skateboarders, not anything else.

"Wow," I say as one of them does a backflip in the air and lands back on his board.

Marshall laughs out loud. "That was the most insincere 'wow' in the history of insincere wows. I wish Brendon were here to call you on it. Come on," he says nudging me with his shoulder. "Let's get out of here."

"We just got here."

"I know, but I'm second guessing it now. First, you're watching a bunch of guys who are better looking than I am do skateboarding tricks I can't do. Second, I mentioned Little Man and now Salted Oreo ice cream is all I can think about." He gets to his feet.

Little Man Ice Cream is a fifteen-minute walk from the skatepark in a building shaped like a giant metal ice cream can in the middle of the block. The patio is crowded with people in parkas licking ice cream cones under flood lights and heat lamps. Indie folk plays through speakers in the pavement. I look at Marshall. "You realize how bizarre this is, right? It's freezing out here."

"That's what the heat lamps are for," he says. "Trust me, ice cream is so much better in the winter. And by winter, I mean actual winter, not whatever happens in L.A. in March."

I'm still deciding what flavor I want when Marshall steps up to the window. Eyes on the flavor list, I follow him up, hear him order half scoops of Salted Oreo and Space Junkie for himself. "I'll have a scoop of Mint Cookie," I say, sliding my eyes toward the girl behind the counter, not realizing that there is a pane of mirrored glass between the flavor board and the open window until it's too late. For half a second I think the girl I see is inside the building. Then I see the scars. Instinctively start to count.

one

two

three

four

five

six

I lose count.

there are too many

I jerk back.

"What's wrong?" Marshall asks.

"Nothing," I say abruptly, eyes pinned to the concrete beneath our feet. "I'll go get us a table." Rattled, I move away from the building. My heart thunders in my chest.

I find an empty table on the other side of the building and slide into one of the chairs. My brain is struggling to process what just happened, to have an opinion about it. But the "it" has no shape now. The image didn't hold because it couldn't. Other than this pounding in my ribcage, there is nothing to go on, nothing to assess.

An ice cream cone appears in my sightline. "Let Little Man help," I hear Marshall say.

I take the cone and try to smile but my lips feel like wax.

"What happened back there?" Marshall asks quietly.

I pick at a hunk of cookie dough with my fingernail. "The mirror," I say finally. "It just caught me by surprise."

"Seeing your reflection, you mean?"

I don't say anything. This is not a conversation I want to have with him, or anyone. *i'm so ugly i can't bear to look*

My ice cream is melting under the heat lamp above us and dripping on my hand.

"Jessa," Marshall says, his eyes pulling at mine. Two fish hooks, trying to drag my insides out. I lick my ice cream, desperate for an activity, anything to keep from looking at him. The mint is real mint, fresh spearmint, the flavor grassy and bright on my tongue.

"I understand the obsession," I say lightly, between licks. "This is really good."

Marshall bites into the top edge of his cone. "It's cool that you just totally changed the subject and are acting like you didn't, but I just want it to be noted that I noted it."

"Noted," I say.

Neither of us says anything after that. A breathy rendition of a Beatles song plays through the speaker at our feet.

"You want to walk and eat?" Marshall asks suddenly.

"Sure. I mean, whatever you want. I'm fine either way."

"Then let's walk," he says, and stands up. As soon as he does he winces and grabs his calf.

"You okay?" I ask, alarmed.

"Yeah. My leg's just been bothering me for the last day or so. I must've pulled something skating." He sits back down to shake it out.

"Are you sure you want to walk?" I ask. "If your leg is hurting?"

"It's either my leg or my eardrums." He shudders. "Talk about things that make my soul sad."

"The music?"

"I'm not sure you can legitimately call this 'music.'"

"This is a Beatles song!"

"No, these are Beatles *lyrics*, presently being massacred by a girl with a ukulele and a fake Irish accent who most definitely lives in Portland with her parents. As soon as we get back to the car I'm blasting N.W.A. We need a least an hour of therapeutic treatment before I take you home."

"Just as long as I don't have to know who N.W.A is first."

Marshall shakes his head. "In three and a half weeks I have yet to introduce you to the most influential rap artists of all time. I have totally failed you."

"Well, then," I say. "You'd better get your head in the game."

Chapter Twelve

Hannah isn't under the stairs when I get to school on Monday morning. Instantly I'm uneasy. She's never not been there.

i should've told her about friday night

The weekend was fine. Good, even. Dad and I went hiking on Saturday, I ate vegetables, I painted my nails. Sunday we went to the movies. I did some homework. Reorganized my drawers. Last night I actually slept, deep and dreamless, until my alarm. But Hannah not being where I expect her to be, that's all it takes to throw me off kilter. As if I've ever been on kilter, in kilter, *is that even a thing?*

I pull out my laptop to work on the English paper I've been putting off. Ten minutes later I'm still staring at the screen. Distracted by everything and nothing in particular, per usual. Hannah still hasn't come.

"Hi, there." It's a man's voice, not Hannah but Dr. I, calling to me from the landing above. "I have a box full of pastries and a hall full of teachers who are watching their weight." He holds up a bakery box. "Want one?"

I do, actually, but that will only prolong this conversation, so I shake my head.

"What're you working on?" he asks.

"English paper," I say dully. "If staring at my screen counts as working."

"What's the assignment?"

I hold up my book. "Twenty-five hundred words on the 'separation of soul and body' in *Dorian Gray*." I remember what Hannah said about Dr. I getting her out of her English paper and have the thought *maybe he'll get me out of mine.* "Due Wednesday," I add.

"'As it was, we always misunderstood ourselves and rarely understood others.'" He smiles a little. "Lord Henry, in the library, with his pipe."

"Impressive. Want to write my paper?" I hear the casualness in my voice and am surprised by it. I normally suck at this, making small talk, but with Dr. I it's weirdly fine.

"But then I wouldn't get to read yours," he says. "You sure you don't want a pastry?"

eat well eat well

"Yeah. I'm sure."

"Well. I guess I'll leave you to it, then." He disappears from view.

dammit why didn't i take the pastry

I thumb through my copy of the novel, eyes skating over the pages. My mind is too scattered to think.

I give up on the paper and head to my locker. At the top of the hall a guy in skinny jeans and a fedora is organizing his books. He glances over as I pass, the way a normal person would. He smiles, I think, maybe he even says hello, don't know, none of it registers. All I see are his scars. More scars than should fit on a face. *are mine that bad?* The boy catches me staring at them, *staring at what, they're not real, there's nothing there*. I jerk my head down. Abandon my locker, head for the bathroom instead.

It's autopilot from there. Eyes on the ground, straight to the handicapped stall on the end. Shut the door so hard it rattles in the frame, fumble with the lock until it fits.

Chest heaving, I suck air in, chemically and dank, cheap disinfectant mixed with public bathroom smells. The smell is terrible and familiar, the smell of *this*, of hiding in bathroom stalls, of being afraid. Of gross things you're trying to make less gross by covering them up without ever getting rid of the muck underneath.

The whirl in my stomach goes sour.

i'm gonna throw up

But I won't, actually, I never do. In eighth grade I learned how to force the issue, stick my finger down my throat until something came up. Mom always let me stay home, even when it was obvious, *it was always obvious*, that I wasn't really sick.

I could do that today. Call my dad from the phone in the front office, tell him I don't feel well. Spend the rest of the day

watching movies on his couch, the volume turned up so loud
I won't be able to think. Maybe I'll feel better tomorrow, but
maybe I won't. Maybe I'll be out the whole week.

and then what?

More of this. This smell, this bathroom, this hollow feeling in my chest.

*here i go down circle road strong and hopeful hearted through the dust
and wind up just exactly where i started . . . HERE*

And all at once I want out of the circle. Suddenly I feel
trapped. The circle is a merry go round. The horses aren't going anywhere. I want to get off.

I yank the lock, push through the stall door, walk straight
to the mirror, look myself in the face.

For a split second I see only the eyes, *my eyes*, blue-green
and anxious; then my gaze shifts and I see the rest. The blond
eyebrows that need waxing. A zit on my forehead I didn't
know to cover up. The scars like pink graffiti on the left side
of my face

so many scars

I force myself to count them, all of them.

Fourteen.

Another wave of nausea ripples through me. I fumble for
the edges of the sink.

"You're okay," the man at the accident said. Not *you will be
okay*, future tense, but it's already happened, present tense, you
already are.

But I wasn't. Not then, certainly not now, hugging a bathroom sink.

dear god please fix me just make me okay

It's my refrain from that summer, the exact words of the prayer I whispered so many times my throat went hoarse. The answer now is the same. Silence. No comment. You're on your own.

"Jessa," someone says, and then I feel a cool hand on my arm. My palms are sticky on the sides of the sink, my tongue like a sock in my mouth. "Are you okay?"

oh-oh-kay

you're oh-oh-kay

I turn. Hannah.

so not okay

Her black eye is all I see. The bruise has crept above her eyelid now. It looks like someone punched her in the face.

"What's wrong?" she asks.

The word *nothing* springs to my lips automatically. The instinctual, self-protecting lie.

"I'm not feeling well," I say instead.

"Like, sick?"

sick in the head

I swallow. Bile stings my throat. "I don't know. Maybe. Do you have gum?"

"I think so," Hannah says, unzipping her bag. As she's digging through the contents, I see the top of a white safety cap, then hear the distinctive shake of a medicine bottle. The

Rite Aid bag I saw in her backpack a couple weeks ago, are these the same pills? *what is she on meds for?* Hannah pulls out a pack of gum. "Here," she says, handing me a piece.

"Thanks." I push the gum into my mouth. "How'd you know I was in here?"

"I didn't," she says. "I just had to pee." She disappears inside a stall. Alone again with the mirror, I go back to staring myself down.

"Did you just get here?" I ask, watch my mouth move with the question. It's my face but it isn't my face. Me, but someone else. This is what it means to dissociate, to disconnect from the self. But which is self and which is other, which is fiction and which is me?

"I've been here since seven," Hannah is saying. "Mr. Tanaka gave me a key to the practice room in class on Friday. Said I could use it before school." Her voice is fast, too fast, staccato, chopped. *how much coffee has she had?* "I think he felt bad about the Logan thing. Which he should, obviously. I meant to leave a note in our spot so you'd know but just spaced. Sorry."

A flush, then the door opens. Hannah comes up beside me at the sink, her face appearing next to mine in the mirror. I stare at her black eye, willing it away. *how long does accepting reality take?*

"What?" she demands.

"Nothing," I say, turning away from the mirror, and from her. "I gotta go. I still haven't been to my locker yet."

"Hey," she calls. "My brother said to tell you he might miss lunch. He's at a doctor appointment right now and doesn't know how long it'll last."

I look back at her.

"Is he okay?" I ask. *do you know we hung out on friday?*

"Yeah, he's fine. He just went to get his leg checked out. He hurt it skateboarding, I guess."

"'Kay," I say, then start to turn away again.

"He says you guys had fun on Friday."

"Oh," I say lamely. "Yeah."

"Why didn't you tell me you were going out with him?" she asks.

"I didn't want to make a big deal out of it. It wasn't a date or anything."

She rolls her eyes. "Yeah, he said that, too."

"It wasn't."

"Whatever it was. I'm fine with it. Just as long as you guys don't get weird about it."

"There's nothing to get weird about," I say. "We're friends, that's it." Then I'm out the door before she can say anything else.

Chapter Thirteen

"Jessa."

I'm hunched over the lab table in fourth period, attempting to burn magnesium in dry ice. I wasn't even sure my chemistry teacher knew my name, but he's calling it out now, no doubt because I'm doing this wrong. My mind is everywhere but here.

I look up. "Yes?"

"You have a call in the front office."

I blink. "A phone call?"

My chemistry teacher looks at the girl standing next to his desk. She has an orange *office aide* sticker on her sweater, a slip of white paper in her hand. The girl nods. "On the main line," she says.

"Who is it?" I ask, fear pinning me in my seat.

something happened something happened that's the only reason someone would call

The girl shrugs. "I didn't answer it. They just sent me to get you. Do you want to take it or not?"

no

"Yes." I force myself to stand up.

"Take your bag," my teacher calls. "The bell's about to ring."

The girl walks with me to the office but we don't speak. She's on her phone and I'm on a loop, *here i go down circle road strong and hopeful hearted through the dust and wind up just exactly where i started*, back on the merry-go-round so I don't spin out, convinced that something awful has happened and I'm fifteen seconds away from finding out.

My hand is shaking as I pick up the phone. The receiver is cold and filmy and smells like perfume.

"Hello?" I say finally, dread ballooning in my chest.

"You have no phone," the voice on the other end says. "I had to resort to desperate measures."

The dread balloon deflates. "Where are you?"

"Still at the doctor," Marshall says. "Wanna come hang out?"

"At a doctor's office?"

"Well, technically it's the hospital, but yes. And I know you hate hospitals, so I'll totally understand if you don't want to come."

"Wait, why are you at the hospital? Are you okay?"

"They're running some tests on my leg. So are you coming? I'm getting you an Uber. It's coming to the gas station on the corner."

"Right now?"

"Uber says six minutes."

"You want me to leave school to come see you at the hospital." My mind goes to my own hospital room, that cold, suffocating cube. No image comes to mind, just a sinking sensation, a heaviness, a dread.

"Only if you want to," Marshall is saying. "But if you don't you have to tell me now because I just hit request. Aaron double A is on his way."

"So I'm just walking out the front door." I flick my eyes around the office to see if anyone is listening to me. Nobody is.

"Sign out first. The sheet's on the counter. That way no one will call your dad. When you get here, take the elevators to the 3rd floor and turn right. You'll see signs for the Heart Institute. I'm in room 312."

"Why are you at the Heart Institute?"

"Because they have the nicest rooms. Hang up the phone now. Aaron is four minutes out and I can't risk my five star rating with a no-show."

"Okay. I'm doing it."

His voice gets quieter. "I'm really glad." Then I hear a click and he's gone.

※

The Uber pulls up at the hospital's front entrance. I can't go in. I can't even get out of the car.

"Take as much time as you need," the driver says help-fully. Aaron double A.

"Thanks," I say hoarsely. "I don't like hospitals."

"No one likes hospitals," he says. "Except doctors. I drive a lot of doctors. Mostly medical students, actually. The doctors take Uber Black."

"Uh huh." I'm watching the automatic door open and close as people come in and out.

"I could park if you want," Aaron says. "I've done that for someone before. I can park and walk you in. I'll end the ride now so it won't be extra." He taps his screen.

"No, that's okay," I say, forcing myself to unbuckle my seatbelt. *your being with me won't help.* My hand is shaking as I fumble for the door handle, eyes locked on the building, my head a cacophony of hospital noises. It's as if my brain is making up for the missing images with an overload of remembered sound. The constant hum, the incessant beeping, voices through walls and through speakers, the squeak and jerk of wheels.

"Good luck," Aaron says as I climb out of the car.

i will walk in, i will go to his room, i will be fine
but what if he isn't fine
he isn't fine
he wouldn't be in the hospital if he were fine
something's wrong something's wrong something's wrong

The lobby is quiet and calm. Nobody pays any attention to me as I pass the information desk and move toward the elevator bank, press the up button, wait for the ding. Room 312 is easy to find once I get to the third floor. I linger outside his room for a few minutes, losing my nerve, until a nurse passes and gives me a funny look and I dart in.

"My day improves," Marshall says, and smiles. He's in bed with his leg propped up on pillows, watching TV. There's a needle in his arm, an IV bag hanging from a metal rack by his bed. And a bruise by his left temple that wasn't there before, *it isn't really there now.* A woman in a fuzzy sweater and horn-rimmed glasses sits in a chair by the window, working a crossword puzzle. Auburn hair like Hannah's, Marshall's ivory skin. A bruise in the exact same spot as his on her check.

am i seeing bruises on everyone now???

"You must be Jessa," the woman says warmly, rising to her feet. "I have heard so much about you. I'm Marianne."

"Hi," I say. "Nice to meet you." I fiddle with the strap of my bag. *i wasn't expecting his mom.* Her warmth is palpable and completely unnerving, like a heat lamp. My mom is nothing like this.

"Well," she says after a minute. "I think I'll go find something eat. Will you two be okay for a half hour or so?"

"So smooth," Marshall says.

His mom swats him with her crossword book. "Would you have preferred: 'Please excuse me, Jessa, my son has ordered me to leave the room as soon as you arrive'?"

"I didn't say you had to immediately bolt."

"Jessa does have to get back to school eventually," his mom says, bending over to kiss him on the forehead. "For the record," she adds, "I was not made aware of this plan until Uber was en route. If asked I will deny all knowledge." But I can tell she's not mad.

"Tell me," I demand when she's gone.

"I was in the mood for some jello," he says, and tries to smile, but it's so painfully fake.

"Marshall."

"The pain in my leg is a clot," he says.

"A clot," I repeat. "Like a blood clot."

He nods. "Deep vein thrombosis is the medical name. Mine's not that big, but it's pretty much the worst type of clot."

"But they can remove or something, right?"

He shakes his head. "There are medicines which they could put directly in that vein to break up the clot, but it's too risky for me because if a piece of the clot breaks off in the process, it could go through the hole in my heart to my brain. So for now I'm on blood thinners, which should keep it from getting bigger or breaking off."

I stare at him. Very little of this is making sense. "So they're just leaving it there?"

"Well, my body should dissolve it eventually. The problem is the hole. For most people a clot like that would get caught in their lungs. But what they're telling me is that mine could take the shortcut through my heart to my brain and if it did, I could have a stroke or . . . die." He takes a quick breath. "The odds of that happening on this one are small, I think, since we know about it, and they're gonna monitor it pretty close."

"So that's good news, then," I say, still confused. "Right?"

"Yeah, for sure. It's great that we caught it." His face isn't a good news face.

"But?"

He hesitates. "They also tested me for this gene mutation, called Factor V Leiden, which it turns out I have. Basically, my body clots way more than it should, which is why I got the clot to begin with. Because there's a pretty good chance that I'll develop another one, even if I'm on blood thinners long term, my cardiologist now wants to close my ASD. That's the medical name for my hole."

"You're having *heart surgery*?"

"Not surgery. They'll go up through a vein in my thigh. I'll only be in the hospital a couple days."

I drop into the chair by the window. My face hurts and feels numb at the same time, like there's no blood in it anymore.

"The procedure is really safe," Marshall is saying, "and quick, and long term it'll just be better because I won't have to think about it anymore. They'll put this little device with two mesh disks inside the hole and then—"

He keeps talking, but I can no longer hear him. Won't let myself hear him, won't let these words sink in because if they do they will lodge themselves in my brain like shrapnel and torture me. Details do that. They give my panic a foothold.

Eventually, his mouth stops moving.

"When are they doing it?" I hear myself ask.

"Tomorrow afternoon," he says. "I should be back at school next week, assuming they feel good about how the clot looks."

"Does Hannah know?"

"Yeah. Mom texted her. She's coming later with my dad. After she finishes practicing, obvi. We can't let my heart condition interfere with that."

"Seriously? She's *practicing* first?"

"Well, to be fair, it's not like the situation is currently an emergency. I get it if she doesn't want to give up rehearsal time to come sit in a hospital room."

I nod but don't say anything.

"What?" he asks finally.

"I don't see how it isn't an emergency," I say. "You're telling me you have a blood clot in your leg that could break off and kill you, and that tomorrow you're having a procedure done on your heart that obviously has to have some risks or else they would've done it already. What am I missing?"

"Nothing. All of that is true."

"So why are you being so calm?" I ask suspiciously.

"I dunno. Maybe you have a calming effect on me." He smiles a little. "I apparently have the opposite effect on people. Hannah told me yesterday that my *looking* at her was stressing her out."

"You do have a fairly stress-inducing gaze."

"Oh yeah?"

"Little bit."

Marshall tiptoes his fingers up my arm. "So you're basically telling me that I make your pulse race."

I punch him in the shoulder. He catches my fist in his hand and his eyes go serious for a sec. "Hey, I know this was hard for you — *is* hard for you. The hospital thing. But I'm really glad you're here."

It takes everything I have not to pull my hand away. Not because I want to, but because what I *do* want terrifies me. I can't let myself acknowledge how much I want him, want *this*, a relationship that has shape and weight and depth, not a boyfriend who lets me hide in his shadow but a boy who sometimes makes my pulse race and always is my friend.

"Me, too," I say finally, and open my fist.

Chapter Fourteen

I'm back at school before the end of fifth period. I come in the building through the front door, carrying a note from Marshall's cardiologist, *Jessa Gray was at a doctor's appointment*, not technically a lie. Doesn't matter anyway; the secretary in the front office doesn't even read it. Slides it into a file, writes me a pass back to class while I try to not stare at the burn on her cheek. If I hurry, I can get to fifth period before the bell. But I don't hurry. I move down the main hall like the floor is made of molasses, fear like lead in my boots. Tomorrow looms like a tornado in the distance, a shark in a coming wave. I want to get it over with, but at the same time I don't want it to come at all. If tomorrow doesn't come then neither does Marshall's heart procedure, and he stays how he is now, *safe*. But if the procedure never happens then Marshall never gets better, and I stay here, in this panic pit. We never get to that day on the other side of all of this where we go on a date and I let him call it a date and his heart doesn't have a hole in it and maybe mine doesn't either anymore. Between that day and this one is tomorrow, a wall I can't see through.

I stop in the bathroom, in and out of the stall quickly, don't let myself consider hiding out, force myself to look in the mirror as I'm washing my hands. The thought *i wish he could've seen how i looked before my accident* pops in my head, but of course there's no way he ever could've. If the accident hadn't happened I wouldn't be here. If things hadn't gone exactly how they went, I wouldn't have needed to move to Colorado, and Marshall and I would never have met. That thought takes the juice right out of my regret.

The fear, though, is unassailable. The dark balls of dread pinball through my brain. This is what anxiety does to a brain, I know that. A barrage of intrusive, unwanted, and distressing thoughts that the person thinking them can't turn off no matter how hard they try, which is exactly what I'm doing right now, trying *not* to think about all the things that could go wrong during the procedure tomorrow, all the ways that Marshall could die. Failing, because when it comes to obsessive thinking, avoidance never works.

The bell rings. My cue to leave, before the bathroom floods with girls. Hannah usually goes to her locker between fifth and sixth so she doesn't have to go again after school, so I go there, to find the one person who I can talk to about the storm inside my head, the one person who will actually get it, who might be feeling the same things, too.

She's bent over, angrily shoving books into her backpack when I walk up, the longer side of her hair hanging in her face. "Hey," I call out, so relieved to see her it makes my throat catch.

But then she straightens up and I audibly gasp. The half moon under her eye has become a dozen bruises all over her face.

"What?" she demands.

"Are you okay?" I ask her, glancing around to see if anyone is staring at her, because even without the bruises I would be staring, *i am staring*, seeing her like this. She looks like she hasn't slept, or showered, or eaten, in days. *did she look this bad this morning?* I have no mental image, no way to be sure, just the absence of a memory of ever looking at her and feeling the way I do right now, concerned and unsettled and a tiny bit afraid.

it's not real i'm imagining it i'm making it up

"I'm fine," she says, going back to her backpack, yanking so hard on the zipper I fully expect it to break. "What's up?"

"I just heard about Marshall," I say, forcing myself not to look away, to act normal, *maybe she looks fine, maybe it's not just the bruises i'm imagining, maybe all of this is in my head.*

"Right. The clot."

"Well, not just the clot," I say, worried suddenly that she doesn't know the rest of it.

"You mean the fact that they're closing the hole? You should be psyched about that. Marshall can stop thinking about it. And so can the rest of us." She slings her backpack on her back. "I just wish it wasn't happening this week. I really don't need another distraction."

I stare at her. "Hannah."

"Sorry." But she doesn't sound sorry. "I just meant it's not the ideal week for family medical procedures, that's all. Obviously, I'm glad they caught the clot."

"So you're not worried about it."

"No. Marshall has literally the best luck of anyone on the planet. Other than the fact that he was born with a heart defect, every single other thing in his life has worked out. So, no, I'm not worried that something will go wrong for him because nothing ever does. I am, however, worried that I'll blow my Interlochen audition, because that's the way things go for me." She slams her locker shut.

She's waiting for me to respond but no words come.

"I'm sorry this is all happening at once," I say finally.

"Yep," she says flatly. Then she turns and walks off.

what has gotten into her?

I'm still standing at her locker when the warning bell rings, replaying our conversation in my head, wishing I could see it, to get the details right. There was something so odd about the way she was acting. Separate from the scowl, the dismissive tone, the preoccupation with herself. There was something else. A not-Hannahness underneath all of that.

she wasn't herself

As soon as I have the thought I second-guess it. Maybe she *was* being herself, maybe I don't really know her, maybe this is who she really is. Maybe this is why she doesn't have any other friends. These thoughts make sense, but I don't buy them. Something is up.

Out of nowhere I remember that prescription bottle I saw in her bag this morning. *what is she taking medicine for?* It could be anything, nothing. But it wasn't nothing when I did it, hid a bottle of pills in my backpack, terrified someone would see them, at the same time hoping someone would so I wouldn't have to carry the secret around anymore, *i'm on anti-anxiety meds.* Looking back I don't know why I was so ashamed of it. By tenth grade I'd realized that half the kids I knew were on Zoloft, but by then I wasn't taking them any more. The headaches and constant dry mouth got to be too much, plus the pills never actually made me feel better. Just sort of numb.

The late bell jolts me into motion, one foot in front of the other until I get to the right door. Psychology of the Artist, my favorite class. The teacher glances at my pass then waves me to my seat where I promptly check out of reality and check into the world where everything that possibly could go wrong with Marshall and Hannah definitely will. My mind making lists and more lists of all the ways that I could lose them, my only two friends, the realest relationships I've ever had.

"One feels as if one were lying bound hand and foot at the bottom of a deep dark well, utterly helpless," I hear my teacher say, and my eyes snap up.

YES THAT IS EXACTLY HOW ONE FEELS

"Vincent Van Gogh wrote these words in a letter to his brother, Theo," my teacher continues, catching my eye for a sec before sliding up the row. "One of many in which the artist discusses at length the depth and darkness of his mental illness. And yet, these same letters suggest that the paralyzing anxiety that afflicted Van Gogh was a crucial component of his creativity. His unique psychological disposition enabled him to see the world in a way that no one else could."

Lucky for him. Anxiety, helplessness, a deep dark well, *check check check*. But my mental illness hasn't made me creative in any sense of the word. I don't see the world differently. Mostly it feels like I don't see the world at all, even now, with my dark mind's eye and my amped-up sight. And what I *do* see, what draws my eye, isn't even *real*. The kaleidoscope of bruises on Hannah's face, my dad's persistent scars, all the things that could go wrong but probably never will. If I were an artist, or an author, maybe I could do something with all of this fiction. Instead I'm just stuck with it, *in* it. My mind caught in quicksand, the more it struggles to get out, the deeper it sinks into the pit.

I WANT OUT OF THE PIT

It's the feeling I had this morning in the bathroom, a sort of mental claustrophobia, *i don't want do this anymore*. Except this time the thing I want to escape is inside me, it is me. Maybe it always was.

I jerk to my feet. My teacher looks at me, eyebrows raised.

"I, uh, have to go to the bathroom," I say.

She nods. "Take the pass."

I take it, an old wooden spoon, even though I know I'm not going to the bathroom and probably won't come back to class.

Once in the hallway, I don't give myself a chance to second guess it, to remind myself of all the reasons I hate therapy, to talk myself out of what I'm about to do. I just walk straight to Dr. I's office and through the door. His secretary looks up from her screen, then frowns.

"Do you have an appointment?" she asks, scanning the calendar on her desk. "Because Dr. I's not here."

but he has to be here

it took everything i had to get here

"No," I say. "When will he be back?"

"Not sure," the secretary says. "He has an appointment right after school, so I know he's still on campus. You can wait, if you want." She gestures to a pair of chairs against the side wall.

I look at the chairs then back at the woman behind the desk. Her hawkish eyes, the *click click click* of her fake nails on computer keys, the powdery smell of her perfume.

"I'll just come back," I say.

She looks back at the calendar, flips the page. "He has an opening at ten fifteen tomorrow. I can write you a pass to give to your second period teacher to leave class."

I nod. "Okay."

"What's your name?" she asks, reaching for a pencil.

"Jessa Gray."

"Grade?"

"Eleventh."

"And where will you be second period tomorrow?"

"Chemistry," I say. "Dr. Geiger."

"Great," she says, handing me the little pink slip. "So we'll see you tomorrow morning then." She goes back to her screen and I think I mumble *thank you* and then I'm back in the empty hall.

I start back toward my classroom. As I turn onto D hall, I see him coming towards me, hands in the pockets of his white coat. My stomach dips. Five minutes ago I was ready to talk to him. In his office, on my terms. Now I feel blindsided. Caught.

"Hello," he says, and smiles.

"I was looking for you," I blurt out.

"Well. Here I am. Everything okay?"

I open my mouth to my answer but my throat clamps shut. So I just shake my head.

"C'mon," he says. "Let's go outside." I follow him out the door at the end of the hall, to the same bench I saw him on last week. "You have your hideout and I have mine," he says, and sits. "I come out here to eat lunch and read." He pulls a worn paperback from the pocket of his coat. *Principles of Philosophy* by Rene Descartes. "You into philosophy?" he asks.

"Not really," I say. *not at all*

"It's a hard sell for high school kids, I know," he says. "But you're all missing out. Descartes in particular is fascinating.

He was a mathematician, not a doctor, but some consider him the founder of modern psychology, because he was one of the first big thinkers to suggest that the mind was independent from the brain."

"What's the difference?" I ask. "Aren't they two words for the same thing?"

"Ha. Ask a dozen doctors and philosophers and you'll get twelve different answers. But for Descartes, it was a resounding no. He believed the mind operated within the physical structure of the brain but wasn't confined by it, because the mind was immaterial, like the soul. That one idea — that the soul and the body are distinct entities that interact somehow in the brain — was the seed that grew into modern psychology." He smiles a little. "But you didn't come out here to talk about Descartes."

I shake my head.

He slips the book back into his pocket and gestures for me to sit.

"Want to tell me what's going on?" he asks when I do.

I stare at my hands.

"Sorry. Loaded question," he says. "How about we start with why you were looking for me."

I scrape at my cuticles. "Because I have to get better," I say finally.

"Okay. Better from what?"

"I have an anxiety disorder," I say finally. "For the last couple years it's been mostly under control, but since the accident

— I was in a car accident two months ago, but you probably know that already, you probably know about the anxiety, too — the panic is all there is." The words are a shaky gush but I don't slow down. "And now my friend is in the hospital and all I can think about are the thousand ways he could die. And maybe if it was just that, the morbid thoughts, the racing heart, the stuff I know how to deal with, maybe I could get past it again, but now, because of the accident . . ." A knot forms in my throat. I swallow it down. "There's other stuff, too."

"What kind of other stuff?" Dr. I asks, his voice super gentle now, and more familiar somehow.

"My mind's eye is messed up," I say, because it's the easier thing to say. "I can't see anything in my head."

"And that's making your anxiety worse?"

"Not just that," I say. The skin beneath my thumbnail tears, stings, bleeds.

Dr. I waits for me to go on. For a couple seconds I consider making something up, something more victim less freak. Finally, I tell him the truth.

"I'm hallucinating," I say hoarsely. "Wounds. On people's faces. Not everyone. Just some people. My dad. Hannah. Other kids at school." *now marshall too.*

"What kind of wounds?"

"Mostly bruises and scars. Sometimes burns or scrapes or scratches. Always on the face. It's been happening ever since my accident — because of my accident, obviously. A way to dissociate from my own wounds or whatever. But, honestly, I'm not even thinking about my scars that much anymore. Seeing them is still hard for me, but I'm not, like, obsessing over them every second the way I was in the beginning. So why haven't the hallucinations stopped?" My voice is rising, panicked, too high-pitched. "I should be getting better, not worse."

"Have you noticed a pattern to the wounds?" Dr. I asks calmly. "You said you don't see them on everyone. So have you paid attention to who you *do* see them on? Why some people and not others?"

"I don't know," I say, irritated. *i need answers not more questions.* "Shouldn't you be telling me?"

"It doesn't work that way, Jessa," he says gently. "My job would be a lot easier if it did."

"Awesome," I say flatly. "You can't help me, either."

"I *am* helping you," he says, and there it is again, that familiar calm in his voice. "I'm telling you that what's happening in your mind isn't random. But you already know that. You said yourself that what you're seeing is specifically connected to your own experience. You were hurt. You're now perceiving other people as being hurt. If I were you, I'd start there."

"I don't understand what you mean," I say, frustrating rising. "Start where, do what?"

"Think like a philosopher," he says. "Figure this out."

"Yeah, I'll get right on that," I say, sarcastic, too sarcastic, *why am i being such a bitch?* My eyes drop back to my lap. "Sorry," I mumble. "It's just— I've tried all the things. Meds, therapy, supplements, a hundred different diets that are supposed to reduce stress. Nothing has ever worked."

He's quiet for a few seconds.

"What do you have going on before school tomorrow?" he asks then.

I shrug. "Why?"

"About a year ago, some students started a support group, open to anyone who felt they needed to come. It meets Tuesday and Thursday mornings at seven-twenty at the recreation center down the street." He looks over at me. "I was thinking you might like to try it out."

thanks no thanks

I start to shake my head.

"The group is completely confidential," he goes on. "The students take that very seriously. Which is probably why the group is so popular. Anywhere from twelve to twenty kids come every week. I'd guess the majority suffer from anxiety, like you, or depression. But others are dealing with bipolar disorder, OCD, eating issues, addiction, self-harm."

I try to let these terms bounce off me, but they lodge beneath my skin. "And they all go to Crossroads?"

He nods. "When the group first started, the administrators assumed it would be mostly alternative school students.

But it's turned out to be a fifty-fifty split between the two pro-grams, and spread out fairly equally among the four grades."

There's an odd sort of comfort in this.

"Why doesn't it just meet here?" I ask.

"The students thought about holding it in a classroom," Dr. I replies. "But for many of the kids who come, school doesn't feel like a safe place to open up."

is any place safe?

"I think it could be really good for you," Dr. I says quietly. "Very low pressure. There's no faculty member there, only students. And no one will expect you to talk on your first visit. Unless you want to, of course."

"I won't," I say quickly.

"So you'll go then?"

There is pretty much nothing I want to do less.

"Yeah," I say finally. "I'll go. Do I just show up?"

Dr. I nods. "It meets in the big room beside the gym. Just make sure you get there on time, because at seven-thirty they shut the door."

"Okay," I say, but I feel my mind changing, the excuses trickling in, the reasons I might not show up.

"How about I meet you there at seven twenty-five?"

"I thought you said it was students only?"

"It is. But getting through the front door can be hard the first time. Sometimes getting to the parking lot is even harder."

so much for those excuses

Eventually, I nod. "Yeah, okay. I'll meet you."

Dr. I points at the wooden spoon peeking out of my bag. My hall pass. It seems like an eternity since I left sixth period. "Do you need to take that back? You've only got five minutes before the bell."

"Probably."

He gets to his feet. "I'll see you tomorrow morning then," he says. Then he gives me a little wave and walks off.

Chapter Fifteen

The rest of the day passes quickly, minutes tumbling past, leaving a snowball of dread in their wake until the bell rings and it's time to go home. I think about finding Hannah again, but for what? Our conversation earlier left me more rattled, not less.

"Hey, Bear," Dad says when I get in the car. "How was your day?"

"Not great," I say, and feel a wall come up between us, the wall that keeps him out. "Marshall's in the hospital," I add, and the wall comes down.

"What? Why?"

"He has a blood clot," I say. "In his leg. And I guess it's really risky for him because of his heart condition—"

Dad frowns. "Marshall has a heart condition?"

"He was born with a hole in his heart," I say. "They were going to leave it there, but now because of the clot, they're putting a device in to close it. Tomorrow."

I'm looking out the window but Dad is looking at me, studying me, gauging my reaction to all of this. We're still parked in the same spot.

"That's a lot to process," I hear him say.

I nod. And then, out of nowhere, but really out of everywhere, I say, "I talked to the school counselor today."

"Oh, yeah? How'd that go?"

"Good. He wants me to come to a support group tomorrow. Before school."

"Are you going to do it?" He's trying to sound so casual but I can hear the hope in his voice.

"I guess."

"I think that's great," he says. I can tell he wants to say something else but he doesn't. Instead, he just backs the Jeep out of the parking spot and heads home.

As soon as we're in the house I'm pulling out the phonebook and looking up the hospital's main line, digging a pen from my bag to write the number down. My eye catches the folded pink paper in the inside pocket. *no boyfriend!!!!* it shouts. I ignore it and dial the number.

The only landline is in the kitchen, but it's cordless so I take it outside as the operator connects me to Marshall's room. It rings four times before he answers. I'm just about to hang up.

"Uh, hello?"

"Hi."

"I should've known it was you," Marshall says, and I hear him smile. "Calling the landline. So vintage."

"Right?"

"Where are you calling from?" he asks.

"My dad's," I say, sitting down on the patio steps. "We just got home. How are you feeling?"

"I'm okay. Bored of sitting here with my leg propped up. How are you?"

"Hey, is your mom with you?" I ask instead of answering.

"No, I sent her home. She's coming back with my dad and Hannah. Why?"

"Will you tell me more about the support group you went to? The one you told me about Friday night?"

"Sure. What do you want to know?"

"I dunno. What it was like. How it worked."

"We basically just sat around a circle and talked," he says. "When new kids were there, the doctor in charge would ask everyone the same question, the way he did on my first day. But most weeks it was more of a vent session. Not so much about our physical issues, but what we were feeling."

"What was the point of it?"

"To feel better, I guess. The doctor in charged used to call it shrinking our dragons. He said that by putting them out there, naming our fears, they'd get smaller. Or less scary at least."

A dragon is exactly what it feels like, my panic. Breathing fire in my gut.

"You still there?" I hear Marshall ask.

"Yeah."

"Why did you want to know about the group?"

I hesitate. "I think I might go to one," I say finally, haltingly. "A support group. Tomorrow morning, before school. Dr. I told me about it. I—I went to talk to him today." These are just words, facts I am reciting, *why is this so excruciatingly hard?*

"What'd you think of him?" Marshall asks.

"Dr. I? He was fine. I'd met him before. Why?"

"People are mixed on him. Just wondering what you thought. The support group sounds cool. Is it the one that meets at the rec center?"

"Yeah. You know about it?"

"Not really. Only that it exists." He pauses. "I'm glad that you're going."

"Yeah. Me, too."

"What made you decide to do it?"

I'm quiet for a few seconds. It's only one word, but that doesn't make it easier to say. "You," I tell him.

"Because I went to one?"

"More like you having a blood clot and needing a heart procedure." I take a breath, *just say it*, pull the band-aid off. "I have an anxiety disorder," I blurt out. "Since before the accident, before the thing with my mind's eye. I get panic attacks, and . . . other stuff, too."

"Like what?"

"Like really dark thoughts I can't stop thinking."

Marshall makes a sound in his throat, a cross between an *ah ha* and an *oh man*. "You're worried about tomorrow."

"So worried," I whisper. This truth is terrifying to speak. It doesn't feel smaller now that it's out there. It feels like the biggest thing there is. "Aren't you?"

"I'm not," he says softly. "I'm a little sad, weirdly, that they're closing it, after I got used to the fact that I'd have it forever. But mostly relieved that I won't have to think about it anymore. And supes disappointed that I won't get a cool Frankenstein scar to show for it."

unlike you, frankenstein barbie

Heat floods my cheeks, fast and prickly. "Yeah, bummer," I say sarcastically.

"I'm an idiot," Marshall says quickly. "Obviously scars are hard for people who actually have them. I just think they're cool. Especially yours."

I don't say anything.

"You won't believe me because you haven't seen them," he says. "But your scars are most definitely the cool kids of all scars. Scar royalty."

I stand up so I'm eye level with the window. The blinds are down so my reflection is impossible to miss. Less clarity of detail than the mirror in the school bathroom, but I can see them still, fourteen lines scattered along the left side of my face.

"I have, actually," I say, with a punch of *take that*. "Seen them. I'm looking at them right now."

"Really? What happened to avoiding mirrors?"

"What can I say? Today was filled with progress."

"Go you," he says. I hear his smile. "I'm really sorry to hear about the anxiety," he says then. "Why didn't you tell me before?"

"It's not something I generally lead with." *or talk about ever with anyone*

"How long have you had it?"

"Since seventh grade."

"You were so young," Marshall says.

"Yeah."

"Are you getting treatment for it?"

"Not anymore," I tell him. "It was pretty bad when it first started. I was pulling my hair out and stuff like that. It freaked my mom out. So she took me to therapy and put me on meds." I fumble for a piece of hair, realize I'm doing it and sit down on my hand. "The therapy didn't help and the meds made me feel worse, but it was easier on both of us if I let her believe that I was getting better. So I started hiding it more . . . twisting my hair instead of pulling it, making myself throw up when I'd have panic attacks so I could pretend I was just sick. Mostly, she bought it. Or she pretended to, so she wouldn't have to deal."

"And your dad?"

"He was here. I don't know how much my mom told him. Not a lot, I'd guess."

"Does he know now?"

"He knows how bad it got. After the accident, I couldn't hide it anymore. It's the reason I'm here, probably. He saw how messed up I was and freaked."

"You're not messed up," Marshall says. "You're human. We've all got our stuff."

Annoyance flares in my chest. "Yeah. Well. You won't have yours after tomorrow. I'm sort of stuck with mine."

Neither of us says anything after that.

"I should probably go," I say finally. "Homework and stuff."

"Yeah. Okay. Good luck at the support group tomorrow."

"Thanks."

I hang up without saying bye and then feel so bad about it I almost call him back. He can't help it that his broken places are fixable. It's not his fault that mine aren't. But the positivity is obnoxious, because it's not actually based on anything real. Sometimes it feels like he doesn't even see the people around him, not really — he just sees what he wants to see. No wonder Hannah gets so irritated when he tells her how awesome she is at piano. Inside she must be screaming *YOU HAVE NO IDEA.* What was it she said about him when we first met? *He likes being the weird guy with the heart defect. It means he doesn't have to try to be anything else.* Meanwhile the rest of us are struggling to be anything other than fragmented, anything other than torn apart.

I go back inside the house.

❊

The next morning, I spend a good twenty minutes trying to talk myself into driving myself. In the end I chicken out. I probably would've bailed on the whole thing had I not told Dad about it yesterday, which maybe subconsciously I did for that very reason, to make sure I'd go.

We pull into the rec center's parking lot at seven twenty-two. Dr. I is sitting on the bench out front, the book he had yesterday in his hands. He smiles when we pull in.

"I'm proud of you for doing this," I hear Dad say.

i don't want to do this

"Thanks," I mumble, and fumble for the door handle, dread churning in the space behind my belly button.

"You made it," Dr. I calls when I get out of the car.

I glance back at my dad. He gives me a super awkward thumbs up.

"I'll see you after school," I say, and shut the door.

Dr. I stands as I walk toward him, pocketing his book.

"You ready?" he asks.

no

I shrug. "Sure."

"Let's do it then," he says, then turns and heads inside. One foot in front of the other, I follow him, on autopilot now, the safest mode, because when I'm on autopilot I do not think. Not about my issues, or Dr. I, or the kids inside the building. On autopilot I just *do*, there is no space even for me to be.

Autopilot takes me through the front door. Then autopilot promptly sputters out. My legs stop moving and I am just standing there in the lobby, sweating. The heat is chugging from the vents. I tug at my scarf.

Dr. I points at an open door nearby. Voices inside, the buzz of several conversations at once. "It's in there."

"Okay," I say, but don't move.

"I'll wait for you in the gym," he says.

I start to shake my head, start to tell him I can't do this, that I'd rather talk to him about my issues than wear them into a room full of strangers my age. But then there are footsteps behind me, and a girl in a puffy green jacket and Uggs is coming my way. I see the scars first, zigzagged and puckered, like a little kid drew lightning bolts across her cheeks with a stick. I blink, hard, willing my brain to behave, but of course it doesn't. The scars stay put.

"Hey," the girl says casually, her boots dragging with every step. "First time?"

"Um. Yeah." I glance over at Dr. I.

"Go on in," he says lightly. "I'll see you when it's over."

"C'mon," the girl says, and smiles. "You can sit by me."

"Be present," I hear Dr. I call from behind me. "Don't let yourself check out."

"I know it's terrifying," the girl in the green jacket says when we get to the door. "Walking into a room like this for the first time, with people you don't know. But this is a safe place. You'll see."

I follow her in and take the seat next to hers. There are a dozen kids seated in twice as many seats arranged in a circle in the center of the room, drinking water from styrofoam cups, bagel halves on little paper napkins in their laps. My eyes hover on their knees, avoiding interaction. I feel myself start to retreat, to pull back from this moment. To check out.

be present

Reluctantly, I pull my eyes up, force my mind to engage. I immediately regret it.

My brain has painted wounds on every face in the room. There's no pattern to it, no method I can see, everyone just looks messed up, from the boy in the beanie with the horrible bruises, to the girl with the braids and the skin-twisting scars, to the boy whose cheeks are burned so badly the skin is nearly peeling off.

i can't do this

Shaking, I drop my eyes to the carpet, where it's safe. My fingers are already in my hair, spinning, making knots, tugging at my scalp so hard it makes my eyes sting. Inside, behind skin and muscles, the walls are coming up, keeping reality out, keeping me in.

"Let's get started," the girl in the green jacket says to the group. The boy nearest to the door gets up to shut it. "As always, what's said in this room stays in this room. The only other rule is honesty. We don't lie to each other. Everyone agreed?"

There are nods around the circle.

"Awesome." She smiles warmly. "I'm glad you guys are here. New peeps especially. Who feels like sharing today?"

"I'll go," a girl to my left says. My eyes are on my knees so I can't see her face. "I'm Amber. I have an eating disorder. Anorexia. I started restricting when I was eleven. Not because I wanted to lose weight or anything. But because not eating made me feel safe." I hear her take a breath. "My dad had – has – a gambling problem. On days when he was winning, he'd bring home steaks and he and my mom would drink champagne and dance in the kitchen. But on days when he was losing, which was most of the time, dinner was whatever I could find in the cupboard. A can of beans. Instant oatmeal. If that."

I look over at her now. She's staring at a spot on the wall across the room. I only see her in profile, but the part of her face I see is covered in fading bruises; streaks of green and yellow from old wounds. "There was so little in my life that I could control," she says then. "Except what I ate. It started as a game, to how little I could put in my body each day. How disciplined I could be. How different from my dad." Her voice catches. I watch a tear slide down her cheek. "My freshman year, I weighed eighty-four pounds. I was hospitalized for anorexia and spent four months in a treatment center. I guess that was a breaking point for my mom, because while I was gone, she left my dad and filed for divorce. Which itself was — is — complicated for me. But for the best, I think." She wipes her eyes, brings her gaze back to the circle. "It's still hard, dealing with my old habits. Stress is a big trigger for me. I'll start restricting without even realizing it, and I'll justify it in my mind, saying I wasn't hungry or whatever. Which is crazy, right? Who do I think I'm fooling? Myself? It's so dumb."

"I do it, too," the boy sitting across from her says, and inside I'm shouting *SO DO I*. The boy's face is a mosaic of colors, red and purple and blue and green, every shade and stage of bruise. "I'll tell myself I'm washing my hands for the tenth time because I got them dirty, or that I'm repeating a certain word over and over again in my head because I like the way it sounds," he says. "I know it's my OCD, but I pretend it isn't, because in a way that lets me off the hook. If it's not a compulsion, then I don't have to stop." His voice breaks a little. He wants to get better, he says then, but he doesn't know how. His OCD is still stronger than he is, a bully he doesn't know how to fight, and the medications his doctor has prescribed have only made it worse. My skin crawls with recognition. *i know what that's like*

As he talks, he picks at his cuticles, *dig dig dig*, until they start to bleed, then he sucks each finger until the bleeding stops. I see myself in this ritual, can feel my hair between my fingers, the tug on my scalp, the tiny burst of relief when I'd pull the strands out. Watching him I'm swept up in sadness. *why do we rip ourselves apart?*

My throat tightens, and again I feel myself disengaging from this moment, from its sharpness, its acidity, its sting.

Eyes back on the boy's face. I force my brain back in.

A girl with braids and combat boots and a pink spider web of scars goes next. She's been coming to this group since sophomore year, she says. Since just after her little brother died of lymphoma. Her parents got divorced eight months later, and she's been splitting time between them ever since. "Not that either of them ever really looks at me anymore," she says softly. "Which is okay. I mean, it hurts, but I get it. It's just hard because I want to talk about him, but my mom just can't, and my dad won't let me even say his name."

Her story slams into me, sucks the air from my lungs. The emotion comes fast, hard, a tidal wave in my chest. I press my palms to my eyes, will the tears back.

"You ready today?" I hear the girl in the green jacket ask. I shake my head quickly, sure she's looking at me, but when I lower my hands her eyes are on the kid two seats down from me. His face is swollen and bloody, like he just walked out of a fight. "Adam?" the girl says gently.

The boy hesitates, then shakes his head. The wounds on his face make it difficult to look at him, so I stare at the buttons of his plaid shirt instead.

"You sure?"

He doesn't look at her. "Yep." The bruise beneath his eye turns a deeper shade of blue. Or did I make that up?

i'm making it ALL up, I remind myself. *none of these wounds are real*

"I'll go," the guy beside Adam says. Other than a thin white scar above his left eye, his face is completely clear.

"Most of y'all know me. I'm Ayo. I'm a senior. I've been coming to this group since the beginning of this year. I was at public school before that, failing most of my classes, getting into dumb fights. I got expelled about a year ago, and it was either this or juvie." He shrugs. "So I came to Crossroads. And from my very first day, things got better. A lot better." He grins. "I'm not gonna lie, a lot of it's because of my girlfriend. Vanessa. We've been together four months. She's in the dance program here." He looks over at Adam. "But the main thing was this group," he says. "Talking about the crap I was dealing with, opening up. I'd never done that before. Put words to it, you know? It made a big difference. 'Cause, like, we've all got stuff, right? What's the point of pretending we don't?"

All eyes are back on Adam. He stares at the carpet, his hands in fists at his sides.

All at once I want to shake him, this kid I don't even know. I want to shake him until he can't hide it anymore, until the truth comes roaring to the surface and he's forced to let it out.

shrink the dragon

And suddenly it's not Adam I'm frustrated with. It's me.

Fast, before I think about it, I put my hand in the air.

"I'll go," I say, ignoring the wobble in my voice. Heads turn in my direction. I stare at my knees. "I'm Jessa. I'm a junior. I was in bad car accident a couple months ago, back in L.A. where I used to live. That's how I got the scars on my face." I almost stop there. A bad car wreck, that's reason enough to be here. I don't have to say anything else.

shrink the dragon shrink the dragon

"I was having a panic attack," I say finally. "In the car. Driving home from a party where I— I'd just found out that my boyfriend was cheating on me." Beside me, the girl in the green jacket sucks in a breath. "The accident wasn't my fault or anything," I say quickly, realizing how it sounds. "The other car ran a red light." The room is completely silent. My foot bounces beneath me.

"Panic is a thing for me," I make myself say. "It's been a thing, for years, since right after my dad left, but I used to be really good at hiding it. At making people believe that I was okay. As long as I looked good on the outside, nobody really questioned what was going on inside. No one cared. And because of that, I could hold it together, sort of. Keep it in. But . . ." My throat goes tight. "I don't have that anymore. Now . . . all of me is broken. Literally. All of me. My brain, my heart—" My hand drifts up to my cheek. "My face."

Moments pass where I'm not speaking. It crosses my mind that I could just leave, right now, get up and walk out, never do this again. I pull my hand back to my lap.

"There's a guy here," I hear myself say. "At Crossroads. We've been hanging out for a few weeks. As friends. And when I'm with him . . . I don't feel as messed up. Not, like, in a denial way, how it used to be. More like maybe the fact that I'm messed up is okay." My voice starts to wobble again. I let it. If I stop talking I might not start again. "But I found out yesterday that he's dealing with some medical stuff and now my panic is out of control again. No one's acting like it's that serious, but I'm convinced something terrible is gonna happen. That–" My throat clamps up, squeezing my voice into a whisper. "He's gonna die."

And then the levee breaks, and I am crying.

The girl in the green jacket lays her hand on my arm. Seconds pass. A minute, maybe two. Tears and snot run off my chin. Someone hands me a box of tissues. "Sorry," I mumble, so embarrassed, awkwardly wiping my nose. "I don't usually do this."

"This is how you deal with it," the girl in the green jacket says. "You cry. Sometimes you scream. You let out whatever it is you're feeling, and you keep letting it out until you can breathe again."

"We've all been there," another girl says.

"Some of us are still there," the boy with OCD says.

I suck in a breath, feel my lungs inflate. My head is filled with static, not thoughts exactly, just noise, as if my brain doesn't know what channel to choose.

"It gets easier," someone else says. Ayo, I think.

And then the baton passes and it's someone else's turn. The girl two seats down from me whose older sister is bipolar and just went off her meds. The others aren't staring at me in pity or disgust. No one is even looking at me anymore. Their eyes are on the girl who's sharing her story now, trying to shrink her dragon, putting it out there for all of us to see.

we've all got stuff

It's so much work pretending that we don't.

The girl who's talking, she's crying pretty hard now. The boy beside her is holding her hand. And in this moment I think I understand what the girl in the green jacket meant when she said this place was safe.

There is shuffling around me. The meeting is over. The circle dissolves as people stand and move their chairs out of the ring. I stay where I am as the room begins to clear. One by one the others head out, back outside, to the real world, to the places where it isn't so safe.

"Hey," a voice says. Ayo, standing beside me with a backpack on this back. "What'd you think?"

"It was cool," I say, then feel like an idiot for being so blasé. "I mean. Not what everyone is going through. That's all horrible. But, like you said — opening up."

"The honesty is dope, right? Sucks that no one ever does it except in here."

"How often do you come?"

"Both days, every week. Most kids bail when they feel like they're better or whatever, but for me, it's like, better isn't a one-time thing. You don't, like, 'get' better, it's more like you *are* better, and then the next day you aren't. But maybe you aren't as bad as you were. You know?"

I smile. "I do, actually." I get to my feet.

"Some of us walk down to the gas station after group," Ayo says when we get to the main lobby. There's a group gathering by the front door. "Candy run. You wanna come with?"

I think of Dr. I, waiting for me in the gym. "Um. I can't today. Next time?"

"That mean you'll be back?"

I hesitate, because I haven't decided yet, and after all the honesty, I don't want to lie to him.

Finally, I nod, and decide. "Yeah."

"Cool," Ayo says. "And, hey, I hope everything goes okay with your boyfriend."

"He's not my boyfriend," I say quickly. Too quickly.

Ayo laughs, and puts up his hands. "Hey, girl. You don't need to convince me." I feel myself flush.

"I'm not really sure what he is," I admit. "I just want him to be okay."

Ayo grins. "See? Gets easier."

"What does?"

"Being honest," he says.

"It still feels pretty freaking hard," I say.

"That's why you're coming back Thursday," he says, flashing another grin as he jogs to catch up to his friends.

Chapter Sixteen

Dr. I is in the gym where he said he'd be, sitting on the bleachers, reading his book. He waves me over.

"So how'd it go?" he asks. I see him see my puffy eyes, the splotches that must be on my cheeks.

"Good," I say vaguely, expecting him to poke a stick at it, *good how?*

"Good is good," is all he says. Then he stands and pockets the book. "C'mon," he says. "Let's walk over."

I follow him out the door, down the rec center's manicured sidewalk, replaying the things I said in the circle, second-guessing them now, worrying I said too much. At the same time, there is a sort of lightness in my chest, as if saying those heavy things somehow let the heaviness out.

"How's that paper coming?" Dr. I asks as we wait for the light. "The one on *Dorian Gray?*"

"It's not," I admit. "I haven't even started and it's due tomorrow."

"Twenty-five hundred words on the separation of soul and body, right?"

"Yeah."

"Want some help?" he asks, and I bob my head because I think he's offering to get me out of it. "I think it's a trick question," he says instead.

"Huh?"

"Your topic. I don't think Wilde believed it was possible to separate the soul from the body. I think that's the whole point of the book."

so much for a way out

"But isn't that the trade Dorian made with the painting?" I ask. "Losing his soul to keep his face?"

"That was the trade he *thought* he was making, certainly. But that's not what he ultimately got. The painting didn't take his soul out of his body. It turned his soul *into* a body — it created a physical representation of something that had only been abstract up to that point. The invisible became visible, bringing Dorian face to face with the terrible truth of who he'd become."

The light changes and Dr. I starts across the street.

"He couldn't escape himself," I say, catching up to him, a weird feeling in my chest as I say it. *neither can i*

"That's part of it," Dr. I. says. "But I think Wilde was getting at something even more nuanced than that. I think he was saying that Dorian couldn't *see* himself — not without the painting. Remember, the novel was as much about art as anything else. I think Wilde was showing his readers that sometimes fiction is more honest than fact."

"More honest how?"

"Consider what happened in the book," Dr. I replies. "The portrait of Dorian started changing, supposedly to reflect the state of his soul— but his soul wasn't actually getting older and uglier. A soul is immaterial, remember? Think about our buddy Descartes. So it *can't* age or get ugly. Only the body can do that. But you walk away from the book understanding that what was on that canvas was more 'true' than the 'real' Dorian, even though, really, the painting was just a symbol of reality, not reality itself."

"My brain hurts," I say dryly.

He smiles. "That means the wheels are turning."

"Ha. You're an optimist."

"Have to be, in my profession. Otherwise the job's too depressing." As we hit the sidewalk, the morning bell rings. "Just don't overthink it," Dr. I says then, stopping at the place where the sidewalk splits. "Your paper. You read the book, you understand the idea. Write from your gut and you'll be fine."

"I think you're overestimating my gut," I say. A kid on a skateboard shoots me a funny look as he wheels past, and suddenly I am hyper aware that I'm openly chatting with the school shrink. "I should get going," I say, pointing vaguely at the building.

"Class."

He nods. Doesn't budge. He seems to sense my sudden awkwardness, my intense need to bail. "Good luck with the paper," he says. "And I hope everything turns out okay for your friend."

I'd momentarily forgotten about Marshall's procedure. The light feeling I left the group with is pushed out by dread.

"Thanks," I mumble, and start across the courtyard toward school.

❈

Hannah isn't under the stairs or at her locker. I didn't really expect her to be here today with Marshall's procedure happening this afternoon, but the fact that isn't she sends me back into a spiral just the same.

I make myself verbalize it. Not to a room full of also-broken people this time; just to one. Myself, in the bathroom mirror, halfway through second period when the panic gets so intense I'm jittery with it, ankle bouncing furiously beneath my desk. Which, in a weird way, sort of feels like progress. The old me would've been frozen with fear, trapped by it, while at the same time trapping *it*, burying the anxiety so deep it couldn't possibly escape. Now I'm wearing it right on the surface, harder to hide, easier to fight.

And fight it I am, or trying to anyway, as I stare at the mirror and watch my mouth move with the words "I'm scared that Marshall will die" over and over again. But this is only half of it, I know that. The *what* but not the *why*. The bathroom is empty so I try to finally do it, *dig deeper*, get down into the dirt like the shrink in the hospital said.

The truth is buried at the bottom, covered in muck.

i'm afraid marshall will leave because every one leaves

He might not walk out the way my dad did, or cheat like Wren, but that doesn't mean I can trust that he'll stay. He might not be a bad guy, but he doesn't need to be. The world isn't safe, or fair.

Then again, the things I'm most afraid of aren't the things that actually happen. It's the things I don't expect that destroy me. My dad leaving. My friends pretending like I didn't exist. Wren cheating. The SUV that ran that red light. I never saw any of that coming, and it came anyway. So maybe, just maybe, if I'm scared that something will happen to Marshall, nothing will.

please don't let anything happen to him
please let him be okay

Instinctively, my eyes flick to the ceiling. And even though I'm pretty sure there's no one up there to hear me, there never has been, and definitely not someone inclined to help, I ask for something else.

please let me get better
let me finally be okay

I mean my scars and the aphantasia and the hallucinations that haven't stopped. But even more than that I just mean *me*, whatever is separate from all that.

Then, not my thoughts but a man's voice, echoing in my head.

"I know it's scary, but you're okay. Do you hear me? You're okay."

My mind scrambles. For a split second I can't place them, these words, they strike me as random and strange. Then my thoughts clear, and I remember him. The man in the white coat who appeared at my window right after the accident and fixed my wrist and told me I was okay, stretching the word out to three syllables, *oh-oh-kay*. The man no one else saw.

why didn't anyone else see him?

I rub my left wrist. It still aches a little, on really cold days. Which is most days, here. Is it possible that the bones were never out of place, that the man never reset it, that I imagined the entire exchange? *Imagined*, code for *hallucinated*, because that's what I'm really asking. Did no one else see him because I made him up?

I squeeze my eyes shut and I'm back there, in the car, glass everywhere, breathing in burnt rubber and old pennies, which I know now wasn't pennies but blood. The man is there, leaning into the car, holding my wrist. His hands are dry, almost papery, and warm on my wrist. I can't see him in my mind, can't see any of it, but the memory replays just the same, a movie on a dark screen.

There are footsteps behind me, someone coming in. "What are you doing?" a familiar voice asks. My eyes spring open. It's Sophie, from the lunch table.

"Nothing," I say, meeting her eyes in the mirror, watching her gaze shift from mine when I do. Avoiding eye contact like I used to but don't so much anymore. She's looking at my scars now, so I look at them, too, but just one quick glance. The flip side of avoidance is rumination, my old back-up plan when avoidance craps out. Fixating on the thing that upsets me, like a record needle stuck in a groove.

"It looked like you were praying," Sophie says bluntly.

"I wasn't praying," I say, and I sound defensive. "I was just thinking."

"About what?"

"My accident," I admit. "And Marshall. He's—"

"In the hospital," Sophie says. "I know. Hannah told us yesterday. That's why I thought you might be praying."

"Oh." And now I feel like maybe I should've been praying. Then again, in a way I sort of was, if it counts as praying when you're not even sure that you even believe in God. "Well," I say, turning around to face her, watching her gaze shift again. I'm about to tell her I need to get back to class when I notice a bunch of fresh scratches down the right side of her face that weren't there last week. "Is everything okay?" I hear myself ask instead.

Sophie shrugs. There are volumes in this.

"What happened?" I ask.

"Nothing," she says. And in her voice I hear a familiar note. The way my own voice used to sound in middle school when my mom would ask how my day went and I'd lie because the truth was too mortifying to speak.

"What brought you in here, then?" I ask.

"It's a bathroom."

"And if you really had to pee you would've gone by now," I say. "I'm sort of an expert at the bathroom hide-out."

Sophie looks away. "I hate second period," she says flatly. "That's all."

"Why?"

She doesn't answer me. She doesn't answer me because she doesn't trust me. Because I haven't given her a reason to. Because she doesn't know that we are the same.

"I used to hate lunch," I tell her. "My friends stopped saving me a seat when my panic attacks started, and everyone else had their regular tables already. So I ate in the bathroom every day pretty much all of eighth grade."

I've never told anyone this. But there it is, the truth.

Sophie is quiet for a few more seconds.

"The girls at my lab table make fun of me," she says eventually, still not looking at me. "They think I don't know they're doing it because my brain can't figure out sarcasm. But it's kind of obvious when the kids at the next table laugh."

"What kind of stuff do they say?"

"That I'm pretty. That they love my clothes."

My heart sinks in my chest. I want to tell her those awful girls don't matter, but what will that do? Some stupid cliché about sticks and stones won't take the sting away, because,

FYI, *WORDS DO HURT.* They freaking hurt a lot. And unlike sticks and stones, it's not our bones that end up broken. It's us.

"People suck sometimes," I say to Sophie instead.

"You don't," she says.

I burst out in a laugh. "Thanks. Neither do you."

"Will you sit with us at lunch?" Sophie asks then. "Since Marshall and Hannah aren't here?"

The invitation catches me off guard. It wouldn't have occurred to me to sit with them. I wouldn't have thought they'd want me to.

"Definitely," I say, and for the first time since I met her, Sophie smiles.

※

Third and fourth period crawl by and then it's lunch time and time speeds up because Marshall's procedure is supposed to start at twelve thirty. I try to be engaged in the conversation at the table, though it's hard without Hannah or Marshall there to referee. In L.A. I always sat with Wren in the cafeteria, at the lacrosse table, crowded with people who liked hearing themselves talk, which meant there were never lulls in conversation or any expectation that I would speak. At this table, there are many pointed questions and even pointier stares and abundant awkward silences that don't seem to be awkward to anyone but me. I tell myself it's exposure therapy and force myself to stay in it, to let it be awkward until it isn't any more. It half works.

"Have any of you ever been to the support group that meets at the rec center?" I ask at some point.

"Is it for Asperger's?" Brendon asks.

I shake my head. "No. Anyone can go."

"I went a few times," the kid at the end of the table says. Everyone is calling him Dash, unclear whether that's actually his name. Heads turn to look at him now. "Dr. I thought it would help improve my social competence."

"Did it?" I ask.

"Mostly it made me realize how much other people lie," he says, and goes back to his food.

"What do you mean?" I ask.

"The whole point of going is to talk about the things you're hiding," he says. "Because that's normal. To hide how you feel. To act like you're okay when you're not okay. To lie."

"Well, it's not really *lying*," I say.

"Yes, it is," Dash insists. "If you feel one way and act like you feel another way, that's lying." His eyes flick around the table. "We don't do that. We don't lie."

"But in the group, people tell the truth," I point out. "That's why they go. To be honest."

"There were fourteen people there the day I went," Dash says bluntly. "There are five hundred and seven kids at Crossroads."

"Being honest is hard," I hear myself say.

"Why?" Sophie asks.

because the truth isn't pretty, pops into my mind, and suddenly I'm thinking about Dorian Gray. He was so desperate to deceive the world about who he was that it literally destroyed him.

"I need to go," I say abruptly, pushing my chair back.

It's twelve twenty-seven by the time I get to the library, which means I only have seventeen minutes until the bell, but for once the time crunch doesn't derail me. I log on to one of the computers and open a blank page and just start typing, don't even bother to pull out my book. *"In his novel,* The Picture of Dorian Gray, *Oscar Wilde suggests that man's attempt to separate his soul from his body will eventually lead to the loss of both. Dorian Gray thought that hiding his true self from the world would set him free, but it actually did the opposite. It made him a prisoner to a lie; a lie that drove him deeper and deeper into darkness and ultimately destroyed him."* I type these words in a flurry then sit back and read them, instantly doubting that they make any sense, but at the same time feeling like there is something in this idea, as bad as I am at expressing it. I grab my copy of the novel from my backpack and start flipping pages, looking for scenes that support my theory, that *The Picture of Dorian Gray* isn't about the desire for eternal beauty or the dark side of decadence, but a cautionary tale about living a lie. Skimming passages with this idea in mind, the story starts to take a different shape. From the very beginning what Dorian wanted was a chance to hide, to tuck the truth away behind a pretty mask. Not because he was a bad person, or even a vain one — not in the beginning, anyway. Before he saw the painting he wasn't even aware of his good looks. More than anything, it seems to me now, he was an insecure person, unsure of his own value beyond his appearance.

i know what that's like

And it strikes me now that I probably would've made Dorian's trade, if I believed it were possible to put my true self on a painting I could hide from the world. But I didn't have a magical canvas, so I tried burying the truth inside me instead, building little mental boxes to hold the things I didn't want anyone to see. The all-consuming panic. The swirling thoughts. The sinking shame. The fear that I'm not good enough, have never been good enough, that if anyone really knew me, they'd leave. Like my dad. Like my friends. Like Wren.

But hiding the truth never diminished it; if anything, it grew uglier in the dark. Just like Dorian's painting under that purple sheet. His shame made him do things he never would've done in the light.

I prop the book open on the desk beside me and keep writing. By the time the bell rings, I'm five hundred words in. I send myself the document, weirdly excited to finish it tonight. Knowing that I will.

It's not until I'm sitting in fifth period half listening to part two of the lecture on Van Gogh's madness that I realize that it's already one fifteen. Marshall's procedure started forty-five minutes ago. My heart picks up its pace. If all goes well, the whole thing should be over by two.

Somehow I sit through the rest of fifth period, and then all of sixth and seventh, without jumping out of my skin. I do, however, get reprimanded by my math teacher, twice, for tapping my pencil on my desk. I'm not used to this, the bubbling, unconfined feeling of anxiety let loose. This isn't a dull whirl behind my belly button, this is a thousand bumblebees buzzing through my veins. Time is creeping slowly again now, every minute feels like an hour I might now live through.

When the final bell rings at three fifteen I sprint across the courtyard to the bank. As soon as I open the car door, Dad hands me his phone.

"Thanks," I say breathlessly, dialing the hospital's main line by heart. Marshall's mom picks up on the second ring. "Hi," I say awkwardly, feeling weird suddenly for calling so soon. "It's Jessa. I was just calling to see if—"

"He just woke up," she says, and I can hear her smiling. I feel a whoosh of relief. "Hold on one sec."

"Hey," comes Marshall's voice.

"Hi. How'd it go? How're you feeling?"

"Better now."

I smile. Then realize Dad is watching me and blush.

"The procedure went great," Marshall says. "They were in and out in an hour. The worst part was the catheter in my thigh - the heart stuff I couldn't even feel."

"So you're okay," I say, and hear my own relief.

"I am."

"How's Hannah?" I ask.

"Dunno," Marshall says. "She's at home, practicing."

"Wait, she's not even at the hospital with you?"

"Long story," he says. "But it's fine. I want her to feel good about her audition. It's important to her."

I physically bite my tongue to keep from saying what I'm thinking, *shouldn't you be important to her, too?*

"So can I come see you?" I ask instead, glancing at my dad, a silent *is that okay?* Dad nods. "Or would that be weird?"

"Guys, Jessa has a hospital gown fetish and can't stay away," Marshall announces to his parents. "Are you cool if she comes by?"

"Ew!" I squeal.

"Sorry," Marshall adds, in a mock whisper now. "Apparently the gown fetish was a secret. Don't tell her I told you."

In the background, I hear his dad laugh. His mom says something I can't make out.

"They say of course you should come by," Marshall says then. "They were just leaving."

"I'm on my way."

Dad drives me to the hospital and drops me off at the heart wing, tells me to call him on his cell when I want to be picked up. My own heart is pounding as I come through the automatic doors into the lobby. Not with anxiety this time, but giddy anticipation, a buzzy excitement for what could come next, if I let it, which in this moment I think I might.

"There she is," Marshall says when I come through his door. "And . . . now I'm realizing I didn't think this through. You look as hot as always and I'm in a purple dress."

"Well, it's the gown I came for after all," I say lightly.

"Creepster."

"Right?"

I drag a chair over to his bedside to sit.

"So I have a question for you," I say, the buzzy feeling so intense I almost wimp out.

"No," Marshall deadpans. "You can't see the back of my gown."

"Ew." I make a face. "I'm being serious."

"Okay. And I will seriously pretend you didn't just make a yuck face when we mentioned my butt. Go."

"To be clear, 'we' were not discussing your butt. But *anyway*." I take a quick, shaky breath. "Will you go on a date with me?"

Marshall's face lights up so quickly it makes my heart hiccup with gladness and relief.

"I guess I'm not the only one who had a change of heart," he says. "See what I did there? Change of heart?"

"Very clever," I say, breathy with the realness of this. The realness of us.

"Will this date involve a lifeless art show and Cowboy Woody khakis? Because otherwise, I'm out."

"Obvi," I say. "Any other requirements?"

"Yes," he says. "You can't bring the wall."

I look at him blankly. "Huh? What wall?"

"The one right there." He gestures at the air between us. "The one you think I can't see."

I stare at the space and it seems to materialize. A wall, made of brick and mortar and fear. A wall I'm not ready to get rid of yet.

"I don't know what you want from me," I say tightly. "I'm not like you. I'm not good at this."

Marshall makes a fist, pretends to punch through the invisible wall. Then he reaches his arm out and lays his palm on my collarbone, and when he does there is a sensation inside me like window blinds snapping up. Every part of me wants to shrink back, to pull the blinds back down, to build the wall back up.

"I want your heart," Marshall says simply. "I want you to trust me with it. I don't think you do yet."

A memory springs to mind. Wren and me in his car, parked somewhere. His hands, so grabby, trying to peel my layers off. *I want all of you,* he whispered in my ear. But he didn't, not really. He never once looked at me like this.

My heart is beating wildly. Surely Marshall can feel it, thumping in my chest.

"It's a mess," I say, shifting in my seat. "*I'm* a mess."

He shrugs. "So am I. So is everyone on the planet." He lifts his hand to my left cheek. My scars prickle beneath his fingertips.

We're both quiet.

"I don't know how it ends," I say finally, pulling away from him. "This. Us. That's what scares me. Not the idea of us. The end of us."

"Maybe there won't be one."

I look at him. "Marshall."

"Okay, so I don't know how it ends, either," he says. "Nobody does. But I know I won't hurt you."

"You can't promise that," I say. I'm thinking about my dad. I'm thinking about the girl with the braids at the support group who lost her little brother. I'm thinking about how broken the world is. I'm thinking about how easy it is to get hurt.

i'm letting fear win

"I can promise I won't do it on purpose," Marshall says then. "And here's what else I *can* promise," he adds, taking my hand in both of his. "When you finally realize that you are far, far out of my league and break up with me, I won't weep loudly and hold onto your ankles." He frowns. "Okay. I can't promise that. But I can *maybe* promise not to do it in public."

I laugh and the fear thins, making space for light and breath.

"That seems fair." I lean over and kiss the back of his hand.

"Speaking of kissing . . ." he says.

"Um. Were we speaking of kissing?"

"In my head we were. We were talking about the two times I tried to kiss you and was denied."

"What! You haven't tried to kiss me once!"

"I'm pretty sure I have. Twice. That day in the rain under the bleachers. And then again at Little Man. I thought about it two more times, but I'm willing to accept that those don't count."

"There was a table between us at Little Man. Kissing would've been awkward."

"So you thought about it."

"I didn't say that. Anyway, it wasn't even a date."

"Uh huh."

I punch him in the arm. He grins and catches my hand.

"I was contemplating a third attempt," he says casually, hand still holding mine. "But it seems kind of obvious now. And there's the whole hospital gown thing, which I know is a turn on for you, but makes me feel kind of unmanly."

"Who says you get to be in charge of the kissing?" I ask, feeling bolder now, but still buzzy and breathy, a tingly feeling down my spine. I slide to the edge of my seat. My knees bump against the hard plastic frame of his bed.

And then, I don't know, my brain sort of shuts off as I move from sitting next to him to leaning over him, one hand in his, the other on the bed behind him, holding me up as I tilt my head down to kiss him on the mouth. I feel him grin as he tugs me closer to him and kisses me back, my hair spilling out over his pillow, probably in his face.

I melt. Literally, that's what it feels like, like my insides are pooling into liquid beneath my skin. His hand is on my shoulder, then in my hair. The arm that's holding me up starts to cramp but I ignore it, don't want this kiss to end.

"My parents will be back soon," Marshall says in a husky voice. "And I don't think my door locks."

I bolt back into my seat. "How soon?" I ask, batting wildly at my hair.

"They said twenty minutes," he says, straightening his hospital gown. It's at this moment that I realize he still has an IV needle in his arm. *i just half made-out with a guy in a hospital bed.* "But knowing my mom," Marshall is saying, "she'll come back early. She can't stand the idea of all these machines doing their jobs. She has to check me herself."

"Check you for what?" I ask.

"Symptoms of device rejection. Chest tightness, dizziness, shortness of breath." He lays a hand on his chest. "Also symptoms of Jessa acceptance, apparently."

I feel my face fall. "Wait, you're kidding right? Kissing you didn't—"

He grins. "Put me into heart failure? Nah. It wasn't long enough for that. But we could try again . . . " He catches my arm with his hand and gently tugs me to him.

"Your parents," I say, giggling, swatting him away. For a second, I'm a stranger in this moment, a foreigner in my own life, because I don't giggle. Fake giggle, maybe, but not real giggle, but here I am doing it, happiness bubbling up inside me, accidentally spilling out.

"Oh, they'll be psyched," Marshall says, but he lets go of my hand. "Their heart-defected son finds romance at last."

"Um. You've never dated anyone before?"

"Does a series of racy instant messages with a girl in a congenital heart defect chat group count?"

I laugh, but it sounds forced. For some reason the idea that he's never done this before freaks me out.

"I had a make-out buddy freshman year," he adds, as if reading my mind. "This girl who used to hang out at the skate park in the afternoons. I think her name was Nicole?"

"You *think*?"

"She kind of mumbled it the first time we hooked up. And then she told me she was moving to New Jersey so it seemed kind of pointless to spend time investigating."

"That's so shady."

"I know, right? If you're gonna hook up with random guys at the skate park, at least have the decency to introduce yourself properly."

"I meant you," I say, laughing. "How long was she your make out buddy?"

"Eh. Not long. A month maybe." He pauses, and his face gets more serious for a sec. "What about you and Wren?" he asks. "How long were you together?"

"Two years," I say. *two years and three months.* "We started dating the beginning of freshman year."

"Why'd you break up?"

"He was cheating on me," I say quietly. "With this girl from school. I found out the night of my accident."

Marshall sucks in a breath. "I'm sorry," he says.

"Yeah."

We're both quiet for a minute.

"So when's this epic first date of ours?" he asks finally.

"Whenever you're better, I guess? When do you get to go home?"

"Tomorrow," he says. "We can probably do it Saturday, as long as you pledge to my mom that we won't engage in any highly aerobic activities."

There's a knock on the door. His parents, coming back.

"How's it going in here?" his mom asks.

"Excellent," Marshall says, his eyes sparkling at me. "Jessa just asked me out on a date."

My face floods with heat.

"Well, that sounds fun," his mom says, smiling.

His dad, bearded and professorial, leans around her shoulder. He's an older version of his son, except with a tangle of silvery scars on each cheek, faded but impossible to miss. Scars that are so realistic looking that they could be real. But if they were, Marshall would've mentioned them to me.

stop staring

I force my eyes to the spot between his dad's eyebrows, my old trick.

"It's a pleasure to meet you, Jessa," his dad says, extending his hand. "I'm Paul Jamison."

"My dad here is a *sansei* in the lost art of the handshake," Marshall says in a mock whisper. "Look at his form!" He bows his head at his dad.

"My son here is a smart ass," Mr. Jamison says mildly as he shakes my hand. "Thank you for putting up with him."

His wife jabs him with her elbow. "Language, Paul!"

I laugh. "It's nice to meet you, too," I say.

His dad looks at his watch. "Well. I should probably leave now, if I want to pick Hannah up as instructed."

"Hannah said she could squeeze me in from five to six," Marshall explains.

"Where is she now?" I ask.

"At home," Marshall says. "Since my parents needed both cars today, she didn't have a way to get home to practice at lunch, so she just stayed home the whole day."

"Oh," I say, eyes darting to his parents' faces, looking for their reaction, not seeing much of one there.

"Hannah's our practical one," his dad says, sensing my question.

what does being practical have to do with it?

"She seems pretty nervous about her audition on Saturday," I say casually.

"Oh, she'll be fine," his mom says, with a funny wave of her hand. "She always is. She came out of the womb like that. Capable. She's barely ever needed us, that one."

"Whereas I remained in the infant stage for a good thirteen years," Marshall says.

224 / LAUREN MILLER

"That's not what I meant," his mom says. "You were both great kids. But you were the one with the delicate heart, both physically and figuratively."

"Wow, Mom. You make me sound like such a stud."

"Studs are overrated," his mom says, leaning over to kiss her son's cheek. "How's that delicate heart feeling by the way? Any of the symptoms Dr. Smith mentioned?"

Marshall shakes his head, but the corners of his mouth turn up just a little. He's thinking about the kiss, and now I'm thinking about it, too.

"Well, I should probably go," I say, reaching for my bag. "I have a paper due tomorrow."

"My dad can drop you off," Marshall says.

"Absolutely," his dad says, reaching for his coat.

I am not especially excited about making small talk with his dad — anyone's dad — for twenty minutes, but don't see a graceful way out of this.

"Thanks," I say, and manage a smile. "That'd be great."

"So Marshall tells us you're from L.A.," his dad says when we get into his car.

"Yeah. I moved here at the end of January," I say.

"How do you like it so far?"

"I like it a lot," I say. "Thanks to Hannah, really. She showed me around my first day and kind of took me in. She's pretty much my only friend in Denver. Other than Marshall, I mean." As I say it, I think about Sophie and the other girls at the lunch table today, it strikes me that maybe I'm wrong about that. "I haven't spent as much time with her lately, though," I add. "She's been really focused on her audition."

"Our little tugboat," Mr. Jamison says, and he sounds proud. "I honestly don't know where she gets it. So determined, so driven. Completely unflappable. And so independent, too." He glances over at me. "I'm glad she found you. She's needed a good girl friend, though she'd never admit it."

i did too

"She's okay, though, right?"

Mr. Jamison frowns. "What do you mean?"

"The pressure she puts on herself. All the stress." I feel weird, like I'm accusing him of not being a good dad or something. I shift in my seat.

But his face relaxes. "Nah. If she were a different kid, I might worry. But Hannah thrives under pressure."

She doesn't seem like she's thriving, not lately. Then again, the way she looks to me isn't the way she looks to everyone else. I'm the only one hallucinating bruises on her face.

Dad looks surprised to see me when I come through the back door. He's hunched over the kitchen table, sketching a wood deck on a blueprint of a backyard. "I was about to head back to the hospital to find you. How'd you get home?"

"Marshall's dad drove me. Sorry I didn't call."

"That's okay. How's Marshall doing?"

"Good, actually." I smile. "The procedure went really great."

Dad smiles back. "I'm so glad to hear it. You were pretty worried, huh?"

I nod. The worry is mostly gone now, but there are bits of it clinging to the back of my throat. I swallow thickly.

"And the support group this morning?" he asks.

I nod again. "It was fine." I fiddle with the strap on my bag. "I think I'll go back Thursday morning, if you don't mind taking me early."

"Of course I don't mind," Dad says. "But what do you think about maybe trying to drive yourself?"

"Yeah, maybe," I say, to avoid making a whole thing of it. "Can we see how I feel on Thursday morning?"

"Sure, Bear." Dad smiles. The scars on his face seem to disappear in the fold of his cheek, and for a second he looks the way he used to, smooth skin, my Dad. My eyes go from his cheeks to his forehead. *weren't there scars above his eyebrows, too?* There aren't anymore. My heart hiccups with relief.

i'm getting better

"I'm almost finished with these plans," Dad says then, leaning back over the table with his drafting pencil. "Want to play a board game or something after?"

"I actually have a paper due tomorrow," I say. "For English. Okay if I use the computer in your room?"

"Of course," he says. "Maybe you can take a break for dinner in an hour or so? I'm making shrimp stir-fry tonight."

I smile. Dad used to make shrimp stir-fry all the time when I was little. He'd put on a red apron and make a paper hat and pretend he was a chef at Benihana in Beverly Hills, where all my friends went for their birthdays but we couldn't afford to go. And all at once I'm struck by the normalness of this moment, the normalness of us. For the first time since I moved to Colorado, this arrangement doesn't feel temporary or strange. It doesn't even like an arrangement at all. It feels like my life. The disappointment that he left five years ago is still there, but it's not the strongest feeling I have anymore. Mostly I'm grateful that he's here now, that *I'm* here, that the story has finally changed.

"I expect an onion volcano," I tell him, smiling as I head down the hall towards his room. "Five slices high, at least."

"Anything for you, Bear," he calls, and I feel my heart squeeze.

Chapter Seventeen

The library is empty when I get there the next morning, early, almost forty minutes before the bell. Dad's printer was low on ink, so I emailed my paper to myself to print here. Two thousand five hundred and eighty words that actually seem to make sense as I re-read them now, one last time before I hit print. The thoughts connect, the thesis builds on itself. It's the best essay I've ever written, which doesn't say a lot, but says something at least.

I went to bed after midnight, exhausted from the mental effort of writing it, and then dreamed for the first time since my accident. Wild, vivid dreams that disappeared as soon as my alarm rang, mental images evaporating into fog, leaving me with vague memories of people and portraits and wounds. Canvas rectangles where heads would otherwise be, strange half-people with portraits for faces, gruesome wounds in bright oil paint. I woke up creeped out but hopeful, because if I can dream, then my mind's eye still works.

The images are gone but the dream has stayed with me all morning, the idea of it, anyway. Souls captured on little canvases, not hidden in attics, but held out for the world to see. I keep thinking, *what if we had that?* What if we could see how people are on the inside, the real, invisible truth, literally painted on their faces? Some people would look hideous, like Dorian. Awfulness telegraphed as ugliness in paint. But most of us would probably just look damaged. Broken in places. Bruised and cut and scarred. In a way, it's what I was afraid of, when I first saw myself in that hospital bathroom. That my messed up face would give me away. Different than Dorian, but kind of the same.

"Jessa," a voice behind me says. I jump a little, startled from my thoughts.

I see the gash on his forehead first. Shiny red on torn black skin. Open and bloody and raw, like someone took a chunk out of his flesh with a knife. It's not actually bleeding — the wounds I see never are — but the cut looks fresh. I hear myself suck in a breath.

"I thought that was you," the guy says, and that's when I see his eyes, the same eyes I saw yesterday morning at the support group, the ones that were blue and happy and bright. They're still blue, but a dull, somber shade. The light has completely gone out. "It's Jessa, right?"

what happened to him?

"Ayo," he says, because I haven't said anything. "From group."

I nod. "I remember," I say. My voice sounds funny. I feel funny. The thoughts he interrupted are still fresh in my mind, and right now I feel as if I'm living my dream. Like this wound I'm hallucinating — am obviously hallucinating, no one would walk around with a gash like that on his head — means something. Like it's *real*.

"Something happened," I hear myself say, and for a second Ayo looks concerned, because he misunderstands. "To you, I mean. Something happened to you. Since yesterday."

Ayo blinks.

"Uh. What?"

"You seem sad," I say dumbly, realizing how moronic I sound. "I thought—," *i thought the wound i'm hallucinating on your face meant that you were really hurting inside.* "Never mind," I say quickly. "Sorry. I don't even know y—"

"No, it's okay," Ayo says. "To be honest, yeah, I'm having a shit day." He pulls out the chair next to me and sits down.

"Is everything okay? I mean, obviously it's not." I'm staring at the gash on his head.

"My girlfriend broke up with me last night," Ayo says. "Out of nowhere. Things were great between us. At least, I thought they were great."

i know how that feels

"You mentioned her yesterday," I say. "At group."

He nods. "Yeah. She's the reason I turned my life around. She's the reason I *wanted* to. But she said it's too much for her, how dependent I am." He rubs his forehead. The wound doesn't budge. The blood doesn't smear. All of a sudden it doesn't look real anymore. It looks like wet paint. I bring my eyes back to his and see desperation there.

i know how that feels, too

He's waiting for me to say something. But what can I possibly offer him, this kid who's older than I am, whose life is so different from mine, whose story I barely know?

"I sucks to be blindsided," I say, because this one thing I know. "To lose the thing you were counting on not to change. And to lose it out of nowhere, when you aren't prepared." I'm talking about my dad, my friends, Wren. I'm talking about the face I took for granted for seventeen years. "It makes you doubt everything. Especially yourself."

"No shit."

We're both quiet for a sec.

"But maybe it shouldn't," I say finally. "Because maybe we're more than the people we date, or the way we look, or the grades we make."

"What the hell are we, then?" Ayo jokes.

I smile a little, half shrug. "Whatever's left, I guess.

✺

Hannah's waiting for me in the hall after first period. "Hey," she says. "You weren't under the stairs this morning." She's all fidgety, almost twitchy, here foot bouncing at lightning speed. *how much coffee has she had?*

"Sorry. I had to print my paper in the library. Is everything okay? How's Marshall?"

"He's fine. I'm fine." She brushes her hair out of her eyes and I notice red, raw patches on the inside of her wrist. She catches me staring. "I haven't been picking it," she says, as if I've accused her. "It's just getting worse by itself. Stress probably. Which is really awesome, since the admissions committee will be watching my hands." Her voice is rushed and choppy, and her eyes are pinging around the hall, like they might bounce out of her head.

"Are you sure you're alright?" I ask, lowering my voice. "You're acting kind of . . ."

"What?" she demands.

weird, I want to say. "Agitated," I say instead.

"I *am* agitated," she says. "I have disgusting eczema on my wrists. It's agitating."

I think back to the first bruise on her face. The little quarter moon beneath her eye that became a half moon, then exploded into a dozen purple splotches across her cheeks. It seems weird, suddenly, the specificity of it. The uniqueness of each injured face. Not just scars and bruises, but gashes and scrapes and burns. If I've been "projecting" like the shrink in the hospital thought, then why hasn't everyone had the exact same injuries that I had? That would make sense. Instead I've been seeing random wounds on random people, wounds that have no connection to my own. But that doesn't mean they aren't connected to something else.

My mind goes back to my dream, to all those little canvas faces, covered in painted wounds. It occurs to me now that the faces around the circle yesterday were painted, too, in a way. Scars on the girl who's come through her darkness. A mosaic of bruises on the boy who's still climbing out. Faces that looked like they belonged to trauma victims. Not the kind of trauma that breaks bodies, maybe, but the deeper kind, the kind that fractures souls, leaving wounds beneath the surface that no one can see. But what if we *could* see them?

How might a soul look if we could stare it in the face?

i'm hallucinating, I remind myself. *because of my accident. because my head broke into pieces and my brain couldn't deal. not because i can see people's souls.*

I give my head a little shake.

Hannah is looking at me funny. "What?" she asks.

"Nothing," I lie. "I was just thinking about your audition. What does a person wear to a music school try-out?" It's the dumbest question ever but it was the only thing I could think of on the spot.

"Concert attire," she says. "Plain black dress and flats." She looks down at her wrists in disgust. "I wish I could wear gloves."

"Why don't you put make up on it?" I suggest. "My mom bought me this hi-tech foundation when I was in the hospital, to cover up my scars. It's made of silicone, I think, and it's super soothing and protective. It's basically like painting on a second layer of skin. It doesn't wipe off unless you use their remover." I see her eyes flick to my scars. "I never used it," I say, because I know what she's thinking. *if it works so well why does your face look so bad?* "Mostly to piss my mom off. But also because the idea of trying to hide them gave me heart palpitations."

"Why?"

"I don't know. Maybe because I was hiding so much already. Sometimes I'd look in the mirror and not recognize myself."

"Your appearance changed that much?"

I shake my head. "I meant before that. Pre-accident. I was such a mess on the inside, and then I'd look at myself in the mirror and not see any of that. And I'd feel relieved. But never happy, because it meant I had to keep pretending, you know? But then the accident happened, and I couldn't pretend anymore. It felt pointless in a way, to even try. Or maybe I just gave up." I force a smile. "It's hard to hide the mess when your face *is* the mess," I joke.

"Hey." Hannah touches my arm. "You're not a mess."

"So, anyway," I say, shrugging her off because my throat is going tight and I don't want to cry. "The make-up. I could come over Saturday morning and help you put it on your wrists, if you want. Not that you need to cover it up," I add quickly. "I just thought maybe it'd be one less thing to think about, you know?"

"No, definitely," Hannah says. "And one less thing for the admissions committee to think about, too." She links her arm through mine. "Thank you."

"I asked your brother out on a date," I blurt out. "I'm telling you because I told you that Friday wasn't a date, and it wasn't, but then yesterday I asked him out." I look over at her, trying to gauge her reaction. "Oh. You already knew."

Hannah rolls her eyes. "It's my brother we're talking about. You think he didn't mention it the first possible second he could?"

The bell rings. Hannah drops my arm.

"Okay," I press. "And?"

"And I'm fine with it. I told you I was fine with it."

"I just don't want it to be weird between us," I say.

"Then don't make it weird," she says. Her eyes jump around my face like water bugs on the surface of a lake.

"Hey. Are you *sure* you're okay?" I ask, catching her hand.

She shakes me off. "I'm fine," she says, flashing a smile that's meant to reassure me but has the opposite effect. Her lip twitches against her teeth. It's the bruises, though, that're the most unnerving. *YOU ARE SO NOT FINE!* my brain shouts. "I'll see you later, okay?" She grabs her bag and heads off down the hall.

I'm distracted through the next three periods, until lunch, until I can go find Dr. I in his hiding spot on the bench by the teacher parking lot. I feel bad for interrupting his lunch break, but he doesn't look all that surprised to see me.

"Hello," he says, and puts down his book.

"Hi," I say. "Do you have a minute?"

He scoots over to make room for me on the bench.

"How's your friend?" he asks when I sit.

"He's great, actually," I say, and feel myself smile. "The procedure went really well."

"That's good news. And how are you?"

I hesitate. "I'm not sure," I say finally. Then I'm quiet for a few seconds, struggling for words that won't sound crazy. "I think the paper I wrote last night messed with my head," I say finally.

"Messed with it how?"

i think i'm seeing souls

hurts telegraphed on faces, painted on skin

"The wounds I've been seeing. My hallucinations. I'm starting to think that maybe the shrink at the hospital was wrong. He said I was projecting my injuries onto other people because I couldn't deal. Which made sense at the time. But now . . . it just doesn't. For one thing, the wounds are different. I don't have bruises or burns or scrapes or gashes. I just have scars. So why does Hannah have two black eyes and a face full of bruises? Why did this kid I met in group yesterday have a giant gash in his head this morning? I never had a gash in my head. And then he tells me that his girlfriend broke up with him and he's really hurting inside, and I'm looking at this cut on his head, which obviously isn't really there, but in a way it *is* there. On the inside. On his soul." It made sense in my brain but now that I'm saying it out loud it sounds completely nuts. I squeeze my eyes shut. "Uh. I don't even know what I'm saying."

"You mentioned that you've been having some trouble with your mind's eye," Dr. I says.

My eyes pop open. "Yeah. But that's separate from this."

"Maybe not." He hands me his book. "Remember the other day when I told you that Descartes believed that the brain was where the soul interacted with the body?"

I nod, turning the book over in my hands.

"Well, he had this whole theory about the pineal gland — it's this little pinecone-shaped gland in the very center of the brain. He thought it was the place where soul and body touched."

"Weird."

"It is a little weird, isn't it? And the idea's been completely debunked. But hang with me for a sec. Descartes also believed that the pineal gland was where the mind's eye resided. Modern medicine tends to focus on the imaginative aspect — the ability to visualize, the thing you're missing — but Descartes had a much grander view of what it means to 'see with the mind.' A view quite a few philosophers still take."

"Grander how?"

"He thought that the truest things about reality could *only* be perceived by what he called the 'eye of the mind.' Never by the senses alone."

"So I'm screwed, then," I say flatly. "Because I'm not perceiving anything with my mind. I'm seeing things that aren't there."

"Wait a second. You just said that the things you're seeing *are* there. You're seeing wounds on people who hurt. The fact that the bruises and scars aren't physically present doesn't necessarily mean they're not real. And the fact that it may feel like you're seeing them with your eyes doesn't mean that you are."

I stare at him in disbelief. "Wait, you're saying it's possible? That I'm literally seeing people's souls?"

"Well, not *literally*," he says. "Souls are invisible, and psychological wounds don't bruise or bleed. All I'm saying is there's no reason to assume that what you're perceiving isn't *true*."

"But *how* am I perceiving it? That's what doesn't make any sense. How could a car wreck do this to my brain?"

"That's a question for a neurologist," Dr. I replies. "I know what Descartes would say, though. He'd say that if you're seeing what you think you're seeing, then it has nothing to do with your brain, because your brain – the organ of soft nervous tissue in your skull – can't perceive Truth. Only your mind can. And your mind wasn't injured in that accident."

I stare at the sidewalk, static in my head. I don't know what he's getting it. Why it matters if it's my brain or my mind or my left thumb.

"Don't check out," I hear Dr. I say. "Stay with me." And in my joints there is a flash of recognition, of deja vu. *stay with me jessa stay with me*

The man from the accident.

He said exactly that.

"These are complicated ideas," Dr. I goes on. "And maybe all this is more than you need right now. But try to stay with me here. There's a point I'm trying to make."

stay with me jessa just another few minutes okay?

I blink, hard, pushing the memory away. I nod.

"You want an explanation for this," Dr. I says gently. "You want a 'how.' But the invisible world doesn't work that way. There isn't concrete evidence. There isn't physical proof. All you have to go on is your own certainty, which takes some measure of trust. In yourself. In Truth itself."

"And if I'm wrong?" I ask hoarsely. "If I'm just hallucinating randomly and it doesn't mean anything at all?"

"I think the better question is what if it *does*."

My mind goes to Hannah. All those bruises. All that hurt. My heart clenches in my chest.

"I should go," I say, and hold out his book.

"Borrow it. See what you think."

I shake my head. "No, thanks. I think I've had all the philosophy I can handle for today."

Dr. I smiles as he takes the book. "Fair enough. But I'm not giving up. I'll make you a philosopher yet."

Chapter Eighteen

Hannah always goes straight to fifth period when she gets back after lunch, so I wait for her by her classroom door. In the middle of the school hallway thirty seconds before class starts isn't an ideal place for a confrontation, but I'm too worried now to put it off. If the bruises on Hannah's face do represent some sort of emotional pain, then she's in a lot of it, and after my conversation with her dad yesterday, I'm pretty sure no one in her family has a clue.

My stomach twists when I see her. For weeks my eyes have been sliding over her bruises, hanging at the edges of her face. Now I can't look away.

"Hey," she says, surprised to see me. "What's up?"

I take a quick breath. "Look. I know you're really anxious about your audition. And you should be, it's a big deal, and I get that. How important it is to you. But I think something else is going on with you, something inside, that you don't want anyone to know."

Hannah blinks. "What?"

I wasn't going to tell her about the bruises. But suddenly it just comes tumbling out.

"I've been seeing things since my accident," I say. "Wounds, on people's faces. Not everyone, just some people. Most people, I guess. At first I thought it was related to my anxiety — I have a panic disorder, I don't think I've ever told you about it, but I do. Avoidance was always my thing — basically, denial — so the doctors thought that's what I was doing again. Hallucinating wounds on other people so I wouldn't have to deal with my own." I pause for a sec, trying to read her expression.

I can't.

"But it isn't that," I go on. "Or, at least, it's not that anymore. What I see when I look at you . . . it's not about my accident or my anxiety. I'm pretty sure it's not about me at all."

Hannah stares at me. "Are you seriously doing this right now?"

I shake my head. "I know how crazy it sounds. Believe me. But—"

She cuts me off. "My brother is in the hospital. The biggest audition of my life is in three days. And you're standing here talking about what you *think you see on my face*?"

"I see bruises," I blurt out. "So many bruises. And I get that now is a crappy time for me to be doing this, but I don't know what else to do. I can't just ignore it."

"Because you see bruises." Her voice is cold.

Doubt sweeps through me. Cold like her voice, and dark.

all you have to go on is your own certainty

"Yes," I say, my own voice shaking. "And I know they mean something. Whether you admit it to me or not."

Hannah just looks at me.

"Say something," I say.

"You should see a doctor," she says. Then she turns and walks into her classroom.

I stand in the hall, staring at her back, more convinced now than ever, because if it was nothing she wouldn't have reacted like that.

but what could it be?

In a way, the bruises are comforting, because they're just bruises. Bruises aren't permanent. Bruises heal. It's not like she's walking around with a gash in her head. Maybe I should leave her alone, let her deal with this on her own, whatever this is. It's what *I* would've wanted, six months ago. If someone had somehow been able to peek through the facade at the soul underneath, my soul, sad and bruised and ashamed. I would've wanted them to put the curtain back down and pretend they hadn't seen anything. I certainly wouldn't have wanted them to drag it out into the light.

But I can't do that. I can't just ignore the fact that my friend is hurting. I can't pretend I don't know. If the bruises were on her skin, I wouldn't just let it go. I'd demand that she tell me who hurt her. I'd rush her to the hospital. I'd get her help.

That's the thing about the invisible world, I guess. Where souls get battered and minds get muddled and hearts get broken again and again. It's a war zone, a disaster area, but no one wants to talk about how messed up things are, so we let each other pretend. We play along, we act like we're all okay. But we're not okay. All the junk we're hiding is right there, right in front of us, right *within* us. The brokenness, and the desolation and the despair. We tell ourselves it'll get better if we just ignore it. But wounds don't work that way. Leave them open, and you'll bleed out.

And yeah, maybe my timing did suck, maybe I should've waited until Hannah's audition was over to say anything. But if I've learned anything from the last couple months, it's that nothing gets better in the dark.

Dad is in a weird mood when he picks me up after school. Quieter than normal, and of course it makes me wonder about his wounds. As he pulls out of the parking lot, I study the scars that twist his stubbly cheeks. They've faded a little, since my accident. At least I think they have. Without a mental image it's hard to be sure. But they haven't disappeared. Maybe that's the thing with scars, maybe they never do. I find myself wondering where he got them. If any of them are because of me.

"You okay?" I ask him.

He glances over at me. "Today's our anniversary. Was our anniversary. Me and your mom."

"Oh. I didn't know you still kept track."

"A wedding date is kind of hard to forget."

His eyes are back on the road now, but I'm still looking at him, his face in profile. I'm surprised at how sad he looks.

but you left her, I want to say.

"You seem sad," I say instead, which is totally unlike me, to probe.

"I guess because I am," he says. "I never wanted my marriage to end. For my family to break apart."

"So why'd you leave?" I ask softly.

"Your mom asked me to move out. I was a struggling landscape designer. I couldn't afford to live in L.A. on my own."

"That's not the way Mom tells it," I say.

Dad sighs. "Yeah. Well. Your mom was always very creative." We stop at a red light and he glances over at me again. "I should've fought harder," he says. "For our family. For you. I wanted you out here with me, full time, but all your mom's talk of disrupting your life made me wonder if I was being selfish, taking you away from your friends."

I stare at him. "You wanted me to live with you?"

Dad looks at me with a mixture of sadness and disbelief. "Of course I did, Bear. You were — are — everything to me."

The light changes and Dad steps on the gas. I'm quiet for a few minutes, staring out the side window, my brain buzzing with about forty different emotions at once.

"I felt so stupid," I say finally.

"Stupid? Why?"

"Because I didn't see it coming. You leaving, the divorce, any of it. And when it happened everyone acted like it was no surprise. Mom's friends, the neighbors, even my teachers at school." Tears spring to my eyes. I wipe them quickly with my sleeve.

"That might be because they all knew your mother," Dad says dryly.

"She wasn't always that bad," I say. "I remember in elementary school, she used to take me to her studio after school and let me do my homework at her drafting table. Most of the other kids in my class got picked up by nannies, even the ones with moms who didn't work. But Mom was always there in the pick-up line, no matter what."

idling in her lexus, the one i totaled on new year's eve

This thought comes and goes.

"You were her priority," Dad says. "Always have been."

"Ha."

"I'm serious. I know she stinks at showing it sometimes, but she's always wanted what's best for you, Bear. The money and the success may have changed her view of me, but not her feelings for you."

"You weren't there, Dad. My anxiety made things messy. Mom hates messy."

"No, your mom hates things she can't *fix*," Dad says. "Your anxiety made her feel like a failure, because she couldn't control it. Ignoring it was easier, I think." He glances over at me.

"You're doing better, though, right? You seem better. The last couple weeks?"

This is my chance to tell him what's going on with me, all of it, to finally fill him in. But starting from the beginning would take too long, and we're almost home. So I tell him the truth that isn't the whole truth, but in a way, kind of is.

"I'm getting there," I say. "I've been talking to the school counselor. It's helping. I think."

Dad smiles. "I'm glad."

Marshall calls the landline exactly ten seconds after I walk through the door.

"How'd you know I'd be home already?" I ask.

"I didn't," he says. "This is the third time I've called."

"Stalker, much?"

"If you were a normal person with a cell phone, I could just text." In the background, I hear piano music.

"Wait, are you home already?"

"Yup. Hence the three calls. Want to come over? We're getting pizza from Beau Jo's to celebrate my whole heartedness."

I want to go, because I want to see him, but there's no way Hannah wants to see me, not after what happened in hall this afternoon.

"I can't tonight," I say. "I have a ton of homework." I should just tell him about my fight with Hannah, about the bruises, the whole thing. It's weird, suddenly, that I haven't, since I've told him everything else. But I can't. Not yet.

"Bummer," he says lightly. "I was hoping we might revisit that conversation we were having in my hospital room before my parents came back."

My cheeks flush. "Maybe we can pick it back up on Saturday," I say.

"You're really hyping this date." I hear him smiling. "Where are you taking me, anyway?"

"A lifeless art show. Then the skate park."

"Don't mock! I planned a perfectly respectable first date. It wasn't my fault I was blindsided two minutes in and had to recalibrate. Admittedly the skate park wasn't my best idea, but I was wearing skinny khakis. The blood flow to my brain was restricted."

"I was serious," I say, giggling. "Well, except about the lifeless part. There's a Van Gogh exhibit at the Denver Museum of Art that looks really cool. Then, after, I was thinking maybe you'd teach me to skate. Which maybe shouldn't involve the skate park, actually, since I will definitely require flat surfaces."

"I accept the itinerary," Marshall says. "Even though you've completely ripped me off. On date eleven I will force you to admit that last Friday was actually our first date and that you had so much fun that you tried desperately to replicate it."

"Who says we'll even make it to date eleven?" I ask. My voice is light, joking, but my chest suddenly feels tight. I don't want to think about the future. I don't want to think about all the ways this could go wrong.

"A boy can dream. Hey, what time are we going on Saturday? We need to figure out transportation. I can't drive for another week, and Hannah needs the car for her audition. Should we bus it?"

"Aren't you going with her to the audition?"

"Can't," Marshall says. "Only prospective students are allowed in the building. Plus, Hannah hates an entourage at these kinds of things anyway. Says it throws her off.'"

"Got it. Well I told her I'd come over in the morning to help her with her makeup. My dad'll bring me. So maybe we could go right after that? What time's her audition?"

"Eleven forty-five, I think. She said she wants to be there no later than eleven-fifteen. It's at Boettcher Hall, close to the museum, so maybe we can just ride with her there, walk to the museum, and then take the bus home?"

"That sounds great," I say. "If she doesn't mind."

"Nah, it should be fine. As long as we don't speak on the ride in. Holy crap, I can't wait for this audition to be over to I can have my sister back. She's been a beast this week."

say something say something say something

"Hey, uh, can we talk about her for a sec?"

"Hannah? Yeah, sure, why?"

"I— I think there's something going on with her."

"What do you mean?"

I could tell him about the bruises, but in a way, it's not about what I've been seeing on her face, not anymore. It's about what I *know*.

"I don't know what it is," I say. "But something's up with her. She's been acting weird. Really weird."

"Yeah, anytime she has a big performance or an audition for something she gets a little crazy," Marshall says. "I guess it makes sense that she'd get even more stressed after her brother with a heart condition found a blood clot in his leg. I don't think it's anything other than that."

"But it's not just stress," I insist. "It's something else. It's like she's—," *hurt wounded broken* "—sad."

Marshall doesn't say anything.

"You still there?" I ask.

"Yeah. I'm here."

"Why aren't you saying anything?"

"I'm not sure what you want me to say," he says hesitantly. "She doesn't seem sad to me."

because you can't see what i see

because you can't see the truth

Now I am quiet. What am *I* supposed to say? I could tell him about the bruises, but then this conversation becomes about me.

"She is sad," I say finally. "Even if you can't see it. I can."

"What does she have to be sad about? If she doesn't get into Interlochen, then yeah, definitely, she'll be crushed. But that hasn't happened yet. And everything is fine with me.

Hannah isn't the type to mope about something, either. It's not in her DNA."

"I don't know what she has to be sad about," I say, annoyed at him for brushing this off. "But I do know that not everybody wears their issues around like a freaking badge of honor."

"What's that supposed to mean?" Marshall sounds stung.

"Nothing."

"You mean me," he says. "You think I do that."

"It's just . . . sometimes I think you're proud of it," I say finally. "Like you *like* having a heart defect, so you can go around telling everyone how broken and messed up you are and feeling really good about yourself for being so open about it. But it's not that simple for the rest of us."

Marshall makes a sound in his throat. "Yeah, because having a hole in my heart has been a real breeze."

"I didn't mean it that way," I say immediately, feeling like a jerk. "I know it's been awful for you. It's just...I dunno. In some ways a heart defect seems less complicated. Because, yeah, it's this one part of you that's damaged, but it's not *you* that's damaged."

"But it is," Marshall says. "Don't you get that? Regardless of whether the muscle in my chest has a hole in it or not, my *heart* is defective, will always be defective, just like everyone else's. We're people, we're flawed. There's no fancy procedure for that."

I'm quiet for a moment, thinking about my own defective heart, the one that's so afraid of getting hurt that it builds walls around itself to keep people out.

"So why doesn't it apply to her?" I ask eventually. "If everyone is damaged, why can't you accept that Hannah is, too?"

"I *do* accept that," Marshall says. "My sister has her issues like everyone else. It's not like her stress level is a particularly healthy. All I was saying before is that I don't think she has some deep sadness she's hiding."

"Maybe you're right," I say carefully. "You know your sister better than I do. But I know what it's like to pretend, to do everything you can to convince people that you're okay. And the longer you do it, the better you get at it, until the act is all you are."

"It's not all you are," Marshall says firmly.

"But it was," I say. "Really, it was. And I'm not saying that Hannah is the same as me. But of course there's more going on with her than you can see on the surface. There always is, with everyone."

"She puts a lot of pressure on herself," Marshall says finally. "She always has. I guess I thought that getting into Interlochen would change that. Take some of that pressure off."

"And when she gets there? Seems like a place like that would only make it worse."

"But it's what she's always wanted," Marshall says. "The one thing. What am I supposed to say, 'Hannah I know you've worked years for this, but I don't think you should go'?"

"Do you really feel that way? That she shouldn't go?"

"No. I don't know. Even if I did. I wouldn't want to stand in her way, or make her second guess it."

"You're a good brother, you know that?"

"Homework!" I hear Dad call from the living room. It's such a dad move, Dad being a dad finally, *my dad*, and maybe someday it'll be annoying, but not yet.

"I gotta go," I tell Marshall. "My dad's calling me." And despite the fact that I have mountains of homework waiting, I'm smiling as I hang up.

Chapter Nineteen

At seven the next morning I'm at the living room window, staring out at the Jeep parked in the driveway, trying to talk myself into driving it. My upper lip is cold with sweat.

"What are you doing in here in the dark?" Dad asks, switching on the light.

"Nothing," I say quickly, turning away from the window. "Is it okay if we go early again this morning?"

Dad nods. "I'll go with you," he says. "But you drive."

"I can't," I say automatically.

"Yes, you can, Bear. But the longer you wait, the harder it'll be for you to believe that."

I start to shake my head.

"The accident wasn't your fault, Jessa. It had nothing to do with your driving. The other car ran that red light because the driver was looking at her phone."

"That could happen again," I point out.

"Sure it could," Dad says. "Just like you could get hit by a bus crossing the street. That doesn't mean it *will* happen, sweetheart. Or that you should live your life in fear that it might."

"I'm just not ready," I say quietly.

"Neither am I," Dad says. "You think I like having my teenaged daughter out there in the world in a car? You think my first response after your accident wasn't 'okay, she's never driving again'?"

"So why are you pushing me to do it?" I ask.

"Because there's something I want for you even more than safety," he says. "I want you to be *free*. Free from the panic and worry, free from all that terrible self-doubt I see in your eyes and blame myself for. But you have to want it, too, Jessa. You have to decide not to let fear win."

Tears spring to my eyes. *he's right*

i've been letting fear win

Not just since the accident. For years, ever since my first panic attack. And I can blame my brain for some of it — generalized anxiety disorder is no small dragon. But *I'm* the one who gave that dragon the throne. Not because I didn't know how to fight it, even though that's what I would've said. But because I was afraid of what fighting it would cost me. Of what being honest would do to the image I'd built. All I had was that image, the facade I'd built to keep the dragon in. It felt like a shield. I couldn't see that it was a cage.

"Okay," I say finally. Shaky, but strong. "I'll drive."

A smile spreads across Dad's face. "That's my girl."

After breakfast we walk out to the Jeep together. In my mind's eye, horrific scenarios play out, versions of my accident with new images subbed in. Dad's Jeep instead of Mom's Lexus, the stoplight at the end of Dad's street, a school bus plowing into my side. Not the accident I had, those images are gone from my head, but the one I could have, will have, *it's going to happen again.* My breath gets shallow. My skin starts to crawl.

"We'll take it slow," I hear Dad say. "You've got this."

unlock the door

climb inside

turn the key

I tell myself that I don't really have to do this now. That maybe Dad was wrong, that maybe I should wait longer before driving again, that maybe I shouldn't ever drive again. But that voice in my head isn't looking out for me, not really. Fear isn't a kind ruler. Avoidance doesn't keep me safe.

The engine rumbles to life, and immediately it's a different experience, because my mom's hybrid barely made a sound when I started it, and the doors didn't creak when they shut.

I shift into reverse and slowly back out of the driveway, heart drumming in my chest, Shel Silverstein on a loop in my brain.

here i go down circle road strong and hopeful hearted through the dust and wind up just exactly where i started here i go down circle road strong and hopeful hearted through the dust and wind up just exactly where i started

Except I don't want to end up where I started, I want to end up somewhere else. The words in my head abruptly stop.

I drive at the speed limit, gripping the wheel so hard my hands cramp. The intersection at the end of the street is up ahead.

red light stop

Somewhere inside a soundtrack is playing on a loop. Screech of brakes, crunch of metal, thud of impact, again and again. My lungs feel like they're about to explode.

"Bear?" Dad says, as the car behind me lays on his horn. The light is green.

"I can't," I whisper.

"Yes, you can," Dad says calmly. "You're already doing it. Press the gas. Go through the intersection. You can pull over up ahead."

The car behind me honks again. Rattled, I punch the gas pedal and the Jeep jerks forward. My heart is ping ponging in my chest.

"But your blinker on," Dad says. "You can pull off into the shoulder here."

don't let fear win

White knuckles on the steering wheel, I shake my head. "No," I say. "I'll keep going. It was the intersection. I'm better now." This is a lie. I'm not better. But somewhere inside I believe that I could be, *I will be*, if I just finish this drive.

I exhale slowly, try to force the fear out. Foot on the gas pedal, speed back up. *i can do this.* Through the intersection, second right, *i can do this i can do this.*

"You're doing great, Bear," I hear Dad say. I want to burst into tears. I'm not doing great. Every second of this is agony, my hands are sweating, my shoulders are so tight they're starting to cramp.

"Thanks," I murmur, not taking my eyes of the road. An eternity later, the rec center comes into view. Seeing it, my muscles let go just a little. I can almost breathe like a normal person as I come through the last intersection and make the turn into the parking lot.

"You did it!" Dad says brightly, as I pull up in front of the building. "See? That wasn't so bad."

I wish I felt his enthusiasm. All I feel is relief that it's over and dread that I will at some point have to do it again.

"I don't want to drive home," I say quietly. Then I grab my bag from the backseat and get out of the car before Dad can turn this into a whole thing. "I'll see you after school," I call just before the door shuts.

I walk to the front door without looking back. Behind me, I hear a door open, and I expect Dad to call out to me but he doesn't. Just the sound of his shoes on the pavement as he walks around to the driver's side, the rev of the engine as he leaves. I try to imagine the disappointed look on his face, but my mind's eye still isn't taking orders yet. It works when it wants to. So far, only when it feels like freaking me out.

There's a paperback on the bench in front of the building. It's lying face down but right away I know it's Dr. I's Descartes book. I look around for its owner but he's nowhere in sight. I'm oddly touched that it's here, that he's here, somewhere. The he came early to check up on me. Then again, I didn't tell him I was coming today. He must've just assumed after our conversation yesterday that I would. Or maybe he's here for someone else, another bruised soul, another kid with a dragon. Either way, I'm glad he came.

Inside the lobby it's quiet, which means that everyone is in the room already. I slip in the room just before the girl in the green jacket pulls it closed.

"I'm glad you came back," she says.

I smile, and it doesn't take the effort it usually does. "So am I."

As I sit, I catch Ayo's eye across the circle. The gash is still on his forehead, but it's not any worse than it was, and he's here. That feels like something. It feels like enough. And maybe if it's true for him then it's true for me, too. I can't drive without panicking yet, and I'm in this awkward place with Hannah, and my brain may or may not be completely effed up, but despite all of that, and maybe actually *because* of it, I'm better than I've ever been.

Dr. I's book is still lying on the bench when the meeting is over. I grab it to return it to him before the bell.

"Dr. I isn't seeing students today," his secretary says when I come through his office door. She doesn't look up from her screen. "He's on vacation until Monday."

"Oh." I look down at the book in my hands. "I have his book."

"You can leave it with me if you want. Or keep it 'til he's back."

"Um. Okay. I'll keep it I guess."

"Great," his secretary says. She couldn't possibly care less.

"Where did he go?" I ask, when what I really want to ask is *why didn't he tell me he was leaving town?*

"Wyoming," she says, just as the phone on her desk rings. I duck out of the office as she picks it up.

I feel oddly thrown by Dr. I's absence. Not that I needed him for anything particular today, but it's weird to me that he didn't mention that he'd be out. And weirder still that his book would still be on that bench if he left it there last week. It dawns on me that he probably loaned to another student to read, the way he tried to pawn it off on me. Now I feel bad for taking it; whoever he gave it to is probably freaking out that they lost it.

There are still a couple minutes before the bell, so I head downstairs to find Hannah. She's hunched over her calculus textbook and doesn't hear me come down.

"Hey," I say.

She doesn't look up. "I can't talk right now," she says.

"I just wanted to apologize for yesterday," I say awkwardly.

She doesn't respond.

"Hannah."

"I accept your apology. Now can you go? I need to concentrate." She still hasn't looked at me.

"Do you still want me to come over on Saturday morning and do your makeup?" I ask.

"If you want," she says flatly.

I make my way back up the stairs, tears stinging my eyes, wishing I could press rewind and take back everything I said to her yesterday. Wishing I could go back to the moment before everything went to crap.

i miss my friend

I try to tell myself that I have Marshall, that he's my friend, that he's enough. But this doesn't ease the aching in my chest. Because he isn't and he shouldn't be. If dating Wren taught me anything, it was that.

At lunch I skip the cafeteria and head out to the bleachers, top row, our spot, Marshall's and mine, and pull out Dr. I's book. *Principles of Philosophy* by Rene Descartes. It even *sounds* boring. I open to the beginning of Part One, "The Principles of Human Knowledge."

1. That whoever is searching after truth must, once in his life, doubt all things, insofar as this is possible.

I've never really sought after anything. Except maybe quiet in my head. The doubt part I've got covered. Particularly when it comes to myself.

I shut the book and stare out at the practice field.

Truth. I've never thought that much about it, really. Not until Dr. I started bringing it up. But the last couple days I keep going back to it, brain buzzing with half-formed thoughts. Wondering if maybe I've been missing the point. If maybe the truth isn't so much the opposite of a lie, but something different, bigger. Harder to nail down, even harder to see. Maybe truth is whatever's permanent. Whatever's left when you take the rest away.

I hear the bell ring from the building. I haven't even touched my lunch.

In fifth period we've moved onto Picasso, but I'm still stuck on Van Gogh, thinking about his very last words before he died. Our teacher wrote them on the board yesterday, and I can still see them there in smeared chalk. "The sadness will last forever." It makes me think about Truth again. It makes me wonder what is true about the world. If sadness is the truest thing about the world, then, yeah, Van Gogh was right, it won't ever go away. But if there's something more true than sadness, *there has to be*, then darkness isn't all there is. There is also light.

Chapter Twenty

"So this is officially a date?" Dad asks as we pull into the Jamisons' driveway on Saturday morning. I made the mistake of mentioning that we were dropping Hannah off at her audition before our date, and Dad really zeroed in on my word choice.

"Yes," I say. "Now can you please control the size of your grin? It's really embarrassing for you."

Dad chuckles. "Sorry. I'm just relieved we're past Wren."

My own smile fades. "I didn't know you didn't like him."

"Well, to be fair, I didn't really know him. I only met him that once." Two Christmases ago Wren and his family came skiing in Vail over Christmas while I was here visiting Dad, and we met them for dinner. I was so preoccupied with what Wren thought of my dad. I didn't consider what my dad might've thought of him. "But no. He wasn't my favorite boyfriend choice."

"Why didn't you say something?"

"Ha. Yeah, like that would've gone over well."

I don't say anything.

"It was mostly how you were around him," Dad says then. "Like you were afraid of messing up."

i was

"I should probably go in," I say. "Hannah's waiting on me to do her makeup."

"Have fun today. Will you give me a call this afternoon, just to check in?"

"Yep. And I put Marshall's number in your phone like you asked." On impulse, I lean over and kiss him on the cheek. It's been years since I've done that. He looks about as surprised as I feel. "I love you," I blurt out, then I shut the door.

The sky is dark like it's about to rain. *so much for learning to skate.* Mostly I just hope it doesn't wreck our museum plans. This is the last weekend of the Van Gogh exhibit, and after talking so much about him in class, I really want to see his paintings in real life.

you could drive their car

no i can't

Marshall opens the front door as I'm coming up the walkway. "Beware, all ye who enter," he says.

"Uh oh. That bad?"

"I'd recommend not speaking unless spoken to. That seems to be working the best. She's up in her room."

"Where are your parents?"

"Dad's hiding in the basement. Mom left a couple minutes ago to get another pair of tights. Unclear what the issue was with the existing pair, but whatever it was apparently warranted ripping them in half."

"Yikes. Was it this bad when she auditioned last year?" I ask.

"Nowhere close.

"But you're still not worried."

"I'm not sure what good worrying would do at this exact moment. Her audition is in two hours."

"How long do we have until she wants to leave?"

"Nineteen minutes." He steps back to let me in. "First door on the left at the top of the stairs."

Hannah's door is shut so I knock lightly. "Your makeup artist has arrived."

A few seconds later the door is flung open. To my relief I see that Hannah doesn't look any worse than yesterday. In fact, she might even look a little bit better, even though the black dress she's wearing is at least a size too big. I'd noticed that she'd lost some weight, but the slim cut of the dress accentuates just how much. Her bruises, at least, aren't any darker than they were.

"Hey," she says, and actually smiles a little. "Thanks for doing this." She waves me into her room. Pale blue walls covered with concert posters and vinyl record covers, a collection of vintage music boxes on a shelf.

"So which do you want to do first?" I ask, fishing my makeup case out of my bag. "Face or wrists?"

"Wrists," she says, dragging her desk chair over to the bed. "So I can get used to it." She sits down on her bed and holds out her arms. Her wrists are angry and red and raw.

I'm quiet as I blot the foundation on with a sponge, taking Marshall's advice. If she wants to talk about the audition, she'll bring it up. Her knees bounces beneath us, shaking the bed. It's that jittery, amped up vibe again, over-caffeinated, over-stressed.

I finish with her wrists. The foundation perfectly matches her skin. "Voila. What eczema?"

Hannah looks down and grins. It's the first real smile I've seen in weeks. "Thanks."

I start on her face. It's weird, touching the bruises with my fingertips as I blend tinted moisturizer onto her cheeks. Weirder still to watch the makeup sink behind her wounds. The bruises seem to spring to the surface, like buoys in the ocean, always on top. I try to ignore them, focus on her actual skin, so I don't put on too much.

"So the big first date's today," she says as I'm doing her eyeshadow.

"Yeah," I say awkwardly.

"How are you feeling about it?"

"A little freaked out," I admit.

"Because it's Marshall or because it's a date?"

"Um. Both, I guess. You guys are my only two friends at Crossroads. If you're leaving next year, I don't want to lose the only other friend I have."

"You won't lose me," Hannah says softly. "Even if I go. We'll still be friends. And you won't lose Marshall, either. Even if you guys break up or whatever, he'll be cool about it. Okay, not *cool*, he's not cool about anything. But he won't let it be weird."

"I just don't want to mess it up. With him or with you. About what I said yesterday, about the bruises—"

"It's fine," she says, cutting me off. My cue to stop talking, clearly.

I finish her eyes then brush on some blush. "Done," I say, stepping back. Except for the nasty purple splotches, she looks really good.

Hannah walks over to the mirror. "Wow. Thanks."

There's a knock on her door. "It's Mom. I have the tights."

"It's open," Hannah calls flatly.

"I got two pairs, just in case," her mom says as she comes in. "Wow, sweetie, your makeup looks great."

"Thanks." Hannah takes the bag.

"Hi, Jessa," her mom says warmly. "Take good care of my son today, okay?"

"Absolutely," I say.

Out of the corner of my eye I see Hannah's face darken. "We'll be down in a sec, okay?" she says to her mom, with a look that says *get out.*

Her mom looks taken aback. "Okay, sweetie. I'll be in the kitchen if you need me."

When her mom is gone, Hannah rips open a package of black tights. "Can you grab my shoes?" she asks, pulling on the tights. "They're in my closest. Plain black ballet flats."

I head into Hannah's walk in closet. It's spotless, more like a commercial for a closet than an actual closet. Her shoes are organized in a cubby behind the door. As I look for her ballet flats, I hear Hannah in her bedroom, opening a drawer. Then that distinct sound of pills against plastic. I peek through the open space at the hinge of the closet door.

"What are those?" I ask, too loud, still inside the closet. Through the crack I see Hannah freeze. I grab the shoes and come back out into the bedroom. Hannah caps the pill bottle, tosses it into her bag.

"Allergy meds," she says, not looking at me.

"Hannah."

"What?"

"Please just tell me the truth."

"It's Adderall, okay?" she sounds hostile now.

"Like, for ADD?" I ask.

"Yes. I have a prescription. It's not a big deal."

then why did you lie about it?

"How much have you been taking?" I ask.

"Can we please skip the interrogation?" Hannah snaps, taking the shoes from my hand. "We need to go."

I follow her out into the hallway and down the back steps, so thrown by the last five seconds that I'm holding my breath.

Marshall and both of their parents are in the kitchen. Their dad is at the stove, scrambling eggs.

"Dad's famous cheese eggs," he says to Hannah. "Breakfast of virtuosos."

"I'm not hungry," Hannah says.

"You have to eat something, sweetie," their mom says.

"No, actually, I don't," Hannah says darkly.

"How about a water at least?" Marshall calls from the fridge. Then he winces, presses his hand to his chest.

"You okay?" I ask in alarm. His mom jerks her head toward him. Hannah goes still.

"Everything alright, son?" his dad asks.

"Yes. Guys. I'm fine. Can we please not make it a red alert when I have heartburn? I'm trying to impress Jessa with my iron physique, but I don't have the will power to kick my SunChips habit, so I'm in a really tough spot here."

"I invite you to consider your breath," Hannah fires back. "I can smell French Onion from here."

"Nice try," Marshall calls, and opens his mouth wide. There's a wad of gum on his tongue.

"You're disgusting," Hannah says.

"You have Dr. Smith's number in your phone, right?" his mom asks Marshall.

"Yep."

"And you promise to take it easy today, right?"

"Yep."

"Can we please go?" Hannah asks. "I know it's not any-one's top priority today, but my audition starts in forty-five minutes."

Their parents exchange a glance. "Hannah, we know it's been a tough week for all of us," their mom begins gently. "But of course your audition is our priority. We know how impor-tant this is to you. We also know how talented you are, and how lucky Interlochen would be to have you. There's no doubt in our minds that you'll get an Emerson this year."

Hannah doesn't look at her. "You ready?" she asks Mar-shall. Marshall looks at me. I nod, so uncomfortable in this moment that I wish I could erase myself from it.

"Let's do it," Marshall says, tossing Hannah the keys.

None of us says anything on the drive in. I stare out the passenger side window, watching the storm clouds rolling in over the mountains, uneasy, a prickly feeling in my chest.

Hannah pulls into the parking lot of the performing arts center and parks. A fat rain drop splats on the windshield. Then another.

"Do you guys want the car?" Hannah asks, looking over at me.

I shake my head. "I'm fine to walk," I say. The rain picks up, heavy and hard, pounding against the windshield.

"We'll take the car," Marshall says. "Why don't you pull closer to the building so you don't get wet," he says to Han-nah, pointing to the covered front entrance, where other cars are dropping kids off. As we join the line, Logan Dwyer gets out of the blue Mercedes in front.

My eyes dart to Hannah. She sees her, too. Her knuckles are white on the wheel.

"You've got this," I say quietly.

Hannah doesn't say anything.

When we get to the front of the line, Marshall hops out of the backseat and opens Hannah's door.

"Just text me when you're done," he tells her.

"You can't drive," Hannah says to him, not budging.

"I'm just gonna re-park it," Marshall says, waving her out of the car.

Hannah hesitates for a sec, then gets out.

"Break a finger!" Marshall calls after her. Hannah flicks him off without looking back. Marshall grins and gets in the car.

"You said you were just re-parking it," I say as he pulls forward, away from the row of parking spaces, toward the exit. "I am," he says. "At the museum."

"No way," I say, shaking my head. "Your doctor said no driving for three weeks. It's been three days."

"The museum is five blocks away. It's fine."

"Marshall."

"Jessa."

"You realize I was in a terrible car wreck, right? That maybe I'm already a little on edge in cars?"

Guilt flashes across his face. "Okay. So I wasn't thinking about that. And now I feel like a total jerk. The problem is, we're on a one way street and the next available place for me to turn around is at the civic center, which is next to the museum." He points. "Right there."

"Can you just get there, please, and park?"

"Yes. And in the meantime, let's distract you." He reaches forward to switch on the radio, turns it way up. Classical music blares through the speakers. "Ugh, but not with this." He punches the CD button, and now it's booming eighties rap.

Panic Zone, don't get your girl in here

A way out in here, a way out in here

The voice is distorted, inhuman, unsettling, the lyrics like spiders beneath my skin. Rain drums against the windshield now, an unrelenting assault.

"This was N.W.A's debut song," Marshall says, turning it up louder. "This is what started it all."

It's called the Panic Zone

that's right the Panic Zone

Some people call it torture, but it's where we call home

I switch off the knob.

Marshall looks over at me.

"Too much," is all I say.

Marshall turns into the parking garage for the museum. The rain abruptly stops.

"Is it weird for me to ask what it feels like?" he asks when we're parked.

"What what feels like?"

"A panic attack. Your panic attacks."

"That song we just listened to," I say.

"No, seriously."

"I *am* being serious," I say. "When I'm having one, every-thing intensifies and speeds up, like a strobe light's going off in my head and an epileptic rabbit is having seizure in my chest."

Marshall laughs out loud.

"Yeah. It feels less than awesome when it's actually hap-pening to you." His features pinch, *doh*, so I flash a smile, the way I used to, a puppeteer tugging the strings, to let him off the hook.

"I shouldn't have laughed," he says as we walk toward the elevators. "An epileptic rabbit sounds terrible."

"Yeah, almost as terrible as that song." I shudder.

"What?! That song is great!"

"Ugh. That song is awful. But rather than debate that with you, I'm changing the subject to your sister. Does she have ADD?"

Marshall's eyebrows shoot up. "ADD? Hannah? She's, like, the most un-ADD person on the planet."

"Is it possible that she has it and you just don't know?"

"No. Why would you ask that?"

I hesitate.

"Jessa. What?"

"She's taking Adderall," I say finally. "She said she had a prescription."

He stops walking. "What do you mean she's taking Adderall? How do you know?"

"Because I saw her," I say. "In her room, before we left."

"Where'd she get Adderall?"

"Maybe she has a prescription, like she said?"

"Yeah, but where would she get one?" His face darkens. "Never mind. I know where she got it."

"Who?"

"Indelicato."

"*Dr. I?*"

"I doubt he's met a kid he hasn't tried to medicate."

"Really? He's never even *mentioned* drugs to me."

"Then you're the exception. He's all about the meds. Sophomore year he tried to put me on Ritalin twice."

"That doesn't sound like him," I say, doubtful.

Marshall shrugs. "Maybe he's different now. But he's the only doctor I can think of who would've given Hannah a prescription."

"I'm worried she's taking a lot," I say quietly. "Too much. I think it might be the reason she's been acting so weird."

Marshall rubs his forehead. "Why would she do something so careless?"

"She's been under a ton of pressure," I say.

"But she puts it on herself," he says. "It's not like anyone expects her to do all the stuff she does. She's the one that wanted to take all those AP classes and do a double certificate in music and music theory. She's the one that wants to go to

Interlochen. None of that comes from Mom and Dad. They're always telling her she's doing too much."

"Maybe it's not about that," I say.

We stop again at the elevators.

"What do you mean?" Marshall asks.

"Sometimes when we have a thing that makes us stand out, we start believing that that one thing is all we have. We don't know who we'd be without it. If we'd be anyone at all."

"Do you feel like that?" he asks.

"I used to. Before my accident. I spent all this time obsessing about my looks, not because I actually cared about how I looked, but because . . ." A grapefruit rolls into my throat. "Being pretty made me feel safe."

Marshall takes my hand. "You're still pretty, by the way. The prettiest girl in this entire parking garage, in fact. But I know that's not the point. And I think you're probably right about Hannah."

I stand up on my tip toes and gently kiss his lips. "You're right, completely not the point."

Marshall kisses me back. "You know what else I was right about?" he asks, sliding his arms around my waist and pulling me closer. "Space."

I look up at him. He smiles.

"It's completely overrated," he says. Then he kisses me again. Behind me, the elevator doors whoosh open.

"C'mon," I say, pulling him into the car. "We're not spending our first date making out in a parking garage."

"Well, obviously," Marshall replies. "Because our first date was last Friday. Level P1 of a parking garage is perfectly acceptable for a second date." But he follows me into the elevator.

We get in line to buy tickets to the museum. There's a giant poster for the Van Gogh exhibit hanging over the window. A self portrait of the artist with the words "Method and Madness" in cursive script. I stare up at the image. On the artist's left cheek, there are four small red lines that look like cuts, or even scars. They're so random that I wonder if my mind is making them up.

"Do you see those red lines?" I ask Marshall, still looking up at the poster. "On his cheek?"

Marshall doesn't answer me.

I drop my eyes but he's not where I expect him to be. He's over by the wall, holding the wall, his face as white as the paint. "What's wrong?" I ask, sprinting over to him. There are tiny beads of sweat on his face. Fear seizes every cell in my body.

"I don't know," he says. "I'm having chest pains. Bad ones. And my arm feels kind of numb."

please god no

"Where's your phone?" I ask in a low voice.

"My back pocket," he says hoarsely, fumbling for it. "Call Dr. Smith. She's saved in my favorit—"

"I'm calling 911," I say, already dialing, my eyes never leaving his face. A crowd has started to form around us. Or maybe the opposite, maybe it's that people are backing away, giving us space.

"What's your emergency," a voice on the other end says.

"My boyfriend just had heart surgery and now he's having terrible chest pains," I say frantically. "We need an ambulance right away."

"What's your name?"

"Jessa."

"Where are you, Jessa?" the voice asks calmly.

"The Denver Art Museum. In the lobby. Please hurry."

"Okay, Jessa, we have an ambulance on the way. I need you to tell me a little more about your boyfriend so the EMTs have all the information that they need. What's your boyfriend's name?"

"Marshall. Marshall Jamison."

"How old is Marshall?"

"Seventeen. He had a procedure done earlier this week to close a hole in his heart. He's been fine since then but a few minutes ago he started having chest pains out of nowhere. And he says his arm is numb." I hear myself. I sound frantic. I am frantic. *this can't be happening*

"Tell them I need the ambulance to take me to Children's," Marshall says weakly.

"The ambulance needs to go Children's Hospital of Colorado," I say into the phone. "That's where his doctors are."

"I'll let the ambulance driver know," the voice says. "Now, Jessa, I want you to stay on the phone with me until the ambulance arrives. How's Marshall doing?"

I look at him. He's sitting on the ground now, eyes closed, sweat dripping down his face.

I hang up on the 911 operator and call Dr. Smith. She answers on the second ring.

"Marshall," Dr. Smith says immediately. "What's going on?"

"He's having horrible chest pains," I blurt out. "I just called 911 and they said an ambulance is on the way. I don't know what to do. What should I do?"

"Jessa?" Dr. Smith asks.

"Yes."

"Is Marshall still conscious?"

"Yes. But it's bad. Really bad. He's so pale and he says his arm is numb and I can tell he can't breathe."

"I'm getting in my car now," Dr. Smith says, her voice low and urgent but calm. "I'll meet you at the hospital. Do his parents know what's going on?"

"No. I called 911 and then you."

"You did the right thing, Jessa. He's lucky to have you. I'll call his parents. I want you to hang up and talk to Marshall. Try to keep him awake, okay?"

"Okay." There's commotion by the front entrance. The shout of male voices. "I think the ambulance is here."

"That's good," she says. "I'll see you both soon." And then she hangs up.

His phone immediately starts ringing with another call, but I ignore it. I drop to my knees at Marshall's side.

"Dr. Smith is meeting us at the hospital," I tell him, my voice shaking. "She'll fix this, whatever this is. Everything's fine." I take Marshall's hand. It's startlingly cold.

"They're over there!" a man yells somewhere behind me. "By the staircase."

Heavy footsteps, people running, the roll of wheels, and all at once I am not here, I am there, at my accident in those horrible seconds before I passed out. When the enormity of what was happening was all there was.

"You're okay," I whisper to Marshall, the same thing the man in the white coat said to me, and I try to believe it, but deep down I don't, because this was the thing I was sure would happen. The terrible thing I was waiting for this whole time. And yes, maybe I'm letting fear win, but how am I supposed to fight it when Marshall is slumped against the wall on the floor, barely conscious, the pain in his chest sending sweat down his face?

"Pain isn't permanent," that's what the man said, the man no one else saw, the man who might not've been real. How am I supposed to believe the words of a person I might've made up? Maybe I'm not okay, haven't been okay this whole time. Maybe Marshall isn't either. Maybe pain *is* permanent. Maybe pain is all there is.

Marshall's chest stops moving.

"Help!" I scream. "Please help he's not breathing!"

The footsteps get louder, they're right behind me now. Three paramedics rush to Marshall's side.

"It's his heart," I tell them, frantic. "He has a heart condition."

"Are you Jessa?" one of the paramedics asks me. The other two are hunched over Marshall. One of them is doing CPR.

I nod.

"Can you tell me what happened, Jessa?"

"He just started having chest pains," I say. "Out of the blue. He was fine before that."

"When did he stop breathing?"

"Just a few a seconds ago," I say, eyes darting to Marshall's pale face. One of the paramedics is pumping his chest.

please god don't let him be dead

"I've got a pulse," one of the other paramedics says.

The other one is shoving a tube down his throat. The third one, the one talking to me, is asking me questions but I can't focus on her, can't think. For several seconds, maybe minutes, the sound cuts out and all I can hear is my own pulse roaring in my ears.

Then Marshall is on a stretcher and they're wheeling him away.

"Can I ride with him in the ambulance?" I ask, jogging to keep up with the gurney.

"Sorry, no," the EMT closest to me says. "Company policy. If the sirens are gonna be on, not even family can ride in the cabin."

family

My mind leaps to Hannah.

Someone has to tell her what's going on, but how? No way she has her phone on right now. And Marshall's parents only have one car right at home, which they'll take straight to the hospital.

i have his keys

i have to go get her

They're loading Marshall into the ambulance now. I watch him disappear into the red box, wonder if this might be the last time I ever see him, vaguely aware of the tears dripping down my face, running off my chin, mixing in with the pouring rain.

When the doors close behind him I turn and sprint toward the parking garage, digging the keys out of my purse as I run. I'm shaking as I start the car but I ignore it, my mind so focused on Hannah, on getting to Hannah, that there is no room for anything else. There is power in this, in having something bigger in my brain than fear.

Thunder rumbles as I pull out of the parking garage, tracing our route back to auditorium. The clock on the dash says it's eleven thirty-seven. Hannah's audition starts in eight minutes. I drive slowly because of the rain, pause a little too long at each green light, but I get there, and I'm fine. As I sprint inside the building I have the thought, *i won't be scared to drive any more.* This one fear, at least, hasn't won.

The hallway is crowded with kids in concert gear, some of them holding instruments, waiting their turns. Heads turn as I jog toward the auditorium, soaking wet and tear stained, completely out of place.

"You can't go in there," someone says as I pull open the auditorium door, but I barely hear them. It's not until that door shuts behind me and my hand is on the next door that it hits me what I'm about to do. I'm about to barge into Hannah's audition, to ruin it, maybe ruin her whole life with this news. I can see her through the crack in the second set of doors, at the piano, on the stage, playing the Phillip Glass piece. The song is coming through the crack, through the wooden doors, muffled but beautiful. I imagine her smiling a little bit.

I take my hand off the door.

I sit against the wall in that space between the doors, and wait. She'll finish this song then play the next one then maybe talk to the people with clipboards sitting on the front row. And then she'll come through those doors and I'll tell her what happened and this whole day will become about something else. But until that moment, today will be about *this*, the music, her talent, all the hard work paying off. And sitting here, listening to her play, I totally get it. Why she's been the way she's been. It was for Interlochen, yeah, but it was also for *this*, her on that stage, being great.

My heart aches at the thought of telling her. I can't imagine speaking the words. What will I even say? I don't even know that much, only that something awful has happened.

When she finally comes through the door and sees me, I don't have to say anything. One look at me, and the color drains from her face.

"What happened?" she whispers.

"He started having chest pains," I say hoarsely, through tears. "I called 911. They took him to the hospital a few minutes ago. Dr. Smith was calling your parents. I came here to get you."

"How bad is it?"

"I don't know. Bad. We should go to the hospital." When she doesn't move I take her hand and pull her into the hall, keep pulling her, all the way to the parking lot, where finally she seems to snap out of it and starts to run.

As we sprint to the car, I'm barely thinking about the fact that I'll be driving. It's already become a non-issue, the least of my worries now, and in a way I'm actually grateful for it, because it's something to think about. Something to keep me from spinning out. Panic isn't an option right now. It just isn't. I won't let it be.

It takes us almost half an hour to get to the hospital, because of the rain. Neither of us says a word during the entire drive. When we get to Children's I give the car to the valet at the ER entrance and we sprint inside.

"I'm looking for my brother," Hannah says to the woman at reception, her voice trembling. "Marshall Jamison. He came here in an ambulance."

The woman types the name into the computer. "He was just admitted over at the Heart Institute. They're prepping him for surgery now. I'll have an escort walk you over." The woman looks at me. "Are you family also?"

"Yes," Hannah says before I can answer. "She's our cousin. But we don't need an escort. I know where it is." She turns and dashes back through the automatic doors.

"You can go through the building!" the woman at reception calls. Hannah ignores her.

I follow her down the sidewalk toward another entrance, the one for the tall L-shaped building where Marshall was on Tuesday afternoon, when I kissed him, when he was still okay.

Hannah doesn't slow down in the lobby. She heads straight to the elevators, presses the button for the third floor.

"How do you know that's where he is?" I ask.

"The operating rooms for heart surgery are all on the third floor. There's a waiting room by the elevators. I'm sure that's where my parents are." As the elevator doors close, she slips a hand in the pocket of her dress, pulls out two round white pills. She doesn't look at me as she pushes them into her mouth and swallows. I feel her waiting for me to say something. I don't.

As the elevator dings, Hannah's eye flick to mine. "I know," she says quietly. "But if I stop taking it now I'll crash, and I can't deal with that right now."

I nod. "Okay."

She grabs my hand and squeezes it. "I'm glad you're here," she whispers.

I see her parents as soon as the doors open, perched on the edge of waiting room chairs. Her mom's eyes are puffy from crying. Her dad is staring into space. There are fresh scratches on both their faces, red and raw, but not deep enough to be permanent yet. Their hope like a shield to their skin, keeping the wounds on the surface, not letting them set in.

Her mom sees us first. "Hannah," she says, rising to her feet. "Thank God. I've been calling you."

Hannah runs to her. "I left my backpack at the auditorium. I don't have my phone. Jessa picked me up."

"Jessa, thank you," her mom says, her voice wobbling like it's taking everything she has not to let it crack. "For everything. Dr. Smith says you did exactly the right thing. Calling the ambulance, then calling her. I'm so thankful you were with him, and that you stayed so calm."

"How is he?" Hannah asks.

Her mom's eyes fill with fresh tears. "We don't know yet. They took him straight into surgery."

Hannah takes the seat her mom was sitting in, next to her dad, and her mom sits down on the other side. They angle their bodies together, a sort of family huddle, and all at once it's too much.

"Do you guys want coffee?" I blurt out. "I'll go get some coffee." I turn and press the elevator button. When the doors don't open right away, I bolt toward the stairwell, tripping over my rain-soaked boots. I feel Hannah and her parents staring at me, but right now I can't get out of this room fast enough.

I take the stairs two at the time, nearly falling twice. The walls of the stairwell are too narrow; they feel as if they're closing in. I burst through the first floor door and am in the atrium again. I spin, looking for somewhere to go. There's a cafe over on one side, a place to get coffee, what I said I was coming down here to do. But I can't go back up there any time soon.

But I can't stay here either. Not in this airy, optimistic room, which at this moment feels like a really sick joke.

A choking sound. The sob I can't swallow anymore, the one that's been lodged in my throat since I was twelve years old, comes hurling out. My shoulders heave with the force of it, the tsunami in my chest. The tears come fast, pouring down my face, dripping off my chin.

My eyes catch a pair of wooden doors at the end of the hallway. Somehow I know it's the chapel. Maybe I saw the sign. I also know somehow that it'll be empty, which is the only reason I go inside.

Chapter Twenty-One

Blurry black words. Tissue thin paper splattered with tears. The Bible was lying open on a chair when I got here, the corner of the page folded down. An invitation, or maybe an omen. I couldn't not pick it up. Someone had underlined the fourth line of Psalm 147. My eyes caught the words and held.

He heals the broken-hearted and binds up their wounds.

WHEN?!? I felt like screaming. *FREAKING WHEN WILL HE DO THAT?!?* I flung the Bible across the room instead. Then I went over to where it landed and got down on my knees and prayed. I'm not sure what I said.

At some point I got up and walked over to this chair, sat down with the Bible open on my lap, and looked up at the stained glass window. My eyes have been there ever since.

I have no idea how long I've been sitting in this chapel. Minutes, maybe hours. I'm cold and my butt is numb but as long as I'm in here I won't know what's happening upstairs, and that's reason enough to stay.

The heavy door opens behind me. Reflexively, I snap the Bible shut.

"Hey, Bear."

daddy

"How'd you know I was here?" I ask, not turning around.

"When you didn't come home this afternoon I called Marshall's cell," Dad says, and then I hear his footsteps on the chapel's hardwood floor. "His father answered, told me what happened. He said you went to get coffees for everyone and never came back." He sits down on the chair next to me. "I had a feeling I might find you here. It's where I hid out when you were in the hospital. The only quiet place."

"Is he—?" *dead*, that's what I want to ask, *is the boy I think I love dead?* But my lips won't form the words. "Was it the clot? Did he have a stroke?"

"No, Bear. He didn't have a stroke. The device they put in Marshall's heart caused some of his cardiovascular tissue to erode," Dad says carefully. "Which basically just means that the wall of his heart wore away where the device was attached, creating a new, much bigger hole. They're trying to repair it now."

I squeeze my eyes shut. "Is he gonna die?"

Dad hesitates. My own heart clenches.

"I don't know," he says finally. "From what his father just told me, he's got really excellent doctors, and they're doing the best they can."

"He was fine this morning," I whisper. Tears roll down my face, drip off my chin. "I mean, I guess he wasn't. But I thought he was." I look over at my dad. He's looking up at the giant stained glass above the wooden altar in the front of the chapel. An angel mosaic made of thousands of tiny pieces of colored glass. I've been staring at it since I came in, thinking about the way my front windshield cracked in the accident, into a thousand small pieces just like that.

"Do you believe in them?" I ask.

Dad glances over at me. "Angels?"

I nod.

"I'd like to," Dad says.

me too

"How come you don't go to church anymore?" I ask. "You used to go all the time."

"I still go," he says. "Just not lately. I wasn't sure you'd be up for coming with me, after you so dramatically vetoed the Christmas Eve service last year."

"Right," I say, remembering the stupid fit I had about it, but not the reason why. There probably wasn't one. Just a need to make things difficult for him, in whatever ways I could. Shame prickles inside my stomach just thinking about it. I was so awful to him.

"Mom's Buddhist now," I say. "Did you know that?"

"I did not," he says dryly.

My eyes well up with tears again.

"I was so lonely," I whisper. "After you left."

His arm sweeps around me and pulls me to him. "Oh, Bear," he says, his voice breaking. "I'm so sorry."

I press my face against his shoulder. He smells the way he's always smelled, like Chapstick and soap. "It wasn't just you," I say into his shirt.

Dad pulls back to look at me. "What do you mean?"

"I prayed every day that my panic attacks would stop. I'd literally beg, over and over, 'please, God, I'll do anything, just make them stop.'" My eyes fill with fresh tears. "And now, it's like, I don't know what I'm supposed to do with that. If I even believe in him anymore. I know you do, but . . . I'm not sure I believe there's someone up there who can freaking 'heal the broken-hearted.' Someone who gives a crap how messed up we all are." My voice catches. "Because right now it doesn't really seem like there is."

"Someone certainly gives a crap about you."

"You don't count."

"I'm not talking about me." Dad looks back at the stained glass window. "People don't walk away from accidents like the one you had. That Escalade was going fifty miles an hour when it hit you. You hit a fire hydrant and spun out into a tree. The fact that you're sitting here now, with scars, yes, but otherwise, still *you* — still able to walk and talk and breathe?" Now *his* voice catches. "Someone was watching over you, I have no doubt about that."

you're oh-oh-kay

"There was a man there," I say quietly. "He came to my window right after it happened and just kind of talked to me . . . told me I was going to be okay. He was wearing a white coat, so I thought he was a doctor on his way home from work. But. . . no one else saw him there. The paramedics said I was alone when the ambulance showed up. There's no way they wouldn't have seen him."

We're both staring at the stained glass window now.

"I could've imagined him, I guess," I say. "But I don't think I did."

Dad takes my hand. "I don't think you did, either."

We're both quiet for a while, staring at the image of the angel, the brightest thing in the room.

"Do you think Marshall has one?" I hear myself ask.

"An angel?"

"Yeah."

"I don't know," Dad admits. "I don't know how these things work. But I know God cares what happens to him. And to you. I know he cares very much."

Tears slip down my cheeks.

"I'm sorry you felt abandoned, Bear," he says quietly, his voice breaking a little. "That's on me. I should've been there for you, and I wasn't. I let you down."

My throat squeezes. "It's okay," I whisper.

"No," Dad says firmly. "It's not."

Except right now it kind of is. I'm still sad about what happened, sad that he left, that we lost four years we otherwise would've had. But I'm not angry at him anymore. Because despite all the crappy things that happened after he left, *because he left*, I came out the other side. Yes, parts of me were broken that maybe wouldn't have been. My confidence, my trust. The bones in my face. But even with all those broken pieces, *because of all those broken pieces*, I ended up here. In this terrible but somehow beautiful moment, holding hands with my dad, praying for a boy who can't help but see kindness and courage everywhere he looks because kindness and courage are what he's made of. Kindness and courage and hope.

"I forgive you," I tell my dad then, and mean it. "So you left. So you aren't perfect. Nobody is."

Dad nods a little, but his eyes stay sad.

"Except me, obviously," I deadpan. "I've been a completely rad human being for the past few years. Daughter of the decade, totally."

This gets a laugh. "You didn't make it easy, did you?" he says, nudging me with his shoulder.

"I learned from the best," I say dryly, and then we look at each other and say "mom" at the exact same time.

"Have you told her what happened?" I ask him.

"Not yet. I came here as soon as I heard."

"It wouldn't mean anything to her anyway," I say. "I haven't even told her about Marshall."

"Why not?"

I shrug. "I haven't told her about much lately. She doesn't ask."

We're both quiet for a few minutes after that.

"So . . . you ready to go back up?" Dad asks eventually. "I'm sure Hannah could use a friend up there."

I fiddle with the Bible again. "I practically had a panic attack in the waiting room. I'm not what she needs right now."

"How do you know what she needs? Have you asked her?"

I don't answer. He knows I haven't. There's also the part he doesn't know, the thing I can't say. That I'm afraid of what I'll see on her face now that this has happened. Not just bruises now, but deeper wounds made of loss and grief.

"Hannah does need you," Dad says gently. "And if Marshall makes it through this, he'll need you, too."

if

I look back up at the stained glass window. "Please don't let him die," I whisper.

Dad squeezes my hand. "Amen," he says.

Then he stands, and pulls me to my feet.

His hand stays in mine until we get off the elevator. I let go when I see Marshall's parents. It seems unfair suddenly, that I'm clinging to my dad when they can't even see their son.

Marshall's mom sees us and smiles. "You found her," she says to my dad.

"Any news?" Dad asks.

She shakes her head. "Not yet."

"Where's Hannah?" I ask.

Their mom blinks, then frowns. "She went to the bathroom, I think." She looks over at her husband. "But that was a while ago, right?"

"I'm not sure," their dad admits.

"I should see if she's okay," their mom says, and starts to stand.

"I'll go," I say quickly. She nods and sits back down. I look over at my dad. "You don't have to stay," I tell him.

"I know that," he says, and sits.

The bathroom is by the elevator. I drop my eyes out of habit, mirror alert, as I push through the door, but then immediately force myself to raise them. To let it be no big deal that I see myself in the mirror, puffy eyes and tear-streaked cheeks, because the way I look doesn't matter even a little right now.

There is no one at the sinks. One of the stall doors is hanging open. The other is shut.

"Hannah?"

No answer.

I bend over and look under the stall doors. No feet in either one. I walk down to the closed door, the handicapped stall. It's locked.

"I know you're in there," I say gently.

There is a long pause. Then I hear the stall door unlock. When she doesn't come out, I go in.

She's sitting cross-legged on the toilet. Her eyes are swollen and puffy. Her cheeks are every shade of bruise.

"Hey," I say. "How long have you been in here?"

She shrugs. "A while."

"Your parents are worried about you," I say.

She makes a sound in her throat and looks away. "I doubt it."

And then I get it.

"This was supposed to be your day," I say.

Her eyes fill with tears. "I'm an awful person," she whispers. "My twin brother is having open-heart surgery right now and I'm pouting in the bathroom because no one asked about my stupid audition."

"I don't need to ask," I tell her. "I heard it. I got there just as you were starting the first piece. You were amazing. Beyond amazing."

Her expression changes from guilt to disbelief. "How could you let me play? If you knew he was in an ambulance, that he could die . . . how could you let me stay in there like that?"

"Because I knew you'd never get it back," I say simply. "That moment, you on stage, being great. All interrupting would've done is ruin an amazing performance. And yeah, maybe we would've gotten to the hospital ten minutes sooner, but so what? It wouldn't have changed anything with Marshall."

Hannah's eyes fill with fresh tears. "I can't believe this is happening," she says.

My own voice catches. "I know." I sit down on the bathroom floor. We're both quiet for a few minutes.

"I used to be so jealous of him," she says finally. "When we were little. I probably would've hated him if he wasn't Marshall and completely impossible to hate. Which is crazy, right? To be jealous of your brother with a heart defect. But I would've given anything to trade. To be the one my parents worried about all the time. Or at all."

"You felt ignored," I say, because I get it. It's the way I felt after the twins were born.

"Ignored implies they knew I was there," Hannah says flatly. "Try invisible." Then guilt pinches her features. "Not that I blame them," she adds quickly. "I get it. The kid with the issues always gets the most attention."

not always, I think. But I know what she means, so I nod. "It still sucks to be the other kid," I say.

We're quiet again. This time it's me who breaks the silence.

"Can we talk about the Adderall?" I ask gently.

Her eyes drop. "I never should've taken it," she says quietly. "I know that. I just thought it would help me be more productive. And it did, at first . . . I'd take a pill and feel super focused. But then it stopped working as well, and when it'd start wearing off I'd feel all foggy and tired. Like I couldn't function."

"So you started taking more."

She nods.

"How much more?"

She hesitates.

"Hannah. How much have you been taking?"

"Sixteen pills a day," she says, staring at her hands. They're shaking in her lap. "The bottle says to take two."

I suck in a breath. "How did you even have that much?"

"Dr. I gave me two refills," she says miserably. "I told the pharmacist I was going out of town and needed to fill all three at once. I figured I only needed it until my audition. I'd stop right after that." Her voice breaks. "I wish I'd never started taking it. It was so stupid. But when Logan took the practice room, I got panicked . . . and I was just so desperate to get in, to get away from them. I would've tried anything."

"To get away from who?" I ask. "Your parents?"

She lifts her eyes to mine. There is so much sadness in them, more than I expect. "You don't know what it's like. Feeling like you're not an actual person, like you're just this category in their heads, 'the healthy kid,' 'the fine one.' Like there's no space in their lives for you to be anything other than that. The only time I ever get their attention is when I'm performing. And even then, it's not like they actually see me. They see some version of me they invented that doesn't even exist."

but i do know what it's like, I want to tell her. *i can see it on your face.* And it strikes me in this moment how fragile the soul is. How little it takes to leave a mark.

"I don't know about your parents," I say softly. "But *I* see you. I see how kind and loyal you are. How funny. How smart."

"I haven't been lately," she says dully.

"That was the Adderall," I say. "That wasn't you."

Her tears spill over. "I was such a bitch to him this week. He was having a freaking metal sponge put into his heart and I couldn't be bothered to come see him. And now . . ." She shakes her head, can't finish the thought. She doesn't need to.

"So you didn't see this coming," I say. "That doesn't make you an awful person. That makes you human. None of us knows what'll happen next. Which, yeah, on one level is terrifying, because it means there will be lots of moments like this, moments when it feels like darkness is all there is. But just because we can't see the light doesn't mean it isn't there, that it isn't right around the corner. And just because we feel alone doesn't mean we are."

"I'm just so scared," she whispers.

"I am, too," I say. "And I'm scared to be anything *but* scared. I'm afraid to believe that he'll get better, because I don't want to be blindsided when he doesn't. But that's not what Marshall would do. Marshall would hope for the best at every second. He'd believe that everything would work out in the end."

Hannah smiles a little. "That little optimistic shit."

We look at each other and burst out laughing, and in the sound of it, I feel a weird kind of power. The kind that punches fear in the face.

"C'mon," I say, getting to my feet, then reaching out my hand to pull Hannah to hers.

The bathroom door opens just as I'm sliding the stall lock.

"Hannah," her mom's voice says.

We both go still. Hannah grips my hand. My heart is in my throat.

"Yeah?"

Her mom appears in the stall door.

"He's out of surgery," she says. "They think . . . they think he's going to be okay."

Chapter Twenty-Two

It's been forty-six hours since that horrible moment at the museum. Thirty-nine since Marshall came out of surgery, thirty-five since he woke up. His parents were with him when he opened his eyes late Saturday night. Hannah was asleep in a chair in the waiting room with me. I left when they came and got her, apologizing that only family was allowed, which made me feel super awkward because of course I didn't expect to rush right in. "I'll call you as soon as I have details," Hannah said as I was leaving. His mom hugged me and whispered, "they're lucky to have you," and my throat tightened so quickly I couldn't tell her she got it backwards, that I was lucky to have them.

I drove myself home from the hospital. When he left around six Dad offered to come back and get me when I was ready to leave, but I told him I was fine to drive myself. We both pretended he wasn't beaming when he handed me the keys.

Hannah called just as I got home. The surgery went as well as it could have, she told me; they'd fixed the tissue damage and closed both holes in his heart. As long as his incision doesn't get infected and he doesn't develop any new clots, he should get to go home in a week, back to school in three. "He's really gonna be okay," she said at the end, her voice thick with relief, and from out of nowhere I had the thought *he always was.*

I slept late on Sunday, and when I woke up Dad was gone. *@ church* the note on the counter said. *didn't want to wake you.* There were pancakes on the table, covered in foil, and juice he obviously squeezed by hand. Last year I would've resented him for the gesture, for trying to win me over with breakfast food, and the thought of how I would've reacted, how I *did* react, so often, crushes me with regret. I couldn't see him, my own dad.

I see him now.

I called Mom while he was gone and told her about everything. The twins were at the park with Carl, so she wasn't distracted for once, and it made me think of those afternoons before they were born when she'd pick me up from school and ask me about my day and then really listen when I told her. But then she asked how my scars were looking and whether I was ready to pick a date to have them "revised" by her plastic surgeon in June. The conversation ended pretty soon after that.

When Dad got home we drove to the mountains to go hiking. I didn't want to at first, just in case Hannah or Marshall tried to call. But Dad insisted. "They mended his heart," he told me. "Let's spend some time on yours." We were gone all afternoon.

This morning they're moving Marshall out of the ICU to a regular room, which means I get to see him finally, this afternoon. Dad said I could stay home from school today, but I came anyway, early, to see Dr. I.

His secretary is eating a muffin at her desk when I walk in. "You're back," she says.

"Is he here today?" I ask, worried for a second that he isn't because his office door is shut.

"Yep. Remind me your name?"

"Jessa," I tell her. "He knows me."

She presses the intercom button on her desk. "A student named Jessa is here to see you. She says she has a book of yours."

A few seconds later, the office door opens and a man in a red sweater and jeans steps out into the waiting area.

"Hello," he says.

"Hi," I say, stepping to the side to let the man pass. He doesn't move. I glance back at the secretary. "Um. Where's Dr. I?"

She and the man share a look.

"I'm Edward Indelicato," the man says. "Dr. I."

I stare at him. "What?"

"I'm Dr. I," he repeats. "This is my office."

"I—I don't understand," I say.

where is dr. i?

"Judy, please hold my calls," the man in the red sweater says. His secretary nods, staring at me, her mouth in the shape of a tiny "o," muffin crumbs on her chin. "Jessa, why don't you come inside my office for a few minutes so we can talk."

I nod dumbly and go in.

"Sit wherever you'd like," the man says when we're in his office, shutting the door behind us. There are diplomas on the wall behind his desk, one from the University of Colorado and the other from Harvard Medical School, both in the name Edward James Indelicato, his name, this man's, a man I have never seen before this moment. A man with thinning hair and bushy eyebrows and dandruff on his scalp. So who was the other guy?

I sit in a chair, avoiding the couch. I won't be here long.

"You're Dr. Indelicato," I say, somehow managing to keep my voice steady.

there is an explanation for this, this is not a big deal

"You seem surprised by that," he says.

"No, it's just— I thought someone else was you," I stammer. "Another teacher."

"What other teacher?"

if i knew that we wouldn't be having this conversation

"I don't know his name," I say. "He's tall, dark hair. He eats lunch on the bench by the teacher's parking lot, out back."

"Why would you think this man was me?"

"I—I dunno. He seemed like a shrink." I think back, try to remember if he ever actually introduced himself to me as Dr. I, but I don't think he ever did.

"So there's a man you thought was me who eats lunch here, at our school, and wears a white coat?"

I nod. "Yes."

The man in the red sweater types something on his keyboard, then swivels his computer screen around to face me. "These are our faculty members," he says. "Do you see the man here?"

I scan the faces on the screen. Longer than I need to. One glance and I know.

My armpits go damp.

"You don't see him," the man in the red sweater says. I shake my head.

"So he's not a teacher here."

"I don't know. I guess not." My mind is reeling, my heart like a jackhammer in my chest.

i made him up

oh my god i made him up

"Well, that's a bit concerning," the man in the red sweater says calmly. He doesn't sound concerned at all. "If there's a man who's been coming on campus and speaking with students who doesn't actually work here. What did you and this man talk about?"

"We just talked." I hear how defensive I sound. "About my anxiety, mostly. He told me about the support group that meets across the street." I realize at this exact moment that I'm still holding the paperback copy of *Principles of Philosophy* in my hands. I hold it up like it's evidence, like it's proof. "And Descartes. We talked about Descartes. This is his book."

The man in the red sweater holds out his hand. I give him the book. He turns it over in his hands. "This is a library book."

"Yeah? So?"

"From a Los Angeles County Library. Didn't you move here from L.A.?"

"It's not my book," I say immediately. "He always had it with him."

"Okay," the man in the red sweater says neutrally.

"He's a real person," I insist, but I sound less certain than before. *how far is the leap from hallucinating bruises to imagining tears to making whole people up?*

"It's possible," the man in the red sweater says. "It's possible that there's a man out there who's impersonating a faculty member, who somehow managed to come onto our campus undetected to eat lunch, and that he did this in order to talk to you about philosophy and tell you about a support group that's advertised on every bulletin board in the building. All of that is *possible*. But it isn't very likely, is it?"

"He never said he worked here," I say stupidly. As if this one fact is the one that matters, that'll resolve the whole thing. "I just thought he was you because he had on a white doctor's coat."

he had on a white coat

There is a sensation in my skull like fogged glass clearing, and all of sudden I see him crisply in my mind's eye. The man who appeared at my window that night. Dark hair, kind eyes, white coat. Peering through a frame of broken glass. The face I haven't been able to picture is there now, as if it'd always been there, the image of him as clear as a photograph in my head. A face I've seen several times in person since then.

it was him

The man at my window. The man I thought was Dr. I.

it was the same guy

"Do you believe in angels?" I blurt out.

The man in the red sweater blinks. "Angels," he repeats.

I hesitate. Then nod.

"Well. I believe there are neurological explanations for why a person might believe she's encountered an angel," the man in the red sweater says carefully. "But no. I don't believe in angels. Just like I don't believe in unicorns. No scientist reasonably could."

"Why not?" I ask.

"Because there's no evidence for them," he says simply. "In thousands of years of supposed angel sightings, no one has ever come up with any concrete proof. What we do know, however — and what we *can* prove — is that the brain is remarkably capable of making things up."

It's tempting to just accept it. That the doctor with the Harvard degree knows better than the girl with the head injury. That the idea that I could've been meeting with an angel is as crazy as it sounds.

But then I remember what the man who might've been an angel said to me.

"The invisible world doesn't work the way the visible world does. There isn't concrete evidence. There isn't physical proof. All you have to go on is your own certainty, which takes some measure of trust. In yourself. In Truth itself."

"There was one at my accident," I hear myself say. "Right after I hit the tree, he appeared out of nowhere in my window. In a white coat, so I thought he was a doctor. He told me I was okay, that the ambulance was on its way. My hand—" My thumb and forefinger catch my left wrist, "—it was pinned under the steering wheel. He popped it back into place."

"How do you know he wasn't a doctor?"

"Because no one else saw him," I say. "And now that I think about it . . . it was kind of weird that he suddenly showed up."

"And based on that, you came to the conclusion that he was an angel."

"Well . . . yeah."

"That's one explanation," the man in the red sweater replies. "Let me propose another one — that the mysterious stranger you thought you encountered that night was a result of the head trauma you'd just experienced. That the reason no one else saw this man was because he only existed in your head." He leans forward on his elbows. "Which, by itself, wouldn't worry me — abrupt hallucinations are fairly common with close head injuries. It can even be a form of neurological self-preservation — the brain's way of keeping you from going into shock. But it sounds to me like you're *still* seeing things, weeks after the fact. And that, Jessa, does worry me."

"No," I say firmly. "I didn't hallucinate him. He was real."

"I'm sure it felt that way," the man in the red sweater replies. "And I can imagine how confusing that might be."

And all of a sudden I'm done here. With him, with this. With always doubting myself.

"I get that you're just doing your job," I say then. "But you have no idea what you're talking about."

Then I turn and walk out, ignoring the look his secretary gives me as I blow past her desk and into the hall, just as the morning bell rings.

There's no way I'm going to class.

I keep moving, not slowing down, through the front door and down the sidewalk to the student parking lot. Thank God I drove today. My hands are shaking as I get in the car. I try to put the keys in the ignition but miss. The keys drop to the carpet.

Skull pressed against the headrest, I suck air through my teeth. The Descartes book is lying on the passenger seat, where I flung it. My bag is upside down on the floor. I reach for the book now, holding onto it with two hands, making sure of it. This one concrete thing.

There's a stirring in my stomach. Panic ramping up.

"I don't know what to believe," I whisper, the confidence I felt in Dr. I's office slipping from me, fear seeping in. As if in response, I hear a voice in my head. *His* voice, the man in the white coat, the man I thought was Dr. I, the man who appeared at my window that night.

"I know it's scary, but you are okay. Do you hear me? You're okay."

Those words have been on repeat since my accident, *you're okay, you're okay, you're okay,* a running pep talk in my head that I've never actually believed, because all the evidence says it isn't true. I'm seeing things, my boyfriend nearly died, and my best friend is addicted to prescription drugs. Nothing about my life in this moment is okay. So either the man at my window was crazy or lying or I missed the point.

It occurs to me now that maybe I misunderstood. That maybe those two words meant something different than I thought they did that night. That maybe *you're okay* was his way of telling me *it won't always be like this.* This is not all there is. Things will get better. This is not how my story ends.

In a way, it's what I was trying to tell Hannah at the hospital on Saturday. *Don't lose hope, it won't always be like this.* Someday those bruises inside you will heal. You can't know when *someday* will come, or what life will look like when it finally does. None of us can see around the corner like that. But in a way it doesn't even matter because *someday* isn't what we have. What we have is *right now,* this moment, when things aren't okay yet, but in a sense they already are, because in the end they *will be*, and as long as that's true, it's enough.

Muscles letting go of bone, the fear releases.

i'm okay

i always was

The fact that I didn't know it yet didn't matter. It didn't make it less true.

And it strikes me in this moment that Marshall was wrong. It's not that we're all broken inside. It's that we're *not*. Brokenness is just like beauty; it's something we wear and carry, and if we let it define us, it will. But we are not our beauty or our brokenness, because souls are not made of beauty or brokenness. Souls are made of something permanent.

Souls are made of truth.

There's a knock on my window. I tense up, prepared to see the real Dr. I, brandishing pills and a straight-jacket. But it's Ayo. Backpack on his back. His face completely healed.

I open the driver's side door. "Hey," I say, my eyes flicking to his forehead, looking for a mark where the gash once was. But his skin is smooth. No trace of the cut, no hint of a scar.

"Going or coming?" he asks me.

"Going," I say. "It's been a rough morning."

"Shit. I'm sorry. Did something happen with your friend?"

"Boyfriend," I say, and Ayo smiles. "And, actually, yeah. A couple days ago. But he's okay now. I'm going to see him this afternoon."

"So he's not the reason you're out here."

I shake my head. Ayo doesn't push.

"How are things with you?" I ask. "Better, I hope?"

He hesitates, and I get my answer. The hurt isn't painted on his face this time, but it's there just the same. Underneath. Within.

I blink, hard, expecting the old gash to materialize, or some new wound. But Ayo's skin stays clear. The hurt doesn't show.

why can't i see it?

My eyes dart around the parking lot. There's a teacher walking to her car. I've seen her before, in the halls. Covered in bruises. Now those bruises are gone.

i don't see them anymore

For a second I am lightheaded. With certainty, with disbelief.

it's over now

Whatever has been happening since my accident has stopped.

Ayo's mouth is moving. He's answering my question. I've forgotten what I asked.

how can it be over when i've only just begun

"Honestly, I don't know anymore," he's saying. "My little cousin got arrested last night, and my grandma — that's who I live with, since my mom split — laid into me, like it was my fault. Said I'm a bad influence, all that. Which, like, a year ago, I would've gotten, 'cause she would've been right. But last few months, things have been so different, and I guess I thought people could see it. That *she* could at least. It's, like, why am I making all this effort if it's not gonna make any difference, you know?"

He's trying to sound matter-of-fact about it, but I can tell that he's really sad. I can tell even though I can't see it. Because somehow, even without it being visible, I sort of still can.

He's waiting for me to say something.

"It *has* made a difference," I tell him. "You aren't the guy you were before. All the stuff you said in group last week about turning your life around. That's what's true."

"So why doesn't she see that?"

"Probably because she's like the rest of us," I say. "We see what we want to see, what we expect to see, instead of what's really there. I don't think we do it on purpose, most of the time. We just get kind of stuck. We start thinking that the way things are is the way they'll always be. But that's not true. It can't be true. Because the world is never still."

Ayo smiles a little. "So things suck and people suck but there's hope."

I smile back. That's exactly what there is. Hope. In car accidents and operating rooms and school parking lots. When we're trudging through the middle place, in the tunnel between *already* and *not yet*. Where the light is visible but we're still in the dark, and the best we can do is believe that eventually we'll get there, someday, and hold each other's hands until we do. There may not be calm or certainty or confidence, but there is hope. That the tears aren't forever. That one day all things will be new.

"Come on," Ayo says then, pulling my door open wider. "If I have to go inside, you do, too."

"Says who?"

"Says me. I'm older than you and twice your size. Get your ass out of that car."

"Do you say this kind of stuff to your grandma?" I ask, reaching for my bag. "Because it might explain her cloudy view."

"You gonna tell me why you were hiding out in your car?" he asks as we walk inside.

"Do I have to?"

"Again: older than you and twice your size. Yes."

I think of how to put it, without getting into the whole thing.

"I guess it's sort of the same thing that's happening with your grandma," I say finally. "Except it was *me* who couldn't see me all that well. I'm different since my accident . . . better. But something happened this morning to make me doubt all of that for a sec."

"That's what you got me for," Ayo says as we reach the school building. "Me, and all the other kids in group. To tell you what's what. To remind you when you forget. Like you just did for me out there. We're like a family that way. The good kind, not the kind most of us got."

"It's hard for me," I admit. "To let people in. My middle school friends bailed when my panic attacks started, and I kind of built a wall after that. Coming to group last week was honestly one of the hardest things I've ever done."

"So what got you there?"

"A friend suggested it," I say. "Not the one who's in the hospital. Someone else."

"Good friend," Ayo says.

I catch sight of my reflection in the window beside the front door. Seeing myself there, *here*, scarred and still a little damaged but okay, I'm swept up in a sense of gratitude for the accident. Not just that I survived it, but that I went through it at all. The wreck itself, the mind's eye blindness, the hallucinations that maybe weren't. Yes, it was awful and hard, and I wouldn't wish something like that on anyone ever, but standing on the other side of it, I also wouldn't go back. The view is so much better from here.

"I couldn't see it," I told the man at my window that night. The car in the intersection, that's what I meant, but there were so many other things I couldn't see.

The beauty in brokenness.

The power of honesty.

The way hope lights up the dark.

I see all of it now.

"Yes," I tell Ayo. "He is."

Chapter Twenty-Three

Hannah meets me in the third floor waiting room after school. Like the gash on Ayo's forehead, the bruises on her face have sunk beneath the surface again, out of sight. There are still bags beneath her eyes, and she's thinner than she should be, but otherwise she looks fine. If I didn't know better, I might believe that she was.

But I do know better.

I know there's more to Hannah's story than what's on the surface. Just like there's more to mine. I could never tell by looking at her that Hannah is amazing at piano or that most of the time she feels invisible or that she's the very best kind of friend. I would have to get to know her to see these things, to see who she really is. And even then, I wouldn't see everything. The soul doesn't put itself on display, which is kind of the magic in it. People aren't flat like canvases, that's the whole point. They're so much deeper than that.

"You ready?" Hannah asks me.

I shake my head. "No." Then I get to my feet and follow her down the hospital hallway to Marshall's room.

"How does he look?" I ask in a low voice.

"Not awesome," she admits. "He's in a lot of pain."

I stop walking. "Should I wait then? I don't want to crowd him if he feels crappy."

"Don't be a wimp," Hannah says.

"I'm not being a wimp! I don't want to barge in there if he needs space."

"When was the last time my brother needed space?" She grabs my elbow and tugs me down the hall.

When we get to his room, Hannah steps back, gestures for me to go in. "Aren't you coming?" I ask.

She shakes her head. "My parents are waiting for me in the cafeteria. I told them, last night— about everything. We're gonna talk now about treatment."

"That's great."

"Yeah. Except they're totally overreacting. My mom was looking online at inpatient programs this morning. Like, actual rehabs. I mean, I want to stop, obviously, but it's not like I'm a full-on addict or anything."

"Han. You've been taking sixteen Adderalls a day, for weeks. It's not gonna be that easy to stop."

She looks away. In my head I see an image of a door slamming shut. "Hey," I say, touching her arm. "It's okay to need help. You don't have to do everything on your own." And the thought *remember that* shoots through my head.

"What if you're right?" she asks quietly. "What if it's really hard and I can't stop?"

"You can," I say firmly. "You've got this. You can play freaking eighth note triplets. You can kick Adderall in the butt."

She smiles a little.

"And if you need backup," I deadpan. "I know Tae-Bo."

This gets a laugh. The heaviness lifts.

"What are you gonna do about your thing?" she asks, lowering her voice. "The bruises and stuff."

"I don't see them anymore," I tell her. "I talked to someone about it, like you suggested. He helped me figure some stuff out." I want to tell her the rest of it, but I don't have the words for it yet. "I think I'm gonna try therapy again," I say instead. "Like, a regular thing, after school."

"I'm proud of you," she says. "For getting help."

"Right back at ya, lady," I say. She smiles.

"Now get in there," she says, nudging me with her hip. Then she turns, heads off toward the elevator, while I stare at Marshall's door and will myself to go inside.

Down the hall, the elevator dings. A whoosh as doors open, another whoosh as they close. I haven't moved. The butterflies in my stomach have tripled in number.

just walk in

"I hear you out there," Marshall calls.

I smile and go in.

"You just had to have one, didn't you?" I say as I come through the curtain. My breath catches when I see him lying there in a hospital gown, his face almost as pale as the sheets, a dorky red wool beanie on his head. I keep talking so he won't hear it, so he won't know how weak he looks and how scared seeing him like this is making me feel. "You couldn't let me be the only one with a Frankenstein scar. Um, nice hat."

"Correction," he says. "I couldn't let you belittle Frankenstein's struggle by comparing those tiny scratches of yours with his."

"Ah."

"I'd shame you right now by showing you a *real* scar," he goes on. "But that would involve exposing my butt, and we're not there yet. I'm not even sure we're at the bad hair day level yet, thus the hat." He smiles his Marshall smile and for a second all I feel is a giddy sort of relief.

But then he shifts in his bed and he winces in pain and I see that he's not as okay as he's pretending to be. I don't see bruises, not with my eyes anyway, not the way I did with Hannah or Ayo or the other kids in the support group. I don't need to. Not anymore.

I just see him.

And, oh, there is so much to see.

Pain, relief, disappointment, excitement, worry, uncertainty, love. Not just one emotion, but a dozen at once. Visible and invisible, conscious and subconscious, physical and emotional, a wild array.

"What?" he asks, because I am staring at him.

"Nothing," I say, and smile. "It's just so good to see you."

Acknowledgements

Every book takes a village. This one took an army.

Thank you to my agent Kristyn Keene, who believed in this story when I wasn't even sure what story I was writing yet, and has championed it – and me – every step of the way.

Thank you to my publicist Megan Beatie, for her optimism and creativity.

Thank you to the scientists and doctors who were willing to lend me their brains and ideas to help make my story better, in particular to the late Dr. Oliver Sacks and his wonderful assistant Kate Edgar for responding to my shot-in-the-dark email about face blindness, to Professor Adam Zeman whose fascinating research on aphantasia and mind blindness kept me going when I was losing steam, and to my dear friends Dr. Anne Drewry and Dr. Noel Salyer for responding to incessant texts from me about medical terminology and doctor lingo.

Thank you to Whitney Davis, Shannon Geiger and Cat Ritchson for being my editors and beta readers and making this book better in innumerable ways with each read. And to Kayli Weatherford for keeping me sane along the way.

Thank you to my parents and to my husband and to the two kids who often took second place to my computer screen as I was writing this, and to the one who was born just as I finished it.

And last but never least, thank you to God for the idea behind his story and for giving me the discipline to write it and the courage to put it out in the world.